Embers

Josephine Greenland, born 1995, is a Swedish-English writer from Eskilstuna, Sweden. She has an MA in Creative Writing from the University of Birmingham and a BA in English from the University of Exeter. *Embers* is her first novel and was written during her MA course. It is based on her own travels in northern Sweden with her brother. The early draft of the story was written at a writing retreat run by the Arvon Foundation, in [...]. She was awarded a place on the course through the [...] Writers' Bursary by Budleigh Salterton Literary Festival. [...] was the winner of the 2019 Bumble Bee Flash Fiction Competition by Pulp Literature and the 2017 Fantastic Female Fables Competition by Fantastic Books Publishing. Her short fiction and poetry have appeared in a number of print and online journals. Josephine currently works as an English teacher in Edinburgh.

Embers

Josephine Greenland

unbound

This edition first published in 2021

Unbound
TC Group, Level 1, Devonshire House, One Mayfair Place
London W1J 8AJ

www.unbound.com

ISBN (eBook): 978-1-78965-104-1
ISBN (Paperback): 978-1-78965-103-4

Cover design by Mecob

Printed and bound in Great Britain by Clays Ltd, Elcograf S.p.A.

For my brother, Christopher

Super Patrons

Gillian Evered
Steve Fenton
Anders Flanagan
G.E. Gallas
David Goddard
Elliot Goodger
Anette Grahns
Christina Greenland
Christopher Greenland
Christopher JH Greenland
Guy Greenland
Jacqueline Greenland
Philip Greenland
Ralph Greenland
Scott Greenland
Nawid Hadary
Elisabet Henell
Nathaniel Holden
Katherine Hughes
Charlotte Johansson
Kate Jones
Ilayda Karadag
Darcy Keeble Watson
Luke Kennard
Carina Kindahl
Imogen Knott
Chris Limb
Eva-Lotta Lind-Jonsson
Ingvar Löfstedt
Beatrice Lönnquist
Lynne Macfarlane
David Marston
Philippa Mills

Emily Nilsson Fornstedt
Emma Norlund
Catherine Norstedt
Kent Norstedt
Helen Norstedt-Girling
Sheila North
Stefanie Octon
Onur Özsoy
Jane Palfrey
Steven Pannell
Andrew Plummer
Ash Prescott
Charles Prosser
Lena Puman
Kerstin Raaber Lundqvist
Margareta Rydå
Nigel Savage
Joel Segal
Par-Magnus Sjostrom
Charlotte Sjöström
Ruth Sjöström
Elin Sjöström Flanagan
Paul Snow
Thomas Southgate
Bronwen Turner
Will Wallman
Todd Waugh Ambridge
Lena Wilhelmsson
Georgina Wright
Dave Young

Foreword

For the sake of anonymity, the names of the key towns and communities in this novel are invented. Svartjokk is based on a real town, where the *Inlandsbana* makes its final stop. All the sights and buildings in the town exist in real life, as does the mining community, referred to in the novel as Järnberget. Mount Dundret is a real mountain outside Svartjokk's namesake, from which one can see the midnight sun. The description of the mining industry and the effects this has on the two towns is all based on fact and aims to depict the true living conditions in this part of the country. Björkliden and Kajava, the communities outside Svartjokk, both exist in real life (although the name Kajava is fictitious), and their connections to the reindeer killings are based on findings from real-life documentaries about the hate crime committed against the Sami. All the descriptions of reindeer abuse in this book are based on true crimes that have been committed in this area, although a few alterations have been made. The concept of the Facebook group is purely fictitious. *Lappland Devils*, the name of the documentary mentioned by Vera, is a reference to a real documentary made by investigative journalists which was broadcast on Swedish TV in 2015, but the programme on which it was shown is different to the one mentioned in this book. The Levinians are based on a religious sect by a different name in northern Norrland and Finland, which is still active today. This book does not intend to openly criticise any of the groups or communities mentioned above, but to tell a story, of both fact and fiction, that depicts some of the realities in northern Sweden.

A Glossary of Swedish Words

Bygdegård – a local, rural community centre.

Fika – a Swedish verb and noun that basically implies 'drinking coffee', usually accompanied with something sweet, that can take place any time during the day.

Inlandsbana – the railway line that runs inland from southern to northern Sweden and stretches over two-thirds of the country.

Joik – a traditional form of song in Sami music performed by the Sami people in the Nordic countries and the Kola Peninsula of Russia. It is usually dedicated to a specific person, animal or place.

Lingon – lingonberry. A small red berry that grows in the forest and is picked in August and early September.

Sapmi – the land of the Sami.

Seit – an object of worship such as a stone, a cliff or a mountain located at strategic places for hunters, fishermen or reindeer herders. They made individual or collective sacrifices at the *seit*, sharing a part of their catch for good luck in future hunts. Reindeer herders offered a coin or other valuable object. A *seit* represents the divine presence thought to watch over particular areas of flora and fauna. The term *seit* has now become a general expression for Sami gods.

Snickarglädje – traditional ornaments carved into wood. Normally appear on porches, doors and cupboards.

Studenten – the celebration when final-year students finish school, normally at age nineteen. Students wear a white and black cap which has their name and their school printed on it. The family construct a poster with a picture from when the student was young. After the ceremony, students have a big dinner at home with family and friends.

Utedass – an outdoor toilet without a sewage system in a red, wooden hut.

Part I

Ring of the Sun

'Just a bit further, please!'

Ellen wanted to yank her brother off his bike. They'd been cycling around Svartjokk all day, criss-crossing through the town centre, darting along the river and through the park. Now, on Simon's insistence, they were rushing along the country road out of the town, the dense pine forest surrounding them on both sides. Her top was plastered against her skin, her yellow hair sticky and damp with sweat under the helmet, and her legs ached from the exercise. The day was so bright it hurt her eyes merely looking straight ahead.

'Ten minutes,' she called. 'Then we must go back.'

Simon nodded and swerved off the main road, heading down the forest track. Ellen lingered by the turn-off, taking the chance to catch her breath. The path, a two-furrow track probably used by tractors, forged dead straight through the pines. She'd be able to keep an eye on her brother from here.

Exactly what it was about this place that excited him so much she struggled to see. The town was like the palm of one's hand, after ten minutes you could navigate it with your eyes closed. It was a transit point, a place you passed through on the way to somewhere else.

There will be plenty to see there, Ellen! Mum had told her. *The mining museum, the local history, the Sami…*

So far, the mining museum was closed. The history museum showed the same kind of How-did-people-live-in-the-past exhibitions with model villages, hunters and stuffed animals that you could see in any town. The Sami, well they'd be with the reindeer in the forest and on the moors. Or did Mum really think they would stand by the station in their traditional clothes, waving at the tourists getting off the train?

She'd booked the siblings in at the Hostel Polaris beside the train station for five nights. Five nights of counting trees and iron ore mines. Perhaps Simon was excited now, on day one, but once the novelty of this place wore off…

Ellen stopped her thoughts. Simon had got off his bike and was kneeling on the ground at the edge of the track.

Had he seen something? An animal, an insect?

'Simon, your ten minutes are up!'

That wasn't true. Looking at her watch, she guessed five or six minutes had gone, and if Simon had heard her, he would tell her so. But what she needed now was his attention and she did not care if her inaccuracy irked him.

'Come on, we need to get back in time for the tour!' She biked over to him and said his name again, louder. Still, he didn't react. In the sun, auburn tones flashed in his straight, sandy hair. She walked up and peered over his back.

There was a dark spot on the ground.

'What is that?' She bent down beside him. Up close, she saw the mark was reddish brown. When she sniffed it, it smelled metallic, like copper.

'Blood?' The word left her lips before she could rein it in. She looked around her. Did an animal get injured on the road? There were no other spots on the ground. The pine trees formed a thick wall on either side of the path and peering through them she saw only darkness.

'A car has been here,' Simon said, his voice flat. 'The grass lining the track is flattened. The car must have reversed and headed back to the road.'

He pointed past her, further down the track. There was a puddle of shiny liquid beneath an overhanging spruce branch, rainbow colours dancing on its surface. Oil.

'Why would anyone drive a car down here?' Ellen said. 'There's loads of roots and stones and stuff.'

'It must be a very old car to drip oil like that,' Simon said. 'And look here.' He pointed at the blueberry bushes in front of them. 'There's blood drops on the leaves.'

There was a dark mark, like a squished berry, staining one of the leaves. Another one further along. And there, a strip of plastic.

'Someone's carried something into the forest, and the plastic bag ripped. Some of the sprigs are broken.' Simon squinted. 'I think I can see a clearing over there.'

'Simon, this isn't the time for playing detective...'

Simon didn't listen. His narrow, fox-like face, already red from all the hours in the sun, was fixed on a distant point beyond the trees. He stepped off the track into the underbrush.

'Wait!'

Her brother stopped. He folded his arms.

Ellen licked her lips. A strange feeling grew inside her, a pulse within her neck, as if she had been stung. She brought a hand to the spot. 'What if...'

What if what? her brother's grey eyes said. Hadn't she been complaining about how dull Svartjokk was?

She looked back from where they'd come. The road was a silver line between the trees.

It wasn't more than twenty minutes back to the town.

'OK, then,' she said. 'But just a quick look, all right?'

Simon nodded and continued. Ellen prodded her neck carefully. The skin was smooth. No tenderness, no swellings from a sting. Yet the pulse was still there, a heartbeat in her spinal cord.

She shook her head. Perhaps it was just the heat. She stepped off the track and followed her brother, blueberry sprigs snapping under her feet.

It wasn't long before the stench reached her nostrils. Rot. Decay.

She covered her nose and mouth. A fly buzzed by her ear and she hit at it with her free hand. The clearing was close. Light filtered through the trees, painting yellow tracks in the moss.

Simon was stepping into the opening. Didn't he smell it?

She quickened her pace. When she reached the light, she froze.

Animal heads were lying in a circle in the glade. Reindeer heads.

They were larger than she'd imagined, maybe twice the size of her own head. They stared at Ellen with their glassy eyes. A fly wandered across a pink tongue hanging from a gaping mouth. She saw teeth, flat and broad, like grey stones protruding from the pale pink gum. Grinning at her.

The animals' antlers had been cut off and laid in a cross. At the centre of the cross was a large, arrow-shaped rock.

Simon had stepped past the heads into the circle. He turned around, taking in the scene, muttering to himself.

Ellen blinked and rubbed her eyes. Scanned the trees and the shadows circling the glade.

Who would do this?

She stumbled forward, failed to spot a root lurking in the undergrowth and fell face forward. Pine needles and dirt in her mouth. She spat them out, wiped her lips, stood up.

Simon was still pacing inside the circle. He'd covered his nose and mouth with his shirt, but he showed no other sign of being affected by the smell. As she watched, he bent down and ran a hand along one of the antlers, fingers curling over the tip. He continued along the line, until he disappeared behind the stone.

'Simon!' Ellen called through her fingers. 'Don't touch them! We have to call the police.' She took a few steps forward, and then it hit her: the death, the stench, the heads. Her stomach heaved dangerously. 'Simon!' She fumbled for her phone.

Her brother appeared around the corner of the rock. He bent down by one of the heads, then picked something from the neck wound and crossed the glade towards her.

'Look, Ellen,' he said, holding out his hand.

In his palm was a fly.

'Simon!' She reeled back. 'The bacteria!'

'It's strange,' he said, voice level. 'All of the flies inside the neck wounds are dead.'

She took a step back. 'We need to call the police,' she said again. 'I'm not doing it here.'

'But I need to investigate.'

'You can investigate when the police come. Please, Simon. We have to get out of here.'

She grabbed his hand, ignoring his protests, tugging harder when he struggled against her grip. He wasn't getting out of her sight this time. Their strides broke into a jog, the jog into a run. When they reached the track, she collapsed by the bikes and her stomach emptied itself. She rolled over onto her back, the taste of bile in her mouth, legs limp as if they'd never be able to walk again, and stared at the distant strip of sky, a blue bridge through the sea of pines.

There was no birdsong, no chirping or tapping. No wind.

From the road a car swished by.

That was all the sound there was.

Departure

It was Simon's fault they were heading north. If not for those beetles he'd dropped on Mum's boss they'd still be at home; Ellen would be going to her morning shifts at the supermarket and spending her free time sketching in town.

Her parents, Niklas and Camilla, told her different versions of what had happened. According to Mum, Simon just overreacted. Her colleagues had seen him all alone in the tree house, dangling his skinny legs over the edge, and wanted to make conversation. When they saw he was making notes on the insects in his jars they became curious. He had all the glass jars lined up by the wall in there, organised from small to large, each with a tape label stating the species of insect. Mum's colleagues were science teachers, and Simon was probably more dedicated to his studies than all their students combined. They began asking questions, and wanted him to come down so he could show them his notebook. Mum's boss reached up to him, asking if she could look at the book, and her hand brushed against Simon's knee. And that's when Simon screamed and knocked the jar over, tipping beetles into the woman's hair. Then, to make it worse, he laughed.

Dad had a different take on it. He said Mum's colleagues had provoked Simon into dropping the jar. There were too many people crowding the kitchen, too many people crowding the lawn. Simon had taken refuge in the tree house as that was the only place where he could shut out the natter. Mum had been irresponsible. She put her own ego first, rather than her son's comfort, and hadn't told her colleagues about Simon's Asperger's. This whole *fika* thing was a massive show-off to say thank you for her promotion.

Dad's complaints took Ellen aback. Normally, he kept a tight lid on his feelings. He could be in an argument with Mum for an hour, and in the next moment talk about the weather or the football with their neighbour. Now he clenched his fists, blue eyes burning with frustration.

Ellen went to her brother, hoping his view on the incident would give her a better understanding of what had happened. Perhaps she could also comfort him. He'd marched straight to his room after the incident, as he always did when he was upset about something, but this time, he'd locked the door. She had to knock three times before he responded, and even then, she had to swear she was alone before he let her in.

Of course, it was a failed mission. Simon told her the facts: the lady had tried to take his book from him and she had touched him, and then he got upset and pulled his hand back and the jar fell over. When Ellen asked him how he felt, he said he didn't feel anything.

No Touch was Simon's Golden Rule. No one could come into physical contact with him unless they were close family, who were allowed to hold his hand if he was upset or pat him on the shoulder if he'd made an Achievement.

If Mum's boss had broken the golden rule, no wonder he tipped the jar.

Ellen knew she wouldn't get any more from him and let it go.

Her mother did not.

'He's overwrought. He needs a holiday,' she announced the next evening. She and Ellen were standing on the veranda in the back garden, laying the table. Dad was in the kitchen, chopping onions for the bolognese. 'He could go with you, Ellen.'

'Me?'

'Mm-hmm.' Mum brushed a stray lock of hair from her face. 'You could both do with a week off. You've never had a holiday alone together. Dad and I can't always trail behind you like guards. Simon is fourteen and a half, he needs a chance to stand on his own two feet.'

'But where would we go?'

'To Svartjokk.'

'Svartjokk?' Ellen froze in her movements, a plate in her hand. She put it down slowly. 'Why?'

'You know why, we've talked about going north for ages.'

'As a family, yes. Not as... not as a way to punish Simon.'

Her mother gave her a wide-eyed stare. 'It's not a punishment, Ellen! You agreed, before, it would be good to go. And you did that school project on the Sami this year. You said yourself you'd like to see where your granddad grew up, and the Sami...'

Ellen bit her lip. It was true. She was curious about her granddad's people. The Sami, the indigenous people of northern Scandinavia, were originally nomads who made their livelihood from reindeer herding. The Swedish settlers who'd arrived in the 1700s claimed the land, pushing the Sami away from the ancient grazing areas. Later, a rigorous assimilation had taken place in an attempt to integrate the Sami with the Swedes. Families had been separated, communities pulled apart, the reindeer herding business decimated. Only a minority of the Sami people kept the tradition going now. Ellen had done her school history project on the assimilation, and the horrid race biology studies that took place in the 1900s, where university professors had measured the skulls of living people to determine whether ethnic groups such as the Sami were biologically different from the Swedes. It was part of a unit her class had done on ethnic minorities. She'd spent hours and hours poring over the Sami collection at the Nordic Museum in Stockholm.

'It would be interesting,' she admitted. 'But why now? Why not next summer?'

'Well, it won't be right now, Ellen. By the time we get tickets and accommodation sorted out it will be mid-July.' Her mother straightened and tucked a lock behind her daughter's ear. 'You know how things have been, Ellen, between your father and me... This incident didn't make it any easier.'

'You mean...'

'It will be good for you. And you're good with Simon – you'll manage.'

'Yes, yes, of course...' Ellen had done excursions with her brother before. The beach, the park, museums, canoeing. At Svartjokk they'd be doing pretty much the same, just further away from home. All you needed with Simon, really, was patience and an open mind. But that would be more easily said than done when they'd be so far from home, and Ellen would have to be responsible for making sure her brother didn't get himself in trouble. 'I have a summer job,' she said. 'They might not give me time off at such short notice.'

For a moment, Camilla seemed about to apologise for something. Her lips fixed into a forced smile. Then her face smoothened, back to business. 'We'll figure that out somehow.' She put her hands on the chair and leaned forward to her daughter. 'Tickets up north sell out fast this time of year, Ellen. If I don't book tonight, they will be gone. You need to decide now.'

Ellen opened her mouth, closed it again. An image of Svartjokk grew in her mind. Open-air mines, deep forests, the lonely mountain Dundret looking down on the tiny buildings and streets below… Reindeer, scampering through the forests and along the moors. Never more than pictures in her imagination. Here was a chance to make those a reality. She felt a tugging sensation in her gut. A curious sense of longing.

'What does Dad think?'

Camilla averted her gaze. 'He agrees.'

'Really?' Camilla usually came up with the ideas, while Niklas went along with them, after a good deal of nagging.

'We think it would be a chance for you to explore your roots. And it would make up for the fact you couldn't go with him to your great-grandmother's funeral.'

Ellen gripped the back of the chair. 'It's quite a lot to take in.'

Camilla leaned over the table and put her hand on Ellen's. 'It's going to be all right, sweetheart.'

Ellen moved her hand away and looked over her mother's shoulder, through the window. She saw her own reflection in the glass: the apple-cheeked face, the line of freckles under her corn-blue eyes and her yellow-white, slightly wavy hair reaching down to her shoulders. Her short, soft frame. Often, she was taken for fifteen rather than seventeen, and Simon… With his skinny arms and legs and knobbly knees, his voice which still hadn't broken, people often thought he was twelve. Ellen tried to imagine the two of them on a train with their rucksacks, on their way to a part of Sweden that was as distant and unknown as another continent.

She shook the thought away, looked beyond her

reflection to her father's tall, hunched-over figure, and went into the kitchen. 'Dad?'

Her father turned to her with red-rimmed eyes. 'Just the onion,' he said. Before his face could betray him, he turned back to his work. The knife cleft an onion in two. Chop, chop-chop.

So he'd heard everything they'd said, Ellen thought.

'Please, Ellen, speak to Simon,' Mum called from outside. 'He doesn't want to talk to me right now.'

Ellen was quite certain it was the other way around.

Simon's door was open, but she knocked anyway. He sat on the bed, working in his *1,000 Brain Sizzling Quizzes* book.

'Yes?' he said without looking up.

She wasn't sure whether to sit or stand. Simon didn't always like it if you made yourself too much at home in his space. If you moved anything as much as a millimetre, he'd look at you sternly, deep lines forming on his brow, until you put it back.

This situation was different. It required sitting down. She perched on the edge of the office chair.

'Simon, we're going on holiday.'

'I don't like holidays.'

'It will just be you and me.'

He shut his lips tight.

She tried to smile. 'This won't be like a normal holiday. We're going to Svartjokk. On the Inland Railway. You know, where Granddad's from. We discussed going there together as a family, remember?'

Simon's pencil scratched against the paper. 'Why are we not all going together now, then?'

'Well...'

Voices from the kitchen. Simon's bedroom was right next to the stairs, and one could easily hear what was being said down below.

'This is all your fault,' Mum said. 'Simon's got worse since Marika left.'

'He didn't need those "lessons" any more,' Dad said. 'He's fine in social gatherings now.'

'You have a strange idea of "fine", seeing he poured insects over Annika's head!' Mum fumed. 'If Marika was still here, it wouldn't have happened.'

'He needs space to grow on his own. Which is why we *both* agreed they should go to Svartjokk.'

'You just don't want the embarrassment of saying your son needs an assistant!'

Ellen closed Simon's door. '*That's* why we're going,' she said.

'Do you mean that they want to divorce?'

She stalled. Kept her gaze on the door, so Simon couldn't see her surprise. 'People don't divorce because of one argument, Simon.'

'But it hasn't been just one argument, they've had one after the other. For years.' Simon folded his arms. 'They're married. They made a vow to stay together until "death do us part". They can't separate.'

'Simon, it doesn't work like that.'

'Has one of them had sex with someone else?'

She put a hand to her forehead. How was she to explain that Simon's behaviour yesterday probably was the tipping point for their parents' relationship? That going away was a chance for Mum and Dad to clear their mess up?

'Mum and Dad would never betray each other,' she said finally. 'They just need time alone to talk this out amongst themselves, and that's easier if we aren't around. It will be more fun for us going alone, anyway. And I think Mum is upset about the beetles, too.'

Simon looked down at his pencil. 'Mum always says things are my fault. But they aren't.'

'Go on this holiday with me then and prove to her you can do things right.'

A whole minute passed. The argument downstairs ceased, followed by their mother calling them to dinner.

Her brother looked her in the eye. 'Can I collect more insects and expand my lab?'

'Of course you can.'

Simon smiled.

Three weeks later, Dad drove them to the station in Kristine-hamn where the *Inlandsbana* started. There was only one train a day, and it left at 8 a.m., so they had to set off at five. They witnessed the first few sunrays peek over the horizon, streaking the Stockholm skyline in peach and violet. Ellen watched the city she loved melt into the brightening clouds until it disappeared, swallowed by the black sea of trees.

In Svartjokk, that sea would be deeper and darker and wilder than any of the forests at home. The town would be an island, surrounded by an expanse of nothing.

And from that nothing came her grandfather.

'I still don't understand why we're going there,' she told her father on the platform. 'You've never been, you never even talk about the place.'

'I went last year.'

'That was a funeral.' Ellen dragged her foot over the flagstones. What a strange year it had been. First Granddad's death, almost a year ago now, and only four months later, her great-grandmother. 'You never visited the house. Why didn't you ask to see it?'

'Ellen…' Niklas warned.

'But it doesn't make sense. You're Great-Granny's closest surviving family and you didn't go to see her home?'

'Enough!' he snapped. 'How many times do I have to tell you? I'm not having this conversation.' Then he bit his lip and sighed through his teeth. 'Sorry, Ellen, I didn't mean…' He turned to her. 'I did speak to the other reindeer herders. Briefly. They told me the house was still there. Empty.'

'But you didn't go.'

'I was busy clearing out Granny's stuff in the care home. It was like a whole Christmas flea market stuffed up in her room. You know all about it.'

No, Ellen wanted to say, *I don't*. But she resisted the urge to ask him more. Every time she mentioned her great-grandmother's or granddad's funeral, or anything Granddad-related at all, Dad got that shifty look in his eyes and quickly changed the topic. He'd always done it, but more so in the last year, leading up to and following Granddad's death. There'd been quarrels over the phone, fewer visits. Judging by the way Niklas shut down after his father's death, not even letting anyone mention his name, it seemed those quarrels had never been resolved.

'Besides,' he continued, 'they had their reindeer to tend to. The day after Granny's funeral they were back in the woods with their animals. October is when they gather the herd in preparation for winter. They wouldn't have had time to speak to me. The Sami lead very busy lives.'

Sami. The word still felt foreign on Ellen's tongue. Her research project had only scratched the surface. There was so much ignorance in southern Sweden about who the Sami were. They were never studied in school. Ellen's classmates only associated them with reindeer and *kåtor*, the traditional Sami dwelling similar to a tepee, and were surprised at first when they learned about her grandfather being Sami, not realising that many of them lived down south now, with 'ordinary' jobs. Not Lars-Erik's family, though. According to her dad, the Blinds had been reindeer herders for well over ten generations. Now, with Great-Grandmother Marit's death, there were no Blinds left in Svartjokk.

'It will be good for us to visit,' she said. 'We can visit her grave. Great-Granny's.'

Niklas nodded, though his face showed no enthusiasm. He ran the fingers of his left hand up and down the palm of his right, a gesture he often made when lost in thought.

Simon's cry broke the tension. 'The train! The train is here!'

He waved at them from the bench where he'd been sitting. He pointed with his Rubik's cube towards a red-and-white train approaching the platform.

Niklas took a deep breath. 'Here we go then.' He put on a smile that didn't quite reach his eyes. 'Have fun.' He pulled Ellen into a hug. It was clingy; his arm squeezed around her neck, pressing her awkwardly against his shoulder. 'Take care,' he muttered in her ear. 'Keep an eye on Simon.'

'Of course.' She squirmed out of his grip and flashed him a smile. 'See you later, Dad.'

He waved his hand slowly, struggling to keep the smile on his face. Ellen hurried on board.

'I am going to draw a map,' Simon announced as they'd taken their seats. He put his notebook on the seat's foldable table and smoothed out a page. 'This is going to be the best trip of my life.'

Wide-eyed, Ellen looked at him. The smiles, the

chuckles, the talking to himself... as if he were five again. Where did all that come from?

It was as if she were sitting by a stranger. Waved off by a stranger, headed for a stranger land.

Somehow, she knew this had been a long time coming.

Weak Left Hand

The rumble of a car made her sit up. A flash of blue, white and yellow, scuffling and bumping down the track.

Police.

Ellen brushed dirt and pine needles off her skin and clothes and stood up. She noticed, for the first time, that Simon was missing. She cursed under her breath. He must have snuck back to the glade while she was calling the police.

She waved her arms at the vehicle.

The car stopped in front of the bikes. A policeman got out.

'You reported a reindeer killing?'

The policeman walked up to her. He was tall and heavily built, with a nose that looked like it had been broken in the past. His large hands hung at his sides.

'They're in the glade.' She pointed into the forest. 'A whole circle.' She remembered the blood and pointed at the black mark on the ground. 'We saw the blood marks first, and oil.' Her hand swivelled to the spruce branch. 'We think someone must have driven here and carried the heads in plastic bags. One of them ripped on a blueberry bush.'

'Heads?' the policeman repeated. 'Heads?'

'They were beheaded. We couldn't see any bodies.'

'Is anyone else with you?'

'My brother.' She looked towards the trees. 'I think he ran back to the glade.'

The policeman gave a slight nod. 'We'd better meet up with him, then.' He motioned to her to lead the way.

Simon was waiting for them as they reached the glade. He leaned against a pine, just beyond reach of the stink.

'You all right there, fella?'

Simon looked the policeman up and down. The fly was still in his hand. In the other was his phone. Ellen tried to catch his eye, mouth at him to drop the insect, but her brother's gaze was fixed on the policeman.

'I'm Constable Virtanen,' the man said. 'I'm here to check what's happened to the reindeer.'

'I have made a few deductions about the killing,' Simon said.

Ellen's inhalation was a hiss. *No, no, no.*

'The antlers have been sawn off by a left-handed man.'

Constable Virtanen studied Simon's face. 'Show me what you mean.' They headed into the glade, Simon leading the way, Ellen trudging along behind them. Her brother held his head high, describing how they came upon the crime scene, with broad, sweeping gestures. He knelt down by a head and beckoned at the policeman to join him. Ellen hovered beside them, conscious of the dead eyes watching her.

'Do you see?' Simon pointed at the antler stumps on the reindeer's forehead. 'The cut is angled to the right, which means it was a left-handed man who did it, because the force travels to the opposite side, like a mirror. If it was a right-handed man the cuts would slant to the left.'

Virtanen's face was as motionless as the trees surrounding them. He didn't even bat an eyelid.

'I took pictures as well to provide evidence,' Simon said.

'Photography isn't allowed at a crime scene, fella.' The man looked at Simon's other hand. 'What's that?'

'A fly.'

Ellen held her breath.

'Can't handle objects from a crime scene without gloves.' The policeman rose. He towered over Simon. 'Throw the fly away and delete the pictures. Now.'

Simon put both hands behind his back.

'Look, fella, you don't want to get into any trouble.'

The policeman made a grab for Simon's phone. Simon swerved out of the way and began to back out of the circle. His foot nudged one of the antlers.

The constable held up a finger to him. 'If you make any more fuss, things will get very serious.'

Ellen stepped in between them. 'Simon doesn't mean to be difficult. He just doesn't like people touching him or taking his things.'

Virtanen strode past her as if she weren't there. He walked right up to her brother, who stood beyond the circle, phone and fly still hidden behind his back, counting to himself.

The policeman grabbed him by the arm.

Simon hit him.

Constable Virtanen sectioned off the dirt track with a strip of blue-and-yellow tape. He tried to confiscate Simon's phone again, but Simon screamed and didn't stop until the man grudgingly returned it. 'We will deal with that at the police station,' he said. Then he pulled down two of the back seats in the car to make room for their bikes, leaving Simon squeezed into the corner.

The station was a brown-brick complex, which, if not for the blue sign reading *Police*, could have been mistaken for a block of flats. People on the street stopped and watched as Ellen and Simon were escorted inside. She imagined what they thought they were seeing. Teenagers caught shoplifting, maybe, or spraying graffiti. Despite herself, she lowered her head and quickened her pace.

They were handed over to a police sergeant. He was older, perhaps in his early sixties, with a heavy-jowled face and thin wisps of grey hair. His headgear, resting on the desk, was flat at the top, with a black rim to shade the eyes – a combination of a bowler hat and cap. The Swedish police emblem on the front glinted in the light shining through the window, flashing gold and sapphire.

'I'm Sergeant Gunnarson,' he said in a calm voice. 'Sit down.' He motioned to two chairs opposite his side of the desk.

Ellen sat down and rested her hands in her lap, pulling at a nail. Constable Virtanen closed the door behind them.

The sergeant asked if they were local to Svartjokk. He asked about their family, their parents' contact numbers and their home address. He asked them about their accommodation in Svartjokk and the hostel contact number. Ellen answered the questions at first, but the officer reminded her it was Simon who had committed an offence, and therefore it was he who should answer the questions.

Simon told him they used to have a great-grandmother who lived in Svartjokk but that now she was dead.

'Did you mean to hit the policeman, Simon?'

'Yes,' he said without hesitation.

'But you did not mean to hurt him?'

Emphasis was on *hurt*. Ellen slowed her breath.

Simon frowned in thought. 'No,' he said finally. 'I did not mean to *hurt* him.'

'Then why did you hit him?'

Ellen's fingers stilled.

'I hit him because he touched me. I don't like strangers touching me.'

Gunnarson pursed his lips and folded his hands in front of him on the desk. 'The policeman tells me you'd taken pictures of the heads. Is that correct?'

'I took pictures of the cuts to the reindeer's antlers. I made deductions about the murderer. He is left-handed.'

The sergeant clicked his tongue. 'Look, Simon, all those observations sound good and true, but you must let the police run this investigation. We can't have civilians, underage civilians at that, playing detective on the side. It could be... disruptive.' He smiled apologetically at the last word.

Simon puckered his lips but lowered his gaze. Ellen couldn't help sighing in relief. The hostel room flicked through her mind. She longed to collapse on the bed and bury her face in the pillow.

'I got this, too.'

Simon pulled out a handkerchief and unfolded it on the desk.

Inside was the fly.

'It has been poisoned.'

Goodness, no, Ellen thought. Wasn't annoying the constable enough? Did he have to get on the wrong side of the sergeant, too?

Her brother leaned back in his chair, arms folded, telltale frown lining his forehead. 'All the flies in the neck wounds were dead. I told the constable this but he was not interested.'

Ellen waited for Gunnarson to tell him off. To glower, maybe put him in a cell for arguing with the police.

'Poisoned?' Something in the man's face changed. It wasn't anger. 'Tell me about the discovery. From beginning to end. Don't leave anything out.'

This time he was addressing Ellen.

She took a quiet breath and let it out slowly. *OK*, she thought to herself, *keep it simple, keep it true*. She cleared her throat, placed her hands around the chair's edges, and began.

When she was done, the officer leaned back in his chair, resting his chin on his right hand.

'Twelve heads, you say?'

'Yes,' Simon said, before Ellen could.

'You are absolutely sure it was twelve?'

'Yes,' Simon said again. 'I counted them two times, and you can see on my pictures that I am right.'

Gunnarson showed no annoyance over Simon butting in. He leaned forward over the table. 'Let me see.' He squinted at the pictures and nodded. 'That is proof enough.'

'What happens now?' Ellen asked.

'Simon deletes the pictures on his phone.' The man eyed the fly and wrinkled his nose. 'And throws that thing in the bin.'

Simon's face tightened. 'According to the Government Crime Registry, authorised by the Department of Justice, it is against the law to delete photography of a crime scene.'

Ellen raised her eyebrows. She knew Simon had a knack for memorising odd pieces of information, but the Government Crime Registry? It was as if he'd known this meeting would happen and prepared his answers in advance.

Again, the sergeant's eyes betrayed no emotion. 'I think we can make an exception for a fly, don't you?' He rubbed his nose with a thumb. 'If you read the entire registry, you will know it also says that the civilian must follow the policeman's orders at all times. If the police don't want any photography at the scene, that's the way it is. And we don't want any of those pictures going up on social media, do we?' He clasped his hands in front of him on the table. 'Now delete the photos, Simon.'

The room held its breath. Ellen didn't dare look at either her brother or the sergeant.

Simon deleted the pictures. Ellen's hands relaxed; she brought them back to her lap.

Gunnarson made Simon show him on the screen that the photos were gone. 'Well done,' the man said. 'Even so, I am giving you a caution.'

'What is that?' Ellen asked.

'It means we will write down you hit a policeman but did not mean to hurt him,' Sergeant Gunnarson said, without shifting his gaze from Simon. 'That it was an accident.'

Ellen tensed as Simon opened his mouth, but just as she thought he was going to correct the sergeant, he closed it again and shrank back in his seat.

'If there are any more problems, we will consider your caution and things will get a lot more serious. Do you understand?'

Simon nodded his head a fraction.

'Good.' Sergeant Gunnarson stood up. 'Constable Virtanen will see you out.'

They were just about to leave through the glass doors when Ellen spotted the newspaper. It lay folded on the table in the foyer. She stopped and picked it up. *Polluted Lake Kills Reindeer*, the headline read. Dated Wednesday 13 July. Yesterday.

Glancing up, she noticed Simon and the constable were waiting outside. She tucked the newspaper under her arm and hurried through the doors.

'It wasn't an accident,' Simon muttered as she joined them. He gave the policeman a deep scowl.

Ellen shushed him. Constable Virtanen didn't turn, but even if he had heard, she doubted he'd show it. She felt his eyes on her as they reached the car park and she and Simon unlocked the bikes. A quiet, penetrating look that gave her the feeling he could hear with his eyes or lip-read at the very least. She wondered how angry he was over Simon hitting him. Her brother's fist had left no mark on the man's face, but she doubted a skinny fourteen-year-old had ever hit him before. He kept watch on them as they crossed the road, the emblem on his cap a third eye glinting in the sun.

When they turned a corner, Ellen stopped and got out the newspaper. 'I picked this up in the foyer,' she said. 'There was an article about reindeer.' She unfolded the paper and held it out for both of them to read. As her eyes skimmed through the lines, her jaw dropped.

Fifty-four reindeer had been found dead on Tuesday by Nilajaure, a lake south of Svartjokk. They'd been grazing around the lake over the weekend, and it was reckoned they were poisoned by the water and died on Monday night. After a headcount, the reindeer herders had confirmed another twelve were missing.

Twelve.

Ellen lowered the paper. 'They must be the same. The heads, and the missing reindeer...'

'Yes.' Simon nodded. 'There is a very high chance the crimes are related.' He took the paper from her and held it up to his face. 'The killer could have removed the twelve carcasses on Monday night, beheaded them Tuesday night, and planted the heads in the glade on Wednesday.'

Ellen put a hand to her forehead.

'Ellen.'

Her brother's voice made her look up.

'We have to find the killer.'

'Have you forgotten what the police officer said?' She leaned in towards him and lowered her voice. 'If we're found meddling, we could get into a lot more trouble. You could go to jail!'

'I would only go to jail if I were accused of deliberately trying to hurt a policeman or sabotage their work.'

'Hitting that constable wasn't far off!' She put her hands on her hips. 'The best thing for us is to put this aside and move on. We have the midnight sun tour tonight, remember? And the trip to the mine tomorrow.'

She shrugged out of her rucksack, zipped it open and held out her hand. 'Give me the newspaper.'

Simon's grip around the paper tightened. He stared at a point just beyond her shoulder.

'Simon?'

Her brother breathed in and out of his nose. Then he said: 'Police Constable Virtanen is a suspect.'

'How?'

'He tried to confiscate my pictures and didn't listen when I told him my deductions.'

'Simon, that's ridiculous.'

'And he ignored the fact that there was another man in the forest watching us.'

'What?'

'You weren't looking. You were too busy explaining to the constable how I didn't mean to hit him and scream and that it was because of my Asperger's.'

'Simon, I was trying to protect you, seeing you don't know how to.'

Simon's lips pouted and he looked away. His hair fell forward, hiding his eyes. 'I took a picture of the man.'

He pulled out his phone and opened the photo gallery. 'He watched us as we got into the car.'

He angled the phone for her to see. In the photo was a man, peering out from behind a tree.

'He was only ten metres from the track,' Simon said. 'The constable saw him when he rounded the car to the driver's seat.'

The picture had been taken on a zoom-in, which blurred the man's facial features. What was most distinct about him was the brown cap he wore pressed down over his head, and his mouth, a thin line shaped like an upside down 'u'. Ellen bit her lip. How stupid she'd been. If she'd looked up, even if only for a second, she would have seen him. Had the shock of finding the reindeer heads really made her that blind?

'Constable Virtanen looked at him for three seconds,' her brother said, 'but I did not know what he was thinking.' He looked at her. 'If someone looks at a person for that long, does it mean they know that person?'

'I... well...' Ellen counted under her breath. 'Three seconds is a long time.'

'A professional policeman would not have left the site without interrogating the man. It is their job to record suspicious behaviour and this was very suspicious.' Simon raised his chin. The movement made the lock of hair fall back. He looked intently at his sister. 'If the constable and the man know each other, it could be they know something about the crime.' He folded his arms. 'We need to launch our own private investigation.'

Ellen closed her eyes. She suppressed a sigh, opened her eyes again. 'Simon,' she said slowly, 'this is exactly the kind of thing I did *not* want us to get involved in. And what about the pictures? Didn't you say they were solid evidence? Without them, how can you...'

'We still have the pictures,' Simon said.

'What?'

'I sent the pictures to you.'

'When?'

'When we got into the car. I did it when the constable closed the boot and made his way to the driver's seat.'

Ellen wanted to shake him by the shoulders. It didn't seem to matter what she told him, it all went in through one ear and straight out the other. Teeth clenched, she pulled out her phone, looking over her shoulder as she did so. The street was empty. It was still boiling, so most people were probably indoors, or by the river. She scrolled through the notifications on the screen, all of them flashing the same five words at her: **Simon sent you a photo, Simon sent you a photo, Simon sent you a photo.**

'How many did you take?'

'Twelve.'

She swiped through each one. Reindeer heads filtered through her vision. A single death, forever copying itself.

Ellen looked at the newspaper in her brother's hand. The reindeer carcass had its head facing away from the camera, tilting downwards into the moss and the blueberry and lingonberry leaves. Had the photographer deliberately taken the photo at that angle?

Had the police officer known she'd spot the newspaper on the way out? Is that why he didn't tell her about the pollution himself?

She closed her eyes and let out a deep breath, struggling to believe what she was about to say.

'You can investigate a little bit. But if it gets too dangerous, if people get angry, you have to stop, OK?'

A grin spread over her brother's face. Before he could break into excited laughter she held up a finger.

'Remember, though, just a little bit. And like you said, it's a private investigation. We only tell people if it's absolutely necessary. Mum *cannot* know.' Ellen took the newspaper and stuffed it in her rucksack, then put her phone in her pocket. She felt the reindeer's stares through her jeans. She was only doing this to keep Simon calm, she reminded herself. At the best possible moment, she would talk him out of it. Yet, a rush of excitement coursed through her body.

She began to walk, the ticking sound of the revolving bike wheels loud in her ears. She did not know the exact way back to the hostel, but Svartjokk was small. You could cycle through the length of it in twenty minutes. The town fanned out from the shadow of Mount Dundret, split in half by the Svartjokk river. The southern side, closest to the mountain, was a neighbourhood called *Andra Sidan*, or 'other side', sporting a colourful selection of timber houses and a little park with trolls and other creatures painted on the stones. The northern side was the main part of the town, with the train station, the town hall and the New Church as landmarks visible wherever you were.

They could see the town hall now, peering at them from the other end of the town square. A nineteenth-century style red-brick building with little turrets on the sides, it was probably the prettiest building in the town. It was where the museum and gallery they had visited that morning were housed. It seemed rather out of place in the grey, barren town square with the concrete shopping centre, where half the shops were closed down. A group of old men sat on a bench by the fountain, staring as the siblings walked by. Ellen was relieved when she and Simon passed under the shadow of the town hall and took a turn to the left. The wooden train station became visible in the distance, and beside that, their hostel.

A thin strip of cloud skirted across the sun then, giving

it a glum frown. Ellen's excitement faded away. She hoped, for Simon's sake, that she hadn't made the wrong decision.

The Mind of a Sleuth

Simon claimed the first book he read on his own was *The Diamond Mystery* by Widmark and Willis. That wasn't completely true, because Ellen had read the first ten pages aloud to him, but she knew that questioning him would only give her a headache. The book told the story of two friends called Lasse and Maja, investigating the disappearance of diamonds from a jeweller's shop. The thief was a sporty health guru who left work each day munching an apple, which he claimed was good for the stomach. He'd hidden the diamonds inside the apples.

Their mother had spent the following week digging rings, brooches and earrings out of the apples and pears in the fruit bowl. When Simon came home from school one day with the next five instalments in the series, she'd buried her head in her hands.

'I like reading about how they figure out the answers,' he explained.

Dad thought the earrings in the pears were amusing. 'It's like playing Fish in the Pond,' he said. 'You dip your hand in, never knowing what you're going to get.' Simon bought more books with the pocket money Dad had given him.

It wasn't long before the whole school knew about

Simon's new-found interest. He asked for puzzle books and problem-solving tasks in maths class, he made Ellen and the two friendly teachers organise treasure hunts just for him. Bags of Dumle chocolates were hidden on the grounds or in one of the buildings, and Simon got one or two challenging clues to help him find the cache.

Soon he became famous at the school for his detective masterclasses at *Roliga Timmen*, Fun Hour, the session that took place at the end of every Friday. Simon presented his classmates with a situation and gave them ten to thirty minutes to solve it, before going through the deduction process with them. The classroom always filled with complaints. Fun Hour was meant to be Fun – it was in the name. The girls danced to 'The Ketchup Song' and mimed, using the teacher's whiteboard pens as microphones, and the boys screamed rock songs at the top of their voices while playing air guitar. It wasn't actually a class. Friday afternoon, two to three, was when the weekend unofficially started, a chance for the kids to wind down and relax after a full, brain-frying week of learning to read, doing addition and memorising Sweden's four largest lakes and Skåne County's four longest rivers.

The school was inundated with complaints. The kids claimed Simon was showing off. He was putting pressure on them when they should be having fun. He was getting special treatment. He was monopolising Fun Hour and turning it into Boring Hour.

The treasure hunts were cancelled. The maths teacher stopped providing extra tasks. Simon was no longer allowed to run his detective masterclass. He was banned from *Roliga Timmen* three Fridays in a row.

Simon drew back into himself. He'd bring a *LasseMaja* mystery or puzzle book with him to the toilet and stay there for over half an hour reading or working. Ellen would knock on the door, urge him to come outside and play. Twice she was met with a firm NO. The rest of the time, with silence.

'Everyone wants to feel special,' Dad told her. 'That they matter in the world and that what they have is important. Your brother is lucky. Only seven years old and he's already figured out in what ways he wants to matter. It takes decades for some, and they get jealous of people like him.'

'Have you figured out how you want to matter?' Ellen asked him.

'Yes, but it took me a long time.'

'How long?'

He looked at the sky. 'Thirty-three years.'

Hostel Polaris was a yellow, three-storey house just down the road from the station. A wooden sign with the name hung on the wall. There was a wide wooden porch with a letterbox on it, and off to the right, a white wooden bicycle shed.

Henrik, the hostel owner, a lean and wiry man with brown hair, was leafing through post as the siblings walked into the yard. He didn't turn to greet them straight away.

Ellen cleared her throat.

Henrik turned. His eyes widened. 'I was expecting you earlier.'

Mentally, Ellen clasped her hand to her forehead. She'd told Henrik they'd be back by five. She glanced at her watch. It was five past six.

'Sorry,' she said, 'we lost track of time.'

Henrik waved her apology away. 'Electrician's here anyway, have to wait for him to finish.' He looked at the bicycles. 'I'll take those to the shed.'

He walked up to them, tucked the envelopes under his arm and placed a hand on each of the handlebars.

'Did something happen when you were out?' His gaze slid downwards. 'You've got yourselves some big scratches.'

Ellen followed his gaze and noticed, for the first time, the cut marks and mosquito bites grazing her legs. The bracken, it must have been tearing and cutting as she ran away... Simon's were twice as bad.

'We were just cycling...' Her grip on the handlebars tightened. Not wanting to look the man in the eye, she stared at the envelopes tucked up against his arm. Half the logo of the Telenor telephone company stared at her in purple letters.

'We were cycling in the forest picking blueberries and saw a suspicious man spying at us from behind a tree.'

Ellen stared at her brother, mouth gaping. *Shut up*, she tried to mouth at him, but Simon wasn't paying attention. He pulled out his phone. 'Can you identify the man?'

Henrik leaned forward and squinted at the photo. His jaw tightened, his thin lips forming a straight line.

Ellen stepped past her brother. 'The man was actually peeing. Simon wandered past his tree looking for berries and the man just burst out at him. Must have thought we were playing a prank or something. Simon got scared and took a photo before the man walked off, he wanted to go to the police.' She looked at her brother. 'Simon has Asperger's, you see.'

Simon's cheeks turned beetroot-red. He clenched his fists in his pockets and stared at the ground. His lips moved but uttered no words.

Then the front door opened. A man in a grey T-shirt and blue work trousers stepped outside. He wiped sweaty locks of pale blond hair from his face and approached the hostel owner. 'I've mended one of the sockets, but there's another two that have gone and the wiring needs replacing.'

He stopped talking when he noticed the siblings. His gaze drifted from them to the hostel owner. 'Did I interrupt something?'

Henrik sighed through his nose and shook his head. 'No.'

The electrician wiped his forehead again. 'I'd best be going anyway.' Gravel crunched under his feet as he left the yard. There was the rumble of an engine coming to life and then a white van drove past them on the road and out of sight.

'I think you should go inside,' Henrik said. His tone was brusque, hushed.

'You don't know who he is, then?' Ellen asked. 'The man.'

'No.' Henrik's eyes flitted out to the street. 'I don't know.' Then he turned and wheeled the bikes to the shed.

Ellen motioned at her brother to go inside.

They had barely got into their room before Simon asked the question. 'Why did you lie?'

Ellen put her rucksack on her bed. She turned to face her brother. Simon stood on the doormat, jacket still zipped, rucksack on his back. He hadn't even taken off his shoes.

'What do you mean, lie?'

'You didn't mention the reindeer and you didn't mention my investigation and you didn't mention Constable Virtanen.'

'I told you to be careful, and the first thing you do is blurt everything out.'

'You said I could investigate a little bit.'

Ellen took a deep breath. She could not lose her temper. 'It wasn't really a lie, Simon.' She unpacked her rucksack. Water bottle, empty sandwich wraps, the Puma jacket she'd never had to use. She sat down on her bed and pulled off her socks. Her toes were blackened with dirt and smelled of sweat. 'Technically, we did bump into that man while cycling. We just skipped the bit about the reindeer. And added the bit about the peeing.' She looked up at him. 'In fact, if not for the reindeer and the constable, that is probably what would have happened, if we had seen him.' She dropped the socks on the floor. 'It was just a white lie, Simon.'

'I don't know what that means.'

'You tell part of the truth, but not all of it. You're not actually lying at all. You're just keeping a bit of the truth for yourself.'

'I don't understand.'

She placed her hands either side of her on the bed. 'Simon, the truth can be dangerous sometimes.'

'Truth means you stick to the facts,' her brother said. 'Truth keeps things in order. Lies chop the truth into pieces and create chaos.'

Ellen pursed her lips. 'Sometimes, Simon, truth causes more chaos than lies ever could.'

He put his bag on the floor and folded his arms. 'Prove it.'

She sighed through clenched teeth. 'I'm not having an argument with you.' She stood up and rummaged through their purple hiking rucksack where they kept all their clothes. Tugged out her sailor-patterned top and the travel towel and walked over to the sink beside her bed. She wetted a corner of the towel and wiped the sweat off her body.

Simon bent to untie his shoes and walked over to his bed, making sure to keep his back turned to her. He sank down on the duvet. Ellen watched him in the mirror. Slowly, as if they were breakable, he pulled out his water bottle, Adidas jacket and notebook, and placed them beside him on the bed. Then he pulled out a tissue from his pocket and rested it on his lap.

Ellen turned around. 'Is that...'

It was. The fly didn't look like more than a speck of dirt from where she stood, but it made her nose wrinkle. 'I thought you threw it away!'

'I tore off a piece of the tissue,' Simon said. 'I stood with my back to you so neither you nor Constable Virtanen saw me tuck it in my pocket and drop the rest of the napkin in the bin.' He ran his finger along the edge of the white paper. 'I am going to keep this for safekeeping.' He folded the tissue and tucked it in at the back of his notebook. 'I thought you would be happy I did so as you agreed we would investigate the crime.'

Ellen hung the towel over the chair by the desk. The cool breeze coming in through the window aired her skin and helped clear her thoughts. Again, she wondered whether it hadn't been a mistake to play along with her brother's whims. They were booked onto tours and excursions every remaining day of their visit, though, and Simon hated changing plans at the last minute. He ought to forget all about the investigation. She just had to be patient.

'Your phone is receiving notifications.'

Simon's voice made her flinch. Blinking, she bent over her bed where she'd tossed her phone.

Missed calls and unread messages.

Mum.

Of course, the police officer had taken their parents' numbers. He must have called them, which meant Mum and Dad would know all about the reindeer by now, and the caution. Another call came in as she scrolled through the messages. Instantly she pressed the red button.

She drummed her fingers against the phone case. News of the reindeer heads would spread. It would be in the headlines by tomorrow. The story she'd given Henrik was about one-quarter truth and three-quarters lies. If there was an article about the reindeer and Henrik read it…

She thought of the hostel owner's eyes, how they'd darkened when Simon had shown him the picture of the strange man.

'Perhaps Henrik knows this guy. He barely looked at the photo and still his expression soured. Maybe he doesn't like him.' Her fingers drummed faster against the phone case. 'Maybe Henrik knows something about what happened.'

She didn't realise she was thinking out loud until she became aware of Simon looking at her. She shifted her feet. 'Just a thought, of course. I don't think we should pry.'

Her brother's stare shifted to a point just beyond her shoulder. The corner of his lip twitched upwards, as if to smile. Then he picked up his notebook and pen and started writing intently.

One wouldn't think he was the same boy as the one who'd left the police station. Complaining, interrupting, hitting policemen in the face. *Isn't that why you agreed to this 'investigation'?* she thought to herself. *You wanted him to shut up, didn't you?*

Looking at him, Ellen was no longer sure. Talking Simon could be annoying. Silent Simon was unsettling.

Standing up, she slipped on the clean T-shirt, picked up her phone and scrolled through the pictures again. The severed heads didn't make her stomach lurch this time. She traced the dead flies in the red, like patterns in embroidery.

A dismembered body had no warmth. She hadn't

touched the heads in the glade, but she imagined the fur bristly like steel wool. No longer a body, but a *thing.*

As she looked, the reindeer was swallowed by black and then a telephone symbol grew onto the screen.

Dad's mobile.

'Hello?'

'Ellen?' Dad's voice was hesitant. 'The police just called.'

Something in his voice told her he was half-expecting her to contradict him, to say there'd been a misunderstanding.

Ellen told him what had happened. It was obvious by his ums and ahs that the police had already covered it all. He didn't ask if she was OK. He didn't ask if she cried or threw up. He asked her: 'What do you want to do now?'

Did he know? Could he tell she was hiding something? But her voice was calm; she was trying to sound all chatty and casual… Yet the feeling was there. A certainty in her gut.

'Simon is curious to know who did it. He asked the police officer loads of questions.' She forced a chuckle. 'Guess it reminds him of *Roliga Timmen.*'

Across the room, Simon's pen stopped scratching.

'But I'll talk him out of it,' she continued, 'you'll see. We've got a tour up Mount Dundret to see the midnight sun tonight, and then we're off to the Aitik mine tomorrow. So those'll be nice distractions. For both of us.' She listened to her father's breathing. 'Tell Mum not to worry.' They exchanged goodbyes and hung up.

'You lied again,' Simon said.

'No, I didn't.'

'You aren't going to talk me out of the investigation?'

Ellen looked at her brother. Simon's eyes were wider than usual. His hands resting on his book were balled into fists.

'No,' she said.

'Then why did you lie to Dad and Mum?'

Simon watched her closely, as if waiting for her to change her mind.

Ellen stood up, grabbed the article and smoothed it out against the desk. Her thoughts drifted back to her conversation with Dad on the platform, to his unease whenever the word Sami was mentioned. She let out the breath she'd been holding. 'What our parents don't know can't hurt them.'

Thunder Mountain

The midnight sun lay in hiding behind Mount Dundret. Nothing could be seen of it but a sheet of rhubarb-coloured light, spreading out around the mountain's roots along the horizon. The sky above was still blue. It was nearing eleven o'clock.

'This is the last day of the midnight sun,' Simon said as they approached the train station. 'Tomorrow it will be under the horizon again for one hour.'

'It's still going to be light outside, though,' said Ellen. 'I don't know how you managed to get any sleep last night.'

Simon shrugged. 'I just close my eyes and decide to sleep.'

'Wish I could've done that.' She had drawn the blinds, drawn the curtains, propped up their rucksack on the windowsill, but nothing could block out the pristine light. It had felt like midday all night long, which gave the town a weird sense of abandonment, as there were no people about. The midnight sun made the world up here uncanny.

The tour bus was already at the station. At eleven, it would take them to the summit of Dundret to see the midnight sun, serve some refreshments and then return to Svartjokk after an hour. Ellen could see people already seated inside. Two men were loading coffee thermoses and boxes into the luggage compartment. One of them looked up as the siblings approached.

The electrician from the hostel.

'I recognise you,' he said. 'From Polaris, yes?' He'd swapped the work clothes for a black shirt and jeans. He stepped into the bus and fetched a sheet of paper from the driver's seat. 'Your surname?'

'Are you the tour guide?' Simon blurted.

'Simon…' Ellen hissed.

'But he is the electrician.'

'Simon, you can't just…'

The electrician silenced her by raising his hand. 'It's OK,' he said, smiling. 'It's a fair question.' His bright blue eyes looked at Simon with interest. 'I am the tour guide for tonight. It's a side job I do during the summer.' He glanced at the sky. 'You are lucky. Did you know this is the last night possible to see the sun? It's been with us for six weeks, but tomorrow it will start setting again.' He glanced back at his paper. 'Your surname, again?'

'Blind,' Ellen said.

'Ellen and Simon?'

Ellen nodded. She waited for the man to tick their names off and let them on the bus. He didn't move. His gaze drifted from the list to the siblings. Curiosity entered his eyes. 'Isn't Blind a Sami surname?'

'Yes.'

'But you aren't Sami?'

Ellen pulled at her hair. 'Our granddad was. We're just… exploring where he came from.'

'And your parents?'

'They couldn't come.' Ellen smiled hastily. 'This is just a holiday for us.'

The electrician's return smile was sympathetic. 'I hope you enjoy your time here in the north, then.' He held out his hand. 'I'm Daniel Johansson.'

Hesitantly, Ellen took it. He had a firm grip, the skin coarse like rope. The man offered his hand to Simon, who declined.

'Where are you from?' he asked.

'Tyrevik,' said Ellen. 'A suburb in Stockholm.'

Daniel nodded and brushed hair out of his face. This close, Ellen noticed it was streaked with grey, and slightly wavy. He got off the bus and edged out of their way. 'Get yourselves inside, it's nice and warm.' He flashed them a smile, revealing perfectly white teeth. 'Hope you enjoy.'

As the bus set off, Daniel explained to the guests that the trip also included a tour and presentation of Svartjokk and its neighbour, the small mining town of Järnberget, which rested on a hill rise, overlooking the bigger town. The route they took was a repeat of the cycling trip they'd done in the morning. Up through Järnberget, past the Mining Museum, then along the hilltop road where Simon had filmed a lorry moving a giant, eighteenth-century house to another part of the town. Daniel explained how the mining was making the ground unstable, forcing the whole town to evacuate. By 2030, old Järnberget would be a husk, and the new Järnberget ten kilometres down the road flourishing. It would be expanded and adjoined to Svartjokk, the two towns forming an Arctic city.

'He speaks too fast,' Simon muttered. 'There's too much information and he's not pronouncing the words properly.'

For once, Ellen didn't shush him.

The bus rolled down the hill, back through Svartjokk. Mount Dundret rose out of the trees like a bear's back, the communication mast on the summit a needle eye blinking at them. Ellen was amazed they stayed on the road at all. For every turn the road took, the back of the bus swung right out towards the edge. She imagined driving this reverse slalom every day. It was a driver's nightmare, and she admired the man behind the steering wheel for taking the turns so calmly.

Mosquitoes and red light met them at the summit. The bus parked by the hill leading up to the ski lodge and lifts. Daniel gave them thirty minutes to wander around. Coffee and cake would be served by the bus.

Ellen regretted not bringing sunglasses. The blood-orange orb squatting on the horizon defied all logic. It seemed brighter than the day sun, a different sun altogether.

'It would have been light outside when the killer struck,' Simon said. He was drawing a map of their surroundings in his notebook. Just off the road beneath the church tower and clump of houses he'd drawn for Svartjokk was a circle. His mark for the killing site. A mosquito sucked blood from his cheek, but he did not swat it away. 'He could have waited two more days, but he didn't. He wasn't afraid of the sun.'

He winced suddenly, then slapped the mosquito. It left a thin trail of blood on his skin.

Ellen shifted her feet and rubbed her arms. She was wearing her wind jacket and hoodie, but she hadn't expected it to be this cold, and the damp in the earth and moss was seeping into her trainers. She shifted to the side, onto a patch of heather. Why hadn't she brought her fleece? Or thicker socks?

Shouldn't sunlight be warm even in evening?

The core of the midnight sun was yellow. A snake

eye winking at her through the red. It reflected against the roofs of a small community at the mountain's roots – probably the skiing village Daniel had mentioned. It mirrored itself in a large lake further to the left. Trees lined the shore like a wolf's shaggy mane.

'I have finished the map now,' Simon said. 'I want cake.'

Ellen looked over her shoulder. People were crowding by the bus. Daniel and the driver had put up the table and were now serving *fika*.

She'd told Simon that drawing a map of their surroundings and studying the plants on the summit was fine. If she let him anywhere near the electrician, though, she knew he'd start asking questions.

She also knew that missing out on cake would make her brother very upset. 'Come along, then,' she said. Hopefully the cake would keep him distracted.

Daniel smiled as they approached. 'You come at the last minute. These are the only ones left.' He pointed at three pieces of cake on a plastic lid. Carrot cake, with a layer of frosting and crushed walnuts. 'One for each of us.' He grinned. He asked what they wanted to drink and then poured coffee for Ellen and herbal tea for Simon.

Strong enough to turn the blood black, she remembered Granddad saying. *Or you won't keep warm over winter.*

She attempted a sip and almost scalded her tongue.

'Don't burn yourself,' the electrician said with a smile.

She looked at him over the rim of her mug. He hadn't put on an extra layer, yet the hairs on his arms didn't stand up on end. She noticed the biceps curling beneath his shirtsleeves as he reached over the table and poured a coffee for himself.

'Have you done this tour for a long time?'

'A few years. It's a nice change to driving around all

day not talking to people.' He gazed at the horizon. 'We're lucky today. No cloud. Perfect end to summer.'

'End?' Ellen repeated. They were only halfway through July.

Daniel leaned over to grab a sugar packet from a small box. She noticed a scar on his forearm, a white square the size of a tennis ball, the tail end of it winding its way down to the main vein by his wrist, long and thin like the contour of a pine. 'This far north, summer doesn't last long. Autumn will be here in a month.' He tore open the sugar packet, poured the contents into his coffee and watched the steam waft up from the cup. 'Summer is like smoke – suddenly it's drifted away. We need to make the most of it while it's here.'

Without blowing on the coffee to cool it, he took a swig. He swallowed immediately, never making a sound. He looked at Ellen. 'So, young tourists, what have you been up to in the lovely metropolis of Svartjokk?'

Ellen chuckled. She put her own cup on the table. It was too hot to hold. She told the man about their day, omitting the reindeer. She'd just finished when Simon added: 'We also met a very unpleasant man in the woods and I took a photo of him, but Henrik the hostel owner didn't tell us who he was.'

Here we go again, Ellen thought. She glared at her brother, but Simon did not look her way.

If Daniel was taken aback by the boy's statement, he didn't show it. The only thing he did was raise an eyebrow and put his half-empty coffee mug on the table. 'Really?'

Simon took out his phone and showed him the photo. Ellen had texted the images back to him before the tour. 'Have you seen him before?'

Daniel leaned forward over the table to check out the picture. He heaved a sigh. 'Yes, unfortunately.'

Ellen's pulse quickened. She rounded the table to stand

beside her brother. 'You have?' None of the other tourists were within hearing, but she still spoke in a half-whisper. 'What's his name?'

'Bengt. Bengt Persson.'

'How do you know him?'

'Electrician, aren't I? I meet many people in the town.' He eyed the siblings thoughtfully. 'Persson wasn't mean to you, was he?'

Ellen and Simon exchanged looks. She searched her brother's face for signs of the disappointment he'd shown earlier, about her lying, but found none. Without moving her gaze from him, she said: 'He did scare Simon a bit, yes.' She finished the last of her cake and brushed off the crumbs. 'What does he do?'

'This and that. I'm not quite sure.' Daniel rubbed his nose. 'But you said you saw him in the forest?'

Ellen nodded.

'I think he's involved in organising those blueberry pickers. The Thai people, you know.'

'I see.' There were Thai blueberry pickers in the woods at home, too. They'd be there the whole day during summer, swiping through the undergrowth with their berry-picking ladles, leaving the bushes naked and bare in their wake.

A mosquito landed on Ellen's cheek and she slapped it off. There were more and more of them by the minute, their high-pitched whining pricking the air. Looking around, Ellen could see the other tourists returning to the bus. Perhaps it was time to get inside.

She made to leave, when Daniel touched her arm. 'Just a quick question. You mentioned your Granddad was Sami, yes?'

'Yes,' Ellen said hesitantly, pulling her arm back.

'Was he from here?'

'Yes, but he moved to Stockholm when he was young.'

'Ah.' For a second, something moved across the man's face, quick and fleeting; a mixture of emotions Ellen couldn't place.

Then he was back to his normal self. 'You can go inside. Be leaving soon.' He started loading the empty cake boxes into the luggage compartment as if the exchange had never happened.

Ellen turned to her brother. Simon was writing in his notebook. The name Bengt Persson, in red ink. Underlined above it was a single word: Suspects.

Ellen opened her mouth to speak, but before she could say anything Simon closed the book and headed into the bus. They didn't talk for the rest of the trip.

That night, Ellen dreamed of the cherry tree. She was picking the fruits with her father, standing on a stool to reach the branches. Dad was on a ladder, basket in hand, his upper body hidden by leaves.

'This is the last summer you'll pick berries off that tree,' a voice said. She looked over her shoulder to her grandfather, reclining in the sun chair on the deck. A book was in his lap, and his sunhat had tipped forward, shading his eyes.

'In three days' time,' he said, 'that tree will die.'

She asked him what made him think such a thing.

'It smells of death.'

A rustle of leaves beside her. Dad, poking his head out from beneath a branch. 'Stop frightening her, Granddad.' He always called his father Granddad in front of Ellen.

'You smell it too, Niklas,' Granddad said. 'Otherwise you wouldn't be insisting on harvesting all that fruit today.'

He glanced at the thermometer on the wall. 'It's twenty-six degrees in the shade. I bet Ellen would rather be at the beach.'

His gaze drifted to her, and she looked away.

Dad scoffed. 'All I smell now is your small talk. Come give us a hand instead.'

Granddad laughed. He took off his hat and put it on top of his book on the garden table. He approached the tree. A spare bucket waited on the grass. He picked it up, and in one swift leap, climbed up the trunk onto one of the branches.

'Ellen,' he called. 'Come up here with me. There's plenty of fruit on these branches.'

She was aware of Dad's gaze as she got off the stool. There was a natural foothold near the bottom of the tree, which she stepped onto. Granddad reached down and helped her up to the branch on the left where he was sitting.

'Look at you, nimble as a monkey!'

Granddad's grip was strong. His hands were like leather, rough and smooth at the same time, his forearms lean and sunburned, veins tightly coiled under the skin. He smelled of sea salt, boat varnish and lavender soap. His eyes were of the sea, vibrant like turquoise acrylic.

She seated herself on his lap, swinging her quarter-full bucket in front of her.

'What do you mean that the tree smells like death?'

'All living matter smells of something. Food, sweat, dirt. Unbrushed teeth. Dead matter smells of decay. Putrid. Not very nice.'

He shifted on the branch and she felt his chin against her hair. 'Death itself is empty. It's the void all dead things leave behind them. It doesn't have a smell.' His left hand entered her field of vision and stroked a neighbouring branch. 'That is the state of this tree.'

She frowned. Leaned over and sniffed the bark. Nothing. She picked a cherry from the bucket. It was a deep burgundy, almost black, and when she ate it, sweetness exploded on her tongue.

Overripe.

'If you still don't believe me, look at the ground.'

She looked. 'There's nothing on the ground, Granddad.'

Grandfather's face split into a grin. 'Exactly. It's half past three, and yet the tree doesn't have a shadow. How's that for an omen?'

Two days later, bad weather drove in from the east. Thunder broke out and lightning struck the cherry tree. It was cleft in two; the bark turned ash grey and all the leaves fell to the ground.

Later, Dad cut off the branches and built a tree house across the stump. 'For Simon,' he said. 'So he has a private place for keeping his insects and plants instead of using the laundry room.' He smiled wryly. 'Mum's had enough heart attacks from discovering beetles in the bedsheets.'

'Did you know the tree would be hit?' Ellen asked.

Dad rubbed his brow with a knuckle.

'Did you smell death on the tree, like Granddad?' She fingered the hem of her dress. 'I think I did.'

'Granddad won't be visiting for a while, El.' Dad chewed on a thumbnail. 'He's got some maintenance issues with the boat; he needs to fix them before he goes fishing.'

She knew that wasn't true. Granddad had sent her a photo via text message that same morning with the caption: *Another inspiration for your drawing?* He'd sailed to Nämdö in the outer archipelago. He spent every minute of his spare time on that boat. He'd named her *Ellen*.

Why would Dad lie and keep Granddad away?

Because he feared that Granddad was right. Lars-Erik's

predictions, or gut feelings, weren't just small talk, but insights. Minuscule glimpses into the future that more often than not turned out to be true.

Blueberry Whispers

She found the article in the *Svartjokk Correspondent* the following morning. Three paragraphs, squatting in a row in the top left corner. *Reindeer Heads Found by Nattavaara Road.* On Thursday 14 July, the police had discovered twelve heads laid out in a circle around a rock three kilometres outside Svartjokk. The location was a known *seit,* of historical and religious significance to the Svartjokk Sami Village. An investigation was being launched to determine if the heads belonged to the twelve reindeer missing from the mass death in the lake poisoning, thought to have taken place over the weekend.

No mention of Ellen and Simon, or the reindeer herder affected. The only name visible was the journalist's, printed in bold at the end. Stina Hansson.

Ellen drummed her fingers against the table. They were in the hostel dining room, a rectangular room with wooden, moss-green walls and chequered curtains framing the windows. She flicked to the front of the paper. *Svartjokk Correspondent, Lasarettgatan 3b.*

Movement in the corner of her eye made her look up.

Laila, Henrik's partner, a buxom woman with glossy, black hair tied up in a bun, stood in the corridor leading to the kitchen. She carried a wicker tray loaded with bread. She looked from Ellen to the newspaper in her hand, and back again. Clicked her tongue.

Had Henrik told her about their behaviour yesterday? Did they both know the man in the picture? Had the woman read the reindeer article and suspected them of lying?

Laila slid the bread onto the tray on the table and picked up the jam bowl beside it, which stood empty.

'How was your trip on the mountain yesterday?' the landlady asked.

'Good, yes.' Ellen gave a brief recap of the trip, mentioning that Daniel the electrician had led the tour.

'I'm surprised you went, considering.'

Ellen grew wary. 'Considering what?'

'The police called last evening. Told us what you'd discovered in the forest.'

Ellen stared into her empty yoghurt bowl.

'Are you sure you still want to stay?'

'Yes, we are,' Simon said confidently.

Laila puckered her lips. 'Well, let me or Henrik know if you change your mind, or just want to talk, OK?'

'We will,' Ellen said, forcing herself to meet the woman's gaze.

The woman held hers, as if to double-check the girl was being sincere. Then she glanced at the clock above the doorway. 'Just so you know, breakfast closes in thirty minutes.' She flashed them a warm smile and bustled back to the kitchen.

When the woman was out of sight, Ellen's gaze returned to the newspaper. She tore out the article, folded it, and stuffed it in her pocket.

'I did some research yesterday evening,' Simon said as he buttered his bread. 'The blueberry pickers stay at the campsite when they're here.'

'Where is that?'

'Down by the river.'

Ellen dragged her spoon around the inside of her bowl. 'How did you find out?'

'I googled *Thai blueberry pickers Svartjokk* and clicked on the first hit. It led me to a website called *Nordic Berries AB*. I concluded that had to be the name of the recruiting company.' Simon put a large dollop of strawberry jam on the bread.

'So you want us to go there?'

'Yes.'

'What about the trip to the copper mine?'

'The tour starts at ten o'clock. It will take fifteen minutes to go to the campsite so the whole visit should not take more than one hour. We will be back just in time.' Simon took a large bite of bread. Strawberry jam stuck to the corner of his mouth.

Ellen leaned forward over the table. 'I told you to keep the investigation small,' she hissed. 'Interviewing people... that's big time. And what if this Bengt Persson sees us?'

'The whole point of going to the campsite is to speak to Persson and his workers.'

'Simon, it's dangerous.'

'If you don't let me go to the campsite, I will hold my breath until I lose consciousness.'

'You wouldn't dare.'

Simon took a deep breath.

'All right, all right!' She held up her hands in peace. 'But we need to be careful, you hear?'

'I am always careful.'

Ellen rolled her eyes and told her brother to wipe the jam off his mouth. They left as Laila returned to clear the table.

Svartjokk campsite lay by the river, on the eastern side of the town. It was sectioned off by a high wooden fence, beyond which lay the reception, a wooden house with antlers above the front door. Opposite it to the right were three rectangular buildings, two of them utility rooms, the third one a shower block. Beyond was a lawn dotted with red huts, campervans and tents. The air, thick and sticky under the clouded sky, tinted everything a hazy grey. A crow soared above, uttering a mocking call: *craw craw, craw craw.*

Daniel was right, Ellen thought. Summer was passing away.

The girl in the reception pointed out the bunkhouse where the blueberry pickers stayed. Bengt Persson had arrived with his van not ten minutes ago. He would be inside, checking everyone was ready to leave for work.

Ellen thanked her and led the way outside.

'This is a bad idea,' she muttered as they approached. 'We're going to get into trouble.'

'Ellen,' Simon said, 'you need to stop fretting. A detective can't look nervous when they are about to interview someone.'

She sighed. She considered telling Simon that she wasn't a detective, but couldn't find the energy to contradict him. Anxious thoughts crowded her mind. Heavy silence crowded the campsite.

Ellen knocked on the door.

From the other side came the muffled sound of footsteps and voices.

Ellen knocked again. 'Hello?'

A young Asian woman opened the door. Her eyes flitted between the siblings.

'We are looking for Bengt Persson,' Simon said.

The woman shrank back. She muttered to herself, avoiding Simon's gaze.

'Could you bring him?'

The woman's face was blank.

Simon tried again, in English. This time the woman scurried away. A man appeared in the hallway. 'What's this?'

Ellen swallowed. Bengt Persson looked even grumpier in real life. His lips were pressed together into a black line. His eyebrows were colourless, the hair sticking out beneath his cap mousy grey. He leaned against the door frame and folded his arms, which were wide and thick as logs.

Even Simon seemed intimidated. He brushed his hair out of his eyes, opened and closed his fists.

Ellen spoke before the man could shut the door. 'We are Ellen and Simon. We saw you on the road yesterday... The country road, I mean, in the forest...' She took a deep breath, eyes looking anywhere but at the man's face. 'We were the ones in the police car, getting a lift. We'd called the police, about the reindeer... perhaps you've read the news?'

The man spat. The saliva landed right by Ellen's foot.

'Did you see the reindeer, in the forest...'

The man placed himself squarely on both feet. His lips turned halfway to a grin. Then he threw back his head and laughed.

If bears had voices, Ellen thought, they would laugh like him. She asked him a second time, but the man did not listen. Instead, he closed the door on them.

The receptionist was crossing the gravel towards the rubbish bins when the siblings approached the entrance. 'He didn't speak to you, did he?'

Ellen narrowed her eyes at the girl. 'You were watching?'

The girl avoided her gaze. 'He's a creep, that one. When you said you wanted to speak with him…'

'Do you have a minute?' Simon asked.

The girl pursed her lips but nodded. She threw the rubbish bag in the bin and led the way inside. Ellen closed the door behind them.

'Is Persson always in a mood like that?' Simon asked.

The receptionist snorted. 'I wouldn't call that a mood. I've worked here two years, you know, and I've never seen him smile once.'

'Do you know if anything happened yesterday, or Wednesday, that would make him grumpier than usual?'

The receptionist shrugged. 'I don't know. I don't go spying on the campers. And they're all in the forest in the day-time, picking.' She began busying around the till: lifting and moving pens, post-it notes and stray papers, straightening a stack of chocolate bars on the snack shelf. Every few seconds she glanced over her shoulder towards the bunkhouse.

Persson could come by any minute. If he saw them in here…

Simon walked up and put his hand on the till. 'We discovered dead reindeer in the forest yesterday. When the police arrived to give us a lift home, we saw Persson watching us on the other side of the road. There was no sign of berry pickers.' He leaned forward over the till. 'Do you know why he would be nosing around down there on his own?'

The girl took a step back. She bent down and lifted a cardboard box onto the table beside her. It hit the wood with a slam.

'I know nothing about any reindeer.'

Simon leaned further forward. 'Are you sure?'

'Why are you going around asking questions, anyway? You're not police.'

'I know.' Ellen stepped in, motioning at her brother to step back. 'But don't you agree it's weird this Persson would be spying on us?' She tried a friendly smile. 'If you tell us what you know, you will help the police with their investigation.'

Perhaps her own lack of confidence showed on her face. The girl burst out from behind the till and gestured wildly at the door.

'Leave. Don't come back here again.'

She almost chased the siblings out.

'That receptionist is hiding something,' Simon said as they walked back into the town centre. 'She must know what Persson got up to last night and is afraid to tell anyone. Perhaps he threatened her and warned her not to tell anyone.'

'Or she genuinely does not know,' said Ellen. 'It would have been the middle of the night, even if she was doing the night shift she might not have seen anything.'

'But the midnight sun was out. Any suspicious behaviour on the campsite would have been visible, and from the reception there is a full view of the grounds.'

Simon came to a halt. He stared at the river. The gravel path they were walking on wound its way along the waterfront before swerving right into the centre, where it merged into an asphalt street.

'We need to go back,' he said.

'Simon, we can't go now.'

'We need to speak to the Thai people. If the receptionist knows nothing, they might.'

Ellen sighed. 'Even if they do, there's no telling they won't react the same as her. If that man was my boss, I'd never dare go telling on him.'

'But if they know something important, they have to give us answers.'

'Simon, you can't expect everyone to give you all the answers just like that.' She clicked her fingers to demonstrate. 'We aren't police, we are kids, and nobody is just going to tell us all their secrets. You need to put yourself in their shoes.'

She expected him to contradict her. To say that you couldn't put your whole self into somebody's shoe, because that was physically impossible for a human body and if it was just the foot, it depended on what size shoe it was.

But her brother said nothing. He looked at his feet. 'Daniel Johansson told us Persson's name,' he mumbled.

'But he didn't know we were investigating.'

Simon dragged his left foot back and forth along the ground. The frown on his brow deepened.

'I think Bengt Persson is more of a suspect than he was yesterday.'

'Why?'

'His left hand. All the time in the doorway he leaned on his left leg, left elbow against the door frame. Right-handed people would favour their right leg and elbow. And when he shooed us away it was with his left hand.' He swung his arms back and forth. 'What have you got in your pocket?'

'What?'

Simon looked at her. 'I have noticed there is a bulge in your left front pocket. Normally you don't keep anything in there. And I noticed an article had been torn out of the newspaper in the hostel.'

Ellen opened and closed her mouth, then sighed in exasperation. 'You're impossible, do you know that?'

'No, I am observant. Can I look at the article?'

Ellen tugged out the folded paper and handed it to him without meeting his eye.

'Why did you take it?' Simon said when he'd finished reading.

Ellen swallowed. She could lie, she supposed, but Simon would notice straight away, and things were tense enough between them. 'It was just a thought, if we had time, that we could go speak to the journalist.'

Simon grinned. 'I think you want to find out the answer to the crime just as much as I want to.'

Ellen folded her arms and looked the other way.

'Let's go to the newspaper office.'

'What?'

'I can let you ask the questions this time.'

'But what about Aitik?'

'I want us to cancel the Aitik trip.'

'But…'

'This is more important.' Simon held up his hand, a sign that she should not interject any further. 'We will speak to the journalist.' He peered at the article. 'The address is up here in the corner.'

Ellen had no choice but to follow him.

Simon led the way straight to the *Svartjokk Correspondent* office. It was two streets from the station, on the first floor of a yellow block, above a hairdresser's shop. The blue cursive logo was written across the windows.

The newsroom was rectangular, low-ceilinged and divided by screens into booths, with a desk and computer in each. A reception was at the front in the left corner. The room seemed empty.

'Hello?' Ellen called.

A head peered up over one of the screens. A woman. She rose to her full height and approached the siblings.

'We're looking for Stina Hansson,' Ellen said.

'You're speaking to her.'

'Oh,' Ellen wet her lips. The woman was short, possibly in her mid-thirties. Square in the shoulders; not exactly slim, but sturdy, solid. Her eyes were a cloudy grey, and peered up at Ellen as if prying for her inner thoughts.

'We read your article about the lake pollution.'

'That was more a stub than an article,' Stina said. 'But yes, I wrote it.'

'We wondered if you have the reindeer herder's contact details.'

The woman raised an eyebrow. 'What do you want with him?'

'We're distant relatives,' Ellen lied. 'We've been out of touch for years.'

'You don't have an address or a phone number?'

'Our surname is Blind.'

Stina Hansson narrowed her eyes. 'There used to be a Blind family here who were reindeer herders.'

'Yes. Our grandfather's family.'

The woman tapped an index finger to her chin. 'So you're related to Marit Blind?'

'Yes,' Ellen said, taken aback. 'She was our great-grandmother. We never knew her. We were told that we were her closest surviving relatives but we wanted to speak to the Svartjokk Sami Village, learn more about her, see if we could get in touch with her extended family.'

'Your parents sent you up alone?' Stina seemed unconvinced.

'Dad couldn't get a week off work this summer,' Ellen lied. 'Please, do you have a contact number? Since the incident, we've been wanting to contact them, but...' She let the sentence hang.

The woman cocked her head to the side. She had a pen in her hand and she brought it to her chin, tapping it against her lip.

'Marit Blind... yes. I wrote her death announcement. Difficult one. There were no names for her "she is survived by" list.' The journalist leaned back slightly, eyes scanning Ellen's face.

'If you want proof that we're related to her I could show you the email from the funeral director on my Dad's email...'

Stina Hansson laughed. 'You are trying hard, girl.'

Ellen blinked. 'What do you mean?'

'I know it was you and your brother who discovered the reindeer. Sergeant Gunnarson told me about it. He wanted your names to remain anonymous, on account of that caution he gave Simon.' The woman turned her gaze to Ellen's brother. 'What did you do, give the constable a clip on the nose?'

Simon stared at the floor. 'He tried to touch me and take my phone and I didn't like it, so I hit him.'

'And now your confidence in the police is so low you want to solve the mystery yourselves?'

Ellen frowned. 'How did you know?'

'Well, Gunnarson didn't say anything out loud, but he – the whole Svartjokk police force...' The journalist paused, carefully considering her words. 'Hate crime committed against reindeer herders and their animals tends to remain unsolved. The culprits are never found.' She relaxed slightly. 'It was also obvious through his body language. The way he avoided my gaze, pursed his lips and looked at me like I was a kid who'd asked her teacher the wrong question.' Stina rolled her eyes.

'So you will give us the reindeer herder's address?'

Stina spun the pen through her fingers. Then she

wrote down a name, address and telephone number on a post-it note on the reception desk and handed it over to Ellen. *Per-Anders Thomasson, Granhyttan, 961 25, Purnuvaare, Svartjokk. 076 – 233 480.* Loopy handwriting, the lower-case letters as large as the upper-case ones.

'Thank you,' Ellen said, tucking the note away in her pocket. 'We will call this Per-Anders straight away.'

Stina Hansson didn't respond. She rested her right elbow on the top of the screen. 'You may want to know about your great-grandmother. Marit wasn't a Blind by birth. She wasn't Sami. Her maiden name was Lahti and she came from Salmijärvi. Her family were East Levinians.' She searched the siblings' faces. 'You know what Levinianism is?'

The word rang a bell in Ellen's mind. She'd come across the term in history at school at some point, she was sure, but its meaning eluded her. She shook her head, as did Simon.

'It's a branch of Lutherism founded by Levinius, a priest who worked here in the 1800s, particularly big amongst the Finnish-Swedish community. Levinius had Sami roots, so many Sami were enrolled into his church after being chris-tened. But they were regarded as impostors by some of the Finnish groups, and those tensions still linger today. When Marit married Nikolaus Blind, her family wouldn't recognise her as their daughter. As far as they were concerned she'd ceased to exist.' The woman scoffed. 'Didn't stop her nephews and nieces from snapping up all her possessions once she'd passed away. If I remember right, your dad wasn't left with more than a couple of thousand kronor and the family bible.'

'You spoke to our dad?' Simon said.

'I may have asked him a few questions.'

'At the funeral? How come you were there? You are not a relation.'

'I invited myself, in a way. Turned up before the ceremony started, explained I'd written the death announcement, they didn't raise an eyebrow. There were so few people there I don't really think they cared. But I didn't go to the wake.'

Ellen remembered the day her father came back from Svartjokk the previous winter. His face was drawn and for the first few days he said nothing of his journey – at least not to her. He'd travelled light and returned light: the only 'new' item he'd brought from Svartjokk was his grandmother's bible, a Swedish translation of the Finnish 1776 edition, which the Levinians used.

'You certainly know a lot about our family,' said Simon.

'I'm a journalist. It's my job to know things.'

Ellen shifted her standing position. 'What does this have to do with us seeing the Sami now?'

Stina let her elbow slide off the screen and folded her hands behind her, leaning against them. 'It means that you have no relatives up here. No blood relations. The Thomassons may have been closest to the Blinds on a friendly basis but family-wise you are alone.' She stepped away from the wall. 'Before you leave, take my card, if you need to talk again.'

She walked to one of the desks halfway down the room and came back with a yellow card.

Ellen hesitated. Something about the woman's eyes had changed. They seemed brighter, not cloudy grey any longer, but silver. Perky and bright.

'You may not get hold of him straight away,' the journalist said. 'They're busy earmarking calves at the moment.' She pressed the card into Ellen's hand. 'You two look after yourselves.'

Her look said she expected the opposite.

'Aren't you going to call him?'

They were back by the river. Further downstream this time, a ten-minute walk from the town centre, not far from the Old Church and the Strand cafe, where they'd stopped for lunch during their cycle ride the previous day before heading into the forest. The water here was calmer, foam heads ducking and diving through the black depths. Across the river, the other-side neighbourhood, *Andra Sidan*, looked at them with its odd collection of houses. There was a strange emptiness to the place, a lack of human presence, similar to the one she'd felt at night. Ellen knew it was Friday, a working day, but even so she'd expected more people to be out and about. She'd noticed the same thing in the town centre – everywhere they'd been. It was as if the houses and buildings were all a facade. As if Svartjokk was... not quite asleep, but hibernating. Escaping from the never-ending daylight of summer, as it then would the never-ending dark of winter.

Ellen rubbed her thumb against Stina's post-it note. Traced the loopy handwriting with a fingernail. Stina's perky eyes seemed to follow her through the blue ink.

'The journalist obviously knows something,' she said. 'No way she got all that information about Marit from writing a death announcement.' She looked at the woman's business card. It was a simple design: her name in bold white letters against a black background, the 'a' in Hansson designed as an @ symbol, the tail of the last 'n' curling upwards in the shape of a quotation mark. *Reporter and Freelance Journalist* was printed in a smaller font underneath, and at the bottom, her email and telephone number.

'I noticed something about the newsroom,' Simon said. He sat on the grass, using his backpack as an underlay, twirling a grass stalk between his fingers. 'There were eight booths in there and only three of them were occupied. The rest were empty.'

'I guess it's a small newspaper…'

'Or they don't have enough money to recruit new employees. They are struggling, perhaps running out of business. Which suggests that the reason she is interested in our investigation…'

'Is because we have a story.' Ellen tapped the business card against her palm. 'If we find proof that the reindeer heads are linked to the lake pollution, if we uncover some sort of conspiracy and she publishes a big article on it…' Ellen closed her hand around the card, '…she could make a name for herself. It's in her interest to help us.' She opened her hand, traced the graphic symbols on the card with a fingertip. 'Maybe helping us get in touch with the Sami is the way for her to learn more about our family. Why else would she know so much about Marit? Researching people you write about in death announcements can't be normal…' She lowered the card, lowered her voice. 'Remember when Dad came home after the funeral?'

Simon's fingers grew still.

Ellen brushed the edge of the card along her jawbone. 'I asked him why he didn't want to take us with him. It seemed like such an obvious thing Dad would ask us…' She pressed the card against her chin. 'If Granddad were alive, he would have wanted us to be at her funeral. He would have taken us there himself, whatever Dad said.' An image drifted into her mind. 'I dreamed about the cherry tree last night. It had no shadow, and then lightning struck and turned it into a skeleton.'

'I had a dream like that, too. Before we went to Svartjokk.'

Ellen looked to her brother. 'You did?'

'Yes. The tree spoke to me and then it slithered and

wriggled until it wasn't a cherry tree any more but an oak with a big knobbly bit shaped like a nose.'

'What did the tree say?'

'That I should go to Svartjokk. But I can't remember the exact words.' Simon let go of the stalk and stared at the water. A breeze sighed along the bank and played with his hair. 'But I did recognise the voice. It was Granddad's.'

'Granddad always talked about the oak tree outside his bedroom when he was a kid,' Ellen remembered. 'He said it kept guard against nightmares.' She rubbed her finger over the post-it note again. The 'n' and 'u' in Purnuvaare were smudged, creating blue streaks along the yellow paper. 'Do you think it's like an... omen?' In her mind she saw Granddad in the cherry tree, pointing at the shadow that wasn't there. The lightning which cleft the tree into a fork, three skeleton branches poking at the air.

'Omens aren't real.'

'But don't you think the dream is trying to tell us something?'

'A dream isn't supernatural, it's brain connections. According to the activation-synthesis hypothesis, dreams are electrical impulses that randomly pull thoughts and imagery from our memories. When we wake up in the morning we construct dreams to make sense of these impulses.' Simon tapped his chin in thought. 'So maybe it is possible that my waking mind projected Granddad's wishes and how they conflicted with Dad's onto the image of the tree.'

Ellen held up her hands in resignation. 'Fine, fine, Mr Science...' She pulled out her phone. It was warm in her hand. 'I guess we'd better make this phone call then.' Still, her fingers hovered above the keypad on the screen. Stina Hansson's story about Marit's family rewound through her mind.

If the reindeer herder invited them to visit him, there'd

be no going back. The investigation would cease being one of Simon's detective masterclasses and become real, physical... a something that involved actual people. They wouldn't be able to throw up their hands and say 'I quit' if things became serious. They would be married to this until the end.

Taking a deep breath, she dialled the number for Per-Anders Thomasson.

Chrysanthemum

Ellen's first memory of Lars-Erik Blind belonged to her mother. They were in the kitchen, making tiger cake. Ellen was churning the batter. Granddad was coming for *fika* and in those days Camilla still baked all sweet treats herself.

'Granddad says I'm like a tiger,' Ellen said. I'm all light and stealthy and I creep up on people and surprise them, like that time when Daddy had fallen asleep on the sofa watching the news.' She spooned up some batter that had stained the rim of the bowl and licked it off her finger. 'Why does he call Simon "Mr Pi", without an "e"?'

Her mother leaned over her shoulder and look at the batter. 'I think you've mixed that quite enough,' she said. She took the bowl and tipped half of it into a second bowl. 'Pass me the cocoa.'

Ellen handed Camilla the cocoa packet and watched her scoop the brown powder up with a 100 ml measure and pour it into the mix. 'Stir this,' she said and pushed the bowl back.

'Granddad never calls *you* anything,' Ellen continued and grabbed another wooden spoon from the drawer. 'He just says Camilla.'

'Oh, he used to call me this and that. He has a name for everyone.' Camilla turned the tap on and waited until the water steamed. She washed out the jug and placed it upside down on the drying rack. 'I remember the first time I met him. He was still married to your grandmother. Your Dad and I were invited for *fika*, although I had to provide the cake since Ingrid wasn't the "baking type".' Camilla rolled her eyes. 'Your granddad answered the door. He looked me up and down and the first thing he said was: *You have frightfully small feet.* And he laughed as if it was a good joke.' She turned the tap off and dried her hands against her apron. Then glanced at the bowl. 'Don't forget to stir.'

Ellen looked at the batter. Streaks of flour were still visible amongst the brown. She churned the mix two full circles.

'That's better,' her mother said. She poured the cocoa batter into the cake tin and topped it with the yellow one. Then Ellen dragged a fork through them to create the tiger pattern.

Granddad arrived an hour later. 'Mr Pi Squared!' he said to Simon, who responded with '9.8696044'. He did his usual trick of magicking ten-krona coins out of Ellen's and Simon's ears.

After cake, Ellen asked what he thought of her mother's feet.

Granddad made a loud guffaw. 'Your mother? She has the prettiest feet in the world! Don't you know that's why your father married her?'

When Ellen asked Camilla in the evening what she would call her grandfather, Camilla said: 'Chameleon.'

'Why?'

'Because Lars-Erik is like a different person every time

you see him. As if he doesn't want to show his real self. As if he's got something to hide.'

After three calls, Ellen left Per-Anders a voicemail. She picked up a stone and flung it into the river, watching the point where it had been swallowed by the water.

Simon asked her what they were going to do next. He dragged his rucksack behind him in the grass.

Ellen looked upstream. There was a church spire visible between the birches. There were only two churches in Svartjokk and they'd already visited the New Church.

She started walking towards it. 'We're going to Great-Grandmother's grave.'

At first, she thought the Old Church was closed. Weeds and foxgloves crept along the length of the gate and the lawn was a knee-deep jungle of grass. The latch, though, hung loose and the church door stood slightly ajar.

It was one of the most colourful churches she'd ever seen. The wooden walls were painted in repeating stripes of blue, red, green and plain wooden beige. The hall was broad and low in the ceiling, flooded with light from the windows on the right-hand side, which were two-thirds the height of the wall. The altar was a rich red, the cloth covering it pure white. The pillars were blue, the preacher's pulpit moss green, and the lid of the organ was engraved with beige flower carvings.

Even the carving of Jesus above the altar seemed to be smiling.

Hanging in the air was the musty smell of wood, mingled with that of paint, which reminded Ellen of Granddad's boat varnish.

'Strange there's nobody here,' she said. She wandered

over to the windows. Through the dirt-speckled glass, she saw tombstones peer up above the grass.

'I'm going to the grave,' she said.

There was no response. Turning, she saw Simon bent over the altar. She crossed the hall to him and looked over his shoulder.

He was leafing through a ledger. A giant tome of a book, as large as both their heads combined.

'Why are you reading this?'

Simon answered without looking up. 'It contains the names of everyone who's been baptised in the *Andra Sidan* parish, along with the southern-lying villages, since 1621. I'm looking for the Blinds.' He turned a page. 'Perhaps I'll find Granddad.'

Ellen pursed her lips. 'What if someone turns up?' She looked to the door. 'You're probably not supposed to be touching that.'

'The ledger belongs to the church, which belongs to the parish, which belongs to the people.'

Ellen rolled her eyes. 'You don't want to see the grave?'

Simon leaned further over the ledger. 'I want to look at this first.'

Ellen sighed. 'Fine.'

Great-Grandmother's grave was easy to find. It was the only one where the grass had been mowed. A bunch of shrivelled chrysanthemums lay by the stone. *Here lies Marit Blind, 1920–2016*, the inscription read.

Ellen knelt down, one foot touching the mowed grass. She imagined her father standing where she knelt now. Dry-washing his hands, reading a speech in memory of a woman he'd never known, of whom he had no memory, save for her dying words. Sharing his condolences with strangers who perhaps asked him: *Where were you at your grandfather's funeral?*

Would he have asked them in return where they were when Lars-Erik was put in the ground?

Granddad's grave had also been decorated with chrysanthemums. She reached out a hand to them, imagining the smooth texture of the petals against her fingers.

'Did you know Marit?' a voice asked from behind.

Ellen whipped her head around.

An old woman stood at the church porch. She had long, white, wavy hair, with a long dress to match. Around her neck hung a chain with a gold cross.

'We so seldom get visitors, it's easy to forget there's people buried here at all.'

She took a trembling step off the porch, using the wall for support, and made her way to the grave. 'Are you her grandchild? Or perhaps great-grandchild?'

Ellen relaxed slightly and stood up. 'Yes. Great-grandchild.'

'You have her eyes,' the woman said. As she came closer, Ellen saw her eyes were sky blue. 'You have come a long way.'

A lock of her hair blew against Ellen's face. It smelled faintly of pollen.

Ellen brushed grass off her shorts. 'Did you know her?'

'I suppose so.' The woman's eyes grew distant. 'We go back a long time.'

'Did you go to the funeral?'

The woman gave a tired sigh. 'It was a long day.'

'Did you know the others there?'

'All the families. The Labbas, the Blinds, the Fjällgrens. The Thomassons.'

'Per-Anders Thomasson?'

'I'm not so good with first names.'

'He is the reindeer herder?'

'All men in Purnuvaare have been reindeer herders.' She gave a knowing smile.

'Were they related to Marit?'

'To her husband, yes.' The woman smiled to herself. 'We are all distant cousins. The Labbas, the Blinds and the Thomassons have lived in Purnuvaare near three hundred years.'

'Which was your family?'

The woman's face fell. 'I never really belonged to any of them. I was an in-law.'

She stepped across the grass and sniffed one of the flowers. 'Aaah, chrysanthemum,' she said and closed her eyes. 'Common for tombstones, but I've always thought it was a hopeful flower. Face all open like that to the sun. It was the young man with the grey-blond hair who brought them.' She opened one eye. 'You look like him.'

Ellen rubbed her nose with her thumb. 'It was probably my father.'

'Is he with you now?'

'No, but my brother is.' Ellen nodded at the church. 'I can introduce you to him, he's just inside.'

The woman held up a hand. 'There is no need...'

'I'm sure he'll want to meet you.' Ellen went back across the yard. 'Wait here.' She headed inside. 'Simon! There's a woman here who knows Per-Anders!'

Her brother was still at the altar. He did not look up.

'She was at the funeral!' Ellen reached him. She almost tugged his shoulder before remembering. No Touch. Her voice dropped. 'Simon?'

Her brother turned to look at her. The frown darkened his eyes.

'There's a woman,' she said again.

Simon followed her outside.

The woman was gone.

Simon looked around the yard. 'There's no one here, Ellen.'

'But she was here.' Ellen pointed at the tombstone. 'Right there, sniffing the flowers.'

'People don't disappear into thin air.'

'Are you saying I'm hallucinating?'

Simon folded his arms. His gaze wavered.

Ellen put her hands in her pockets. 'Did you find Granddad's name in the ledger?'

'No.'

'No?'

'There was no name.'

'You didn't miss it?'

'I never miss details.'

Simon walked back to the gate.

A wind picked up. It bent the chrysanthemums over the tombstone so Marit's name was hidden.

Ellen pulled her hair behind her ears. 'I guess we'll leave, then.'

Phi Hua Khat

Ellen's silhouette protruded like a knife from the bicycle's bulky shadow as she and Simon cycled into the hostel courtyard. They parked the bikes by the wooden wall. Ellen's hair was still damp from the swim, yet her neck and chest were sticky with sweat from the ride back. The sky was clear, but the air was heavy with humidity.

It was too hot to be outside.

The shrill sound of a drill met them as they entered the hostel.

Daniel is back, Ellen thought. Looking over her shoulder, she glimpsed the electrician's white van peering around the corner of the wall.

'The power's off.'

Ellen turned. Her brother flicked the light switch to the ceiling lamp, on and off. The hallway remained dark.

'Does that mean I can't have a shower?'

'Let me check with Daniel.' Ellen edged past her brother and headed for the kitchen.

Daniel was bent under the kitchen work-table when she entered. His hand was inside a hole in the wall, below which dangled a power socket. As she watched, he pulled a bunch of multicoloured wires out of the cavity, connected to a thicker, grey wire.

She knocked lightly on the open door. 'Hello?'

The electrician turned. His face lit up. '*Hej*, Ellen!' He pushed himself to standing and wiped dust off his face. Sweat glinted on his hands. He looked her up and down. 'You been for a swim?'

Ellen nodded and tucked a lock of hair behind her ear. Her gaze darted to the other sockets around the room. 'How long will the power be off?'

'Ah.' Daniel wiped his hands on his trousers and surveyed the empty socket. 'An hour at most. One more of these and I'm done.' He gave a lopsided smile. 'Then I'll leave you in peace.' He went down on his knees and returned to his work.

Ellen tapped her fingers against the drawer by the door.

Daniel put his weight on his right knee and angled his torso to face her. 'There something you wish to say?'

Ellen stalled. She had not intended to ask him anything. Her body sagged against the door frame. The voices of Stina Hansson and the old woman swirled around her mind; there was no room left in her brain for more information. What could Daniel give her, anyway?

The lie she'd told him last evening crept forward to the tip of her tongue again. She almost spat, to be rid of it. How many times would she have to lie before this was over? How many more lies were needed to find a truth?

'It's not about that photograph, is it? You haven't been looking for Bengt Persson?'

She raised her eyebrow at his words. Tried to keep the surprise off her face. 'What, no, why would we?'

A shadow passed over the man's face. 'You haven't read the news?'

She shook her head, tried her best to look nonplussed.

'Reindeer were found dead in the forest.' Daniel leaned back on his heels, raised his head slightly to get a better look at her. 'Did you see them?' His voice rose a notch as he spoke.

Ellen decided to take advantage of the opening he'd offered. The less lying she had to do, the better. 'We saw the police when we were biking in the forest, but they told us to go back.'

'And you saw Persson there, too?'

She gave the barest of nods.

The electrician stood up. For a moment, it looked like he would rush forward to hug her. Ellen took a step back, forgetting the drawer behind her. Its wooden edge bit into her spine.

'Are you sure you're OK, Ellen?'

'Yes.'

'You don't want to go home?'

'How can I? We're booked in here, we've paid…'

The man took a step forward. He stood with his back to the windows, face sheathed in mute shadows, yet somehow his eyes smouldered, like blue embers. He opened his mouth to speak.

Before he had a chance to, the front door opened, footsteps came down the hallway and Henrik entered the kitchen. He carried shopping bags in his hands.

He gave Ellen a blank look. 'What are you doing here?'

'Oh, I was just wondering how long the power cut will last.' She brushed her hair out of her face.

Henrik raised his eyebrows, then looked up at the dark ceiling lamps. He cursed under his breath. 'I'd forgotten that…'

He lifted out a milk carton from the shopping bag and scowled. 'These had better not go off.'

Daniel caught Ellen's eye. *Go*, he mouthed.

She edged around the drawer and hurried out of the kitchen. She didn't retreat to her room straight away. As the men's voices rose from behind the kitchen door, she lingered, ears pricked.

'... service equipment needs replacing,' came Daniel's voice. 'It hasn't been changed since '62, it isn't safe.'

'You think I can afford to close down the hostel for a month? This is the busiest season of the year. Our loss...'

Henrik's voice rushed on. Ellen stepped across the hallway and dashed upstairs. By the time she'd told Simon about her conversation, and what she'd overheard in the hall-way, the lights were back on.

'Don't go to the shower yet, Ellen,' her brother told her as she took her towel.

'I'm dripping with sweat, Simon.'

'I have been thinking a lot.'

'Since when do you not?'

'This is special. We are detectives now and we cannot rest until the case is solved.'

She bit her lip, swallowing the words she wanted to say, motioning at him to continue.

'I did some research last night—'

'Again?' she said before she could stop herself. Grimaced. 'Sorry.'

'I did a Google search on *Nordic Berries AB* and found an article published by *Svartjokk Kuriren* in May 2015. The company was called Svea Exports in the past, but it closed down because of a controversy. The berry pickers had to pay a lot of money to come to work here but their salary was much lower than they had been told and they earned way below the living wage. They could not pay off their debts at home or support their families and so two workers committed suicide. They were found hanging from trees in the forest.

'Persson was a project leader in Svea Exports. But he was not imprisoned and only paid a fine, and then he was allowed to start a new company: Nordic Berries.' Simon fished his mobile out of his pocket. 'The article is here, you can read it.'

He handed her the phone and watched as she scrolled down the screen.

'This article doesn't mention Persson by name,' she said.

'No,' he admitted.

'We can't jump to conclusions.'

'But we know that Persson works for Nordic Berries...'

'Simon, I'm tired. It's been a very long day and we've spoken to a lot of people. Now, I'm going to have a shower and then I'm going to rest, and you should do the same.'

'Ellen, we only have four nights and three days before we go home. I do not think we have time to rest.'

'We are not detectives, Simon! Just two teenagers pretending we are something we're not. Now please, take your socks off and wash your feet, I can smell them even from here.' Without looking her brother in the eye, Ellen stood up, flung the towel over her shoulder and left the room. She turned on the shower to max and waited for the hot water to numb her thoughts.

The image of the old woman would not leave her. She stood there, white gown swaying gently around her bony frame, imprinted on the inside of the girl's eyelids.

Ellen pushed her fist against the tiled wall. Her words to Simon ran round and round in her mind like a hamster wheel. She tried to convince herself they were true. Each time, her brother's words retaliated. Denying her, challenging her. Reminding her that she did not hate what they were doing. She loved it.

In the end, Simon won their argument again. At seven o'clock, the siblings left the hostel and walked to the Svartjokk campsite. People could be seen in the utility rooms preparing dinner, and others were queuing outside the showers. Down by the water's edge, a family were grilling hotdogs and marshmallows on sticks over an open fire. Two kids were in the water, throwing a ball between them.

'See?' Ellen whispered. 'Loads of people. Zero chance we'll pass through here unseen. Someone will tell that girl in the reception, and we will get kicked out and referred to the police...'

'Calm down, Ellen. If you stop behaving like that, we may not be seen. I know you like being here because you always participated in my Murder Mystery games at *Roliga Timmen* in school.'

Ellen scowled and kicked a stone.

No activity could be seen at the blueberry pickers' bunkhouse. All the blinds were drawn.

Simon knocked on the door this time. He clutched his notebook under his arm.

It was the same woman who answered the door. Her eyes widened in recognition.

'We would like to speak about the reindeer incident that happened yesterday,' Simon said in perfectly pronounced English. 'We wondered if you knew anything. Can we come inside?'

The woman stared from Simon to Ellen and backed away, her eyes widening, mouth gaping.

'Simon, I don't think she understands English.'

'Please, can you let us in?' her brother tried in Swedish.

'Please,' Ellen added, clasping her hands together.

The woman began closing the door. The siblings would have been left on the porch, failed again, if another woman hadn't appeared in the hallway.

'You want talk?' she asked in broken, yet confident Swedish. She was younger than the first woman, with long hair tied back into a ponytail.

'Please, just for a little bit,' Ellen said to her.

The woman whispered into her friend's ear. The older woman eyed the siblings thoughtfully, tapped her fingers against the doorframe a few times, before disappearing back inside.

'Bengt not here,' the young woman said when she'd gone.

'We don't want to speak to Bengt,' said Simon.

'No?'

'We want to speak to you,' said Ellen. 'All of you.'

'About what?'

Ellen cast an eye around the campsite. The family by the water were still grilling. Further down, she saw a boy playing with a dog. No sign of the receptionist girl, or other staff. But she was not taking any chances.

'Can we speak inside?' she asked the woman.

The woman let them in. A white hallway led straight to a kitchen further down, in which she could see people moving around. To either side of them were two narrow hallways which she assumed were dormitories. Trainers, boots and coats littered the doormat and entrance. A dank smell hung in the building, reminding Ellen of unwashed socks.

The Thai woman looked them up and down and folded her arms. 'You come early, speak with Bengt, he tell you go away.'

'Yes,' Ellen admitted. 'We wanted to speak with you but did not know Bengt would be here...' Her words died away. Under the woman's stare, she felt all her confidence, all her arguments, melt into nothing.

As if sensing her thoughts, the Thai woman continued. 'Bengt say, not speak to anyone. He say, if boy and girl want talk, I call staff.'

She took a step towards the siblings, forcing Ellen to back into the door. Ellen bit her lip. What had they expected, coming here? That just because the blueberry pickers were foreign they would hand over information on a silver plate? Nobody in the town, old or young, foreign or not, had any obligation to tell them anything. For all Ellen knew, Bengt Persson might be waiting in the kitchen or one of the bedrooms, ready to spring upon them any moment.

'Is your name Malee?' Simon asked.

It was hard to say who between Ellen and the young woman showed the most surprise.

'Suchada Sirapreesi, nickname Malee, from Udon Thani, a rural province in the middle of Thailand. You have come to Svartjokk picking berries eight summers in a row, and you started when you were twenty. That makes you twenty-eight.'

The Thai woman gaped at Simon as if he'd said he lived on the moon. She tugged at her ponytail.

Unperturbed, Simon produced his mobile phone. 'I read it in this article, about two berry-picking companies called Svea Exports and Nordic Berries. It is two years old, it says you are twenty-six here, but I just did the simple maths calculation. You work for Nordic Berries right now.'

It was the article he'd shown Ellen in the afternoon. Ellen stared at the tiny print, the letters little ants against the white screen.

'You talk here about the working conditions of the company. You were paid thirty kronor per litre, which isn't that much if it is a dry season and bad for berries. Even on a good day, you would not earn more than two hundred kronor. That would equal six thousand kronor per month at the very most. Bengt Persson does not treat you well, so if he's been up to something bad and you know about it, it is in your interest to tell us.' He lowered the phone. 'Have you heard about this incident?' He opened his rucksack and produced the newspaper cut-out from *Kuriren*. He let Malee hold it. 'Do you know if Bengt did something on Wednesday night? Did any of the workers here see something suspicious?'

Ellen folded her arms and dug her fingers into the folds of her Puma jacket. She wanted to shake her brother by the shoulders. They'd agreed to bring the newspaper article with them, but not to present it in this manner. Once again, her brother had agreed to her instructions and then discarded them the next minute.

Malee fingered the edges of the newspaper, staring blankly in front of her. For a moment, she seemed to have forgotten the siblings altogether. Then finally, she looked Simon in the eye.

'You know Bengt?'

'No,' Simon said, 'but we saw him in the forest. We were the ones who discovered the reindeer and called the police, and when we got into the police car I saw Bengt watching us.' And then, as the finishing touch to his presentation, he showed Malee the picture of Bengt in the forest.

'Why you want know this?' Malee's voice was hushed and sharp and she stared at the floor as she spoke. She tugged at her ponytail so vigorously Ellen thought the whole thing might come off.

Ellen glanced towards the kitchen. The people there were watching them. 'Can we speak somewhere more private?' she whispered.

The woman followed her gaze and nodded. She led them down the hallway to the right and knocked on the fourth and last door. 'Hello,' she called.

There was a muffled reply from inside.

Malee opened the door and motioned for them to follow. It was a bedroom with a bunk bed in each corner. A middle-aged woman with short hair sat on the bottom bunk in the far-right corner. When the siblings sat down opposite her she cringed and dug her nails into the mattress. Ellen noticed they were rimmed with blue. Crow's feet sat at the corners of her eyes. One of her eyebrows appeared to have been singed, with only a few hairs remaining.

'Sunan,' Malee said, and spoke quietly to the woman in Thai.

The older woman clasped her hands together and brought them to her face. Her voice was hushed, her words running rapidly into one another. Her right foot twitched nervously.

'Sunan was out on Wednesday night. She saw some scary, come back here very frighten.'

Malee sat down beside the woman and whispered in Sunan's ear. The older woman responded, her face tense as she spoke.

'She was in forest,' Malee translated. 'She was make a phone call home to her children. She stand on little forest road. A car turn onto track and she hide behind the trees. It passed her and stop further down. A man got out, he take things out of car.'

'What kind of things?' Simon said.

Malee asked, but the older woman shrugged. 'She not know.'

'What about the man,' Ellen's brother continued. 'Did she see his face? Was he tall, short?'

'Sunan did not see his head at all, because he bend forward. Only see his body. She say he look like Phi Hua Khat, headless ghost holding his head in his hand. He so scary, she ran away and not look again.'

'There's no such thing as ghosts,' Simon said. 'Especially not ghosts driving cars.' A muscle by his eye twitched.

Ellen gave him a pointed look. 'What happened next?' she said.

'Sunan come back here, tell me everything. She say we not tell Bengt. Bengt cannot know she bike at night.'

'Bike?' Simon repeated. 'She biked all the way to the forest? Why?'

Malee eyed the old woman. 'Sunan make phone call.' Her voice was guarded when she spoke.

'Why bike so far just to make a phone call? Couldn't she just call here in the bunkhouse?' He crossed his arms. 'You are hiding information.'

Ellen held up a hand at her brother to silence him. After all his efforts to win Malee's trust, was he really going to break it just as quickly? 'Do you make these phone calls often, Sunan?' she said softly.

'Two to three time a week,' Malee translated.

'And is that all you do? Or do you have another reason for coming to the forest?'

Sunan was silent. She glanced at the younger woman, muttered a few words, defiance on her face. '*Mai chai*,' she said. 'No,' Malee translated.

'Are you sure?' When further silence followed, Ellen asked another question. 'Did the ghost look like Bengt?'

Sunan shook her head again. 'Bengt tall and fat.' She motioned with her arms to emphasis Bengt's width. 'This man tall, not fat.'

'Did you see any plastic bags in the car?' Simon asked. 'Or antlers?'

Both women looked at them with confusion. 'Antlers?' Malee repeated.

'Horns.' Ellen gestured with her hands, putting them to her head. 'Animals have horns on their heads, but for reindeer they are called antlers.'

'Ah.' The younger woman's eyes lit up in understanding, and she explained to the older woman.

Sunan frowned and shook her head vigorously. 'No, no, no.'

Ellen assumed that answered their questions. 'Did you see any blood?'

'I don't know.'

'Did he see you?'

The old woman stilled. She looked straight into Ellen's eyes. 'Don't swing your foot to look for splinter.' She spoke in English as if through a mouthful of hair, drawing out the words, over-pronouncing the 'er' in 'splinter'. Then she exchanged words with Malee.

Malee's smile was apologetic. 'She want to know if you are police? Or police children? She does not understand why children come asking her questions. She worry.'

'What colour was the car?' Simon asked, as if she hadn't spoken.

Sunan addressed them in English again. 'Wall have ear, door have eye.'

'She did not answer my question.'

'Look.' Malee sighed exasperatedly. 'Most ghosts in Thailand are good, kind… Very popular, they in TV show, children love them…' She swallowed. 'But see one like this, come without warning, it means they want something. Phi Hua Khat never want anything good.' She pulled her hands into her knees. 'Everyone know it is bad sign. Talk about it is bad more.'

'We are doing an investigation and we need all the information we can find,' Simon said. 'Did Bengt find out about the man/ghost?'

This time, Malee answered without translating the question to Sunan. 'He saw Sunan was upset and made her tell why.'

'By force?'

Malee's silence spoke for itself. Then, without warning, she stood up. 'I think it is best you leave.'

Simon blinked. He began to protest.

'We have tell you everything. You cannot stay here any more. Is not safe.' Malee went and opened the door. 'Go, now.'

'Please give us your phone number,' Simon said. He thrust his book and pen at her. 'In case you think of anything else to tell us.'

For a moment, Malee looked like she wouldn't take them. Then, her expression softened, and she scribbled a number down at the bottom of the page. She was just about to show them out when the older woman spoke up. Malee turned to her, asked her a question as if to confirm what the older woman had said. Then she turned to the siblings. 'It was red.'

'What was?' Ellen asked.

'The car. Sunan just remember, she tell me.'

Simon took the notebook back from her and noted the detail down. *'Kob khun krup,'* he said to the women.

Malee's eyes widened in surprise. She opened and closed her mouth, body frozen.

Sunan smiled at the boy. She returned the words, hands moving to her chin in prayer.

'What did that mean?' Ellen said once they'd left the campsite and started back on the main road towards the town centre. 'Khobbun...'

'*Kob khun krup*,' Simon corrected. 'Thank you, in Thai. A man says *krup*, a woman says *ka*.'

'You picked that up from the internet?'

Simon didn't answer. His gaze had grown distant. 'I think the man she saw was Virtanen.'

'We cannot say for sure...'

'He was tall.'

'Virtanen isn't the only tall man on earth.'

'But she confirmed it wasn't Bengt, which means we have two suspects, and I think they know one another. Here is what I think happened. The killer opened the back door, one of the heads must have rolled out of the bag during the drive and fallen on the ground. Sunan saw him pick up the head, his own must have been blocked by a tree, because the midnight sun was out and it would not have been dark. And it means one more thing.' He looked at his sister. 'We have a witness.'

Ellen scowled. She was about to tell him she doubted a policeman even as brusque as Virtanen would betray his profession like that, when something vibrated inside her pocket. Mum, she thought in alarm, but when she pulled the phone out an unknown number flashed on the screen. 'Hello?'

'This is Ellen Blind?'

Her heart leaped to her mouth. 'Yes?'

'You wanted to see me.'

She suppressed a laugh. That was a severe understatement. 'Is this Per-Anders Thomasson?'

'Meet me tomorrow,' the reindeer herder said. He gave her a time and place, and then he hung up. She remained with her phone to her ear for a few moments, before letting out a deep breath.

'Tomorrow,' she whispered. 'Tomorrow...'

Hidden in the Railway Man's Hut

That night, as she lay with her head under the pillow to block out the light, Ellen's thoughts drifted back home, to Tyrevik. It was pouring with rain outside and she was sitting with her brother on the floor in the lounge. She was fourteen, he was eleven; she spent most of her time analysing text messages from her classmates and figuring out whether a boy in her class liked her or *liked* her; Simon spent most of his time trying to convince her she was wasting hers.

'Solve this mystery with me,' he kept telling her, and prodded her shoulder with his pencil.

'I don't want to solve your mystery.'

'I have designed it especially for you.'

'I thought you'd stopped doing those.'

'I created one hundred mysteries. I only got to present thirty-three at *Roliga Timmen*.'

'You were only copying Cluedo games at *Roliga Timmen*.'

'Only fifty of them were Cluedo games. The rest, I designed on my own, and they are more advanced.'

'So you thought you would force me to do the rest of them?'

'Yep.'

Ellen rolled her eyes. 'You know I hate maths.'

'This isn't maths. It is logic.'

'Well, then, I hate logic too!'

'That is illogical. No one can truly dislike logic.'

'Try me.'

Her brother pushed his notebook across the floor to her. 'Take a look at this story.'

She read the loopy text. Her eyes widened.

A rich family lived in a round house. One evening after dinner, their mother was found dead in the bedroom. The daughter said she was playing with her dolls. The son said he was playing outside in the garden. The maid said she was dusting corners. The butler said he was watching the son. And the chef said he was baking the pies. Who killed the mother?

Automatically, Ellen looked to the open doorway leading into the hall. She could just make out the door frame leading into the kitchen, which lay just next to the lounge. Their parents' voices could be heard from there, bickering.

'Simon, where on earth did you get this from?'

'I told you I made it up myself.'

Ellen raised an eyebrow. She drummed her fingers.

'I found them on the internet but I made adaptions.'

'So what is the point of this?'

'To create and solve a mystery ourselves. It will be like Lasse and Maja but for adults. Now give me an answer to the riddle.'

Ellen was about to shoot the book back at him, but did as he asked. She frowned. 'It's obviously the maid.'

'Why?'

'You can't dust corners in a round house.'

'Very good, Ellen, very good. But what about the chef?'

'What about him?'

'Why would he be baking pies after dinner?'

'Maybe he was making them for the next day?'

'It is still a bad alibi and sounds suspicious to me.'

A trace of a smile flitted across Ellen's lips, but she hid it by cupping her chin in her hand.

'Why haven't you mentioned the father?' she said.

'Ah.' Simon said.

'What do you mean, ah?'

'Why do you think I didn't mention the father?'

'Because you forgot? Because he is innocent? Because he discovered the body?'

'What motivation would the father have for killing the mother?'

Ellen shrugged. 'I don't know…' Her gaze flitted up to the doorway. The arguing in the kitchen had ceased. 'Maybe they didn't like each other.'

'Or maybe because of inheritance.'

'As in getting the money?' Ellen pulled a hand through her hair. 'I'm still not convinced about the daughter, though. No one can confirm she stayed in the room, she could have crept down and killed the mother with… I don't know, a candlestick.' She met her brother's eye. 'You haven't even said what the murder weapon was.'

Simon grinned at her.

'What?' she grumbled.

'You are enjoying this just as much as I am.'

She shrugged. 'I just pointed this out because you missed it. And why does the daughter have to play with dolls, that's sexist.'

'It is fun to find out mysteries about people.'

Ellen watched as her mother strode out of the kitchen and left through the front door. She shrugged again. 'I guess it depends.' Camilla was probably going to water the plants at the front. She always did that when she was angry and almost always ended up drowning the poor things.

'Normal people are so confusing and impossible to understand,' Simon said. 'In mystery games you decide in what ways they are confusing, so maybe if one solves a hundred mysteries, one becomes better at understanding normal people.'

Chameleon, Ellen thought. Camilla might have aimed that word at Granddad, but now she was the one behaving like a chameleon, having all these arguments with Dad and then acting as if nothing had happened.

Perhaps there was some truth in what Simon was saying. Creating all these theories about fictional characters, there was control in that. You could decide what was real or not, what was a lie and what was truth, in what ways people behaved like chameleons and why they did it.

It stirred something in her, a mixture of anticipation and curiosity, and something verging on delight.

Per-Anders Thomasson arrived at the train-station car park at nine thirty. He drove a battered Saab, steel grey, with a Sami flag sticker on the back window.

He wound down the window and poked his head out. 'Ellen and Simon?'

The man in front of Ellen matched the voice on the phone. His face was pale, red-brown hair receding on his scalp, which was smooth and pristine like an egg. His eyes were a neutral grey, sunken, framed by shadows, hidden behind thick, dark eyebrows. The kind of face which melted into the surroundings if you passed it on the street, that you forgot before you even set eyes on it. His gaze, though, stuck with you. An invisible line fired from his irises and hit her between the eyes, hauling her in.

He beckoned to them. 'Get in.'

Ellen rode shotgun, Simon taking the seat behind her.

'Thank you for agreeing to see us.'

The man shrugged.

'I expect it's not often you take strangers out to your lands like this.'

'It's not my land. It is its own. I borrow what I need and give back.'

'Oh.' Ellen licked her lips. 'I tried to call you several times... I expect you've been very busy.'

He grunted.

'I'm sorry about the reindeer. It must have been very hard for you.'

'It's as it is.'

This man was impassive enough to make a stone seem emotional. Ellen watched the river pass under them as they crossed the bridge onto Nattavaara road. 'Where are you taking us?'

'Depends on what you want to know.'

'What does that mean?'

'I could show you the house where your grandfather was born. I could show you the care home where your great-grandmother spent her last years. I could take you to the calf marking by my house.' A moment's pause. 'I think your father wanted me to show you your roots.'

Ellen raised an eyebrow. 'You spoke to my father?'

'He called me. To tell me you might try to get in touch while you were here.'

'So that's why you said yes on the phone yesterday.'

Not a single muscle in Per-Anders's face twitched.

Ellen leaned her head against her headrest. Another secret. What had her father ever told her that was true? She shifted on her seat. 'How do you know my dad?'

'I met him at the funeral.'

Marit Blind's funeral. No Sami had been present at Granddad's burial. 'So, you exchanged numbers or something?'

'I gave your father my phone number if he ever wanted to speak. This was the first time he's called.'

'Did you know my great-grandmother?'

'Everyone in Purnuvaare knows one another.'

'What was she like?'

Per-Anders shifted his grip on the steering wheel. 'She saw people for what they were, and treated them accordingly. I didn't know her very well; she kept to herself a lot, but my father knew her better. He was best friends with Lars-Erik, before he left. It seemed to me Marit had a big heart. There was always a sorrow hanging over her. I think, the rest of her life, she pined for her son.'

Ellen nodded, her face grave. 'She died only four months after him.'

'It affected your father too, when he was here.' Per-Anders glanced at her. 'He carried the same sorrow. Seemed conflicted. Torn.'

Ellen picked at a thumbnail, biting her lip. Again, the image of her father waving her off in Kristinehamn floated up before her eyes. His expression seemed almost tortured; unsure whether to keep quiet or speak out... about what? Suppressing a sigh, she buried her hand in her lap. 'Dad never mentioned you.'

'He wasn't up here very long. It was a rushed visit. That was an intense day for him.'

'Could you show us the lake where the reindeer were poisoned?'

Ellen whipped her head around. Simon did not look at her. His gaze was on Per-Anders: focused, decided.

'Why do you want to see the lake?' the reindeer herder asked calmly.

'I want to see the place where the reindeer were poisoned, so I can find out more clues. I'm investigating the crime.'

Per-Anders's expression was guarded. He glanced at Ellen. 'You did not say this on the phone.'

Ellen looked down at her hands as heat rushed to her cheeks. In the voicemail, she'd only said who they were and that they'd discovered the heads of his reindeer in the forest. How could she possibly have mentioned Simon's plans?

'Simon doesn't mean to be so blunt,' she said quickly. 'I'm sorry. I've told him to stop treating it like a murder mystery.' He must have forgotten what she'd told him at breakfast: don't be too direct. She'd let him ask the questions at the bunkhouse, but this situation was different. Per-Anders was the owner of the stolen reindeer, he would feel his animals' wounds as keenly as if they were his own. If Simon was too direct, firing off the questions straight from the paper, he could come across as uncaring.

She turned around to look at him, searching for an understanding in those bright, earnest eyes. As the morning sunlight sliced through the trees and hit the car, Simon's irises flashed, switching from cloud grey to dazzling silver.

He leaned forward between the two front seats, his hair brushing against his sister's shoulder. 'What happened to the bodies after they were decapitated?'

Per-Anders glanced at him in the rear-view mirror. 'They were put in a hut not far from the lake.'

'I want to see both the hut and the lake.'

Per-Anders slowed the car down. He pulled in at a parking space on the side of the road, turned the engine off, pulled down the window, and twisted in his seat to face Simon.

'What is your interest in this case? I know you discovered the bodies, but it's in the hands of the police now.'

Simon's jaw tightened. 'I think the police are hiding something.' He explained about the flies, about Constable Virtanen's lack of interest and how he had hit him, how the sergeant had forced him to delete his pictures but he'd secretly sent them to Ellen.

'Virtanen's behaviour is very suspicious and I want to know how much he knows,' he finished.

'Why?' the reindeer herder asked.

'Because it's wrong how they're treating this and it should be put right. Lots of animals have died. I like animals.'

Per-Anders surprised Ellen then by smiling. The first open, genuine smile he'd given them since they met. It made him look ten years younger. Then his expression grew serious again and his eyes fixed on the road.

'The police are collecting the bodies from the hut this afternoon.'

'Take us there,' Simon said. He met his sister's gaze for a second. 'Please.'

Ellen wished Per-Anders would say no. But the man simply nodded and started the engine, as if that had been his plan all along. She hoped he didn't notice her unease.

They stopped only ten minutes' drive from the killing site, on another forest track delving into the trees from the road.

Ellen shrank into her seat. She only got out when Per-Anders, without a word, opened the door for her. She glanced around as she emerged. For all she knew, it could have been the same track. There were the roots, shimmying through earth, weed and grass. There were the blueberry bushes, the spruce branches hanging over the track. Sunlight cut through the pines from the right, a thousand yellow knives slicing the air.

She pulled her Puma jacket tighter around her and folded her arms. There was a chill in the air that hadn't been there the previous mornings. 'What is this hut you're taking us to?'

'It was one of the lodges for the railway workers who built the first train tracks here in the 1800s. From Kiruna to Gävle, Svartjokk to Luleå. Connecting north to south, forest to coast. They slept in huts like this one to be close to work.'

'So you just came across the bodies by accident?' Accident. She regretted how offhand the word sounded.

'No.' The reindeer herder locked the car and started walking down the path. 'I knew they were there.'

'How?'

'My gut told me.'

After ten minutes, the sound of a stream reached their ears. They ducked under a spruce branch, pushed through juniper bushes which grew over the track, and arrived at a small clearing in the forest. A steep rise loomed ahead of them. Pines and spruces formed a ridge on the top, and below them was a sheer, thirty-metre drop to rocky ground. Gushing over the edge of the ridge was a narrow tail of water. It formed a pool at the bottom, no more than an arm's length wide, and tumbled through the blueberry bushes and bracken.

Tucked in at the foot of the rise, where the ground was less steep and covered in moss, was a small hut. It had a grass roof and a porch that once must have been painted white, but was now ash grey, with flakes of paint peeling off the wood. The wooden boards for the walls were rotten, and weeds were winding their way through the gaps. A birch sapling had even nestled its way in between the planks. A few metres away from the hut was a stump for chopping wood. The face of the log was stained black.

A foul smell curled on the air, mingling with the dank scent of moss, dew and mud. Putrid, like that of the glade, except this time it was at least ten times as strong.

Ellen made a gagging sound and covered her nose and mouth with her shirt.

'We think the animals have lain here since Tuesday,' Per-Anders said, watching her. 'They're bloated and have started to release gases. I wouldn't recommend going inside.'

'I want to see them.' Simon took a step towards the hut. He also held his shirt to his face, but he showed no sign of being affected by the stench.

'You will learn nothing from going inside that I can't tell you.'

'I asked to see the bodies and I won't leave until I have seen them.'

The reindeer herder watched Simon carefully, then he nodded and led the way to the hut. Ellen hesitated, but when Simon looked over his shoulder at her, she relented and followed them.

'Only take a quick look,' Per-Anders warned. 'If you're squeamish, it's best to look away.' His gaze was on Ellen.

She straightened her back and put on what she hoped was a brave face. 'I'm fine.'

Per-Anders opened the door.

At first, all Ellen could see was darkness. Then her eyes adjusted and she made out the pale, bloated shapes of animal carcasses. Black liquid oozed out of their behinds, their skins had ruptured and something white wriggled in the putrid flesh.

Maggots.

Ellen threw up. She didn't even have time to turn around.

There was a creaking as Per-Anders shut the door. His boots came into view and then a hand touched her shoulder.

'Let's get away from the stink.' The reindeer herder guided her away from the hut and had her sit on a stone by the stream.

'My son was just like you, when we came here yesterday.' Per-Anders knelt on his haunches and pulled a stalk of grass through his fingers. 'He sat here ten minutes before he was ready to move on. I've never seen his face that pale.'

Drops of dew came off the grass and settled on the man's fingertip. He smoothed the drops out between his fingers, then looked over his shoulder. 'You can see where the bodies have been dragged, from the stump to the door.'

He pointed towards the hut. Now, Ellen made out black marks like ski-tracks in the earth.

'Four days,' she said, and surprised herself at how weak her voice was. 'How come the police haven't been here yet?'

'They were supposed to collect the bodies yesterday. For reasons I don't know, they postponed. It happens.'

Ellen thought of Constable Virtanen and her fingers tensed. She looked up to the ridge. The sun turned the sky between the trees yellow.

'They really got the reindeer down this slope?' she said. 'Surely they didn't drag them...'

Simon, who'd walked up to them and stood digging the heel of his shoe into the ground, fidgeted at her word choice. She could just imagine what he was thinking: *'They' is unspecific and suggests there were several killers and we have evidence from a witness that there was only one person present. Furthermore, 'they' doesn't specify gender.*

'They' was gentler than 'killer'. It put the crime at a distance, made it less real.

Per-Anders looked at the stalk in his fingers. 'The animals weren't dead.' He gazed over his shoulder to the ridge. 'They were led down here alive.' Dropping the stalk, he rummaged inside his jacket pockets. 'I found this by the lake.'

In his hand was a piece of cord. 'They were led down here with a rope around their necks. Their brains would have been addled by chlorine, so they would not have put up any resistance.' A mosquito landed on his lip. He pinched it between his fingers. Blood oozed out of the grey body, wetting the tip of his thumb. He wiped the thumb clean on the moss.

'It would have taken a strong man, or several strong men, to lead the reindeer down here and haul their bodies inside the hut,' Simon said. His face was hidden behind his notebook, and he tapped his pen against the edge of the book.

Per-Anders nodded. 'The carcass of a full-grown reindeer weighs up to three hundred kilos.'

'Did you see any dead flies?'

Per-Anders frowned. 'Flies?'

'I found them in the neck wounds of the heads,' Ellen's brother said. 'Little black dots stuck in the flesh, every single one dead.' He tapped his pen against the book again. 'I believe the chlorine must have killed them.'

Per-Anders looked to the carcasses. 'Maggots are the only creatures still alive in this area.' His face was sad.

'Maggots can survive a relatively high concentration of chlorine if it's through indirect exposure,' said Simon.

'Will you take us to the lake?' Ellen asked. She didn't want to stay by the hut any longer than necessary.

Shadows moved in Per-Anders's eyes. He rose. 'I will take you there.'

He held out his hand and helped Ellen up. His grip was

a lot stronger than she'd expected. The movement caused her head to spin and she gripped his arm to steady herself.

'Are you sure you want to continue?'

'Yes.' The firmness of her voice surprised her. 'You agreed to take us here, remember?' She caught Simon's eye. 'We're not leaving.'

Per-Anders's jaw seemed to tighten. Then it relaxed, and his face went blank.

Without another word he led the way up the ridge.

The climb was challenging. There was a tiny animal path through the bracken winding up the right, less steep side of the rise, but it was almost invisible beneath the underbrush and Ellen tripped several times. As if that wasn't enough the ground was still wet with dew and her trainers grew damp within minutes. By the time they reached the top she was sweating. She took off her jacket and tied it around her waist.

Then she gasped in wonder.

The lake at the end of the slope was shaped like a figure eight, with an extra tail curling in around the trees. Its right side was veiled in the shadow of the forest, the left side bathed in sunlight. Stretched out between the trees, not far from the waterline, was a tape similar to that the police constable had used to block off access to the glade. It flashed in the morning light, seeming more like a ribbon of electricity than plastic.

'I didn't realise the lake was so small.'

'It is Nilajaure,' Per-Anders said. His breathing was normal and he wasn't sweating at all.

'I read that many place names in Sapmi are named after people,' Simon said. He copied Ellen, tying his Adidas jacket round his waist.

'Lars-Nila Thomasson,' Per-Anders said.

'Your ancestor?' asked Ellen.

'The first reindeer herder to settle in Purnuvaare.

1786.' The lines in the man's face deepened. 'Two days ago, this whole area stank with chlorine. It is not so bad now.'

He led the way down the slope.

Ellen walked alongside him. 'How long will it take to sanitise the lake?'

Per-Anders grunted. 'The Natural Environment Agency haven't been clear on that point.'

'What have they done so far?'

The reindeer herder took a large step over a fallen branch. 'They've already dredged the lake at its mouth. The mud has been covered with cloth and a layer of sand to thicken it. Eighty per cent of the lake's bottom has also been covered with a sediment which stops the bleach from leaking into the rest of the lake and spreading down the streams. But bleach has already done damage. None of the villages in the area can use their tap water.' His expression hardened. 'It might stay like this for six weeks.'

Ellen imagined how her mother would cope that long without tap water. Camilla would have packed their belongings and had them evacuated within a week. 'How did you discover the pollution?'

Per-Anders slowed his pace. 'Reindeer were missing. We had rounded them up for calf marking and were about sixty animals short. We retraced their tracks; we knew they'd been around the lake for a few days. We came and… there they all were.' He gestured around them. 'From a distance, it looked like they were sleeping.' He shifted his feet, blueberry sprigs snapped.

Ellen waited for him to continue. When he didn't, she stepped over the fallen branch, coming closer to him. 'Then what happened?'

'We took care of them.' He nodded to himself as he

spoke. 'The police were taking too long. We hauled them onto trailers ourselves. It took all five of us.'

'Five?'

'Me, my brother, my son, my brother's sons.' He looked out towards the lake. 'It was so quiet, not a single waxwing or sparrow. There were dead crows on the ground that must have died after eating the carrion. There were foxes, and ferrets, even a badger.' He pulled his hand over his nose. 'It felt like we were the only beings alive on earth.'

Ellen looked around her. They couldn't hear the stream from here. The lake was as blank as a mirror. Not a single ring from water insects stirred its surface. From above, she felt the stare of the pines. There was no wind, the air was still; the crowns of the pines glared down at her, motionless. The forest felt oddly crowded. Not because of the trees, but because of them: Ellen, Simon, Per-Anders. They made Nilajaure feel crowded. They were intruders.

'And yet,' Per-Anders continued, oblivious to Ellen's discomfort, 'things are growing here.' He bent to the ground. 'Here is cloudberry. They will be ripe for picking within a week.'

Ellen and Simon bent down beside him. Peeking up through the moss were bright orange berries.

'Cloudberries are known as the gold of the north,' Simon stated.

'But surely they will be inedible now?' said Ellen.

'Perhaps.' Per-Anders straightened. 'But it shows the ground hasn't died. The land hasn't given up.'

'Do you have any idea who could have done this? Anyone with a reason to hurt you?'

Per-Anders gave a wry chuckle. 'I've angered many people throughout the years.'

'But to go to the trouble...' Ellen gazed back up the

ridge. 'Dragging the reindeer up and down that hill, planting the heads at that *seit…*' She looked back to the reindeer herder. 'There was purpose to this crime. It was planned.' She looked at the lake. 'They knew this was a regular watering hole for your reindeer. They polluted this lake for a reason. They wanted to kill your herd.'

She held the reindeer herder's gaze. He stood perfectly still. 'Who do you know who would want to destroy your life that way?'

Per-Anders didn't answer straight away. He began walking towards the tape strung up between the trees. 'Parts of the herd have gone missing before. Two or three animals at a time, gone without warning. Mostly in winter. One or two weeks later they were found, dismembered, disposed of in carrier bags. This was two years ago.' He stopped by the tape, waved off a mosquito drawing near. 'Then there were five. Six. Gone in springtime, just before the calves were born. Again, dismembered in bags.' He turned and looked up the ridge. 'Now it seems all those killings were a rehearsal.'

'Did you find out who did it? The other killings, I mean?'

Per-Anders put his hands in his pockets. 'I had my suspicions. I made them known. But it never works pointing fingers around here. People only hate you more for it.'

'Who did you suspect?'

'The scooter tracks and the blood drops led me to Kajava. It's a village, not three miles from here.'

'I did not see it on the map,' Simon said.

'You wouldn't,' said Per-Anders. 'Not on an ordinary road map. Really, it's an outlier to another village, Björkliden, just off the main road. To get to Kajava you have to go through Björkliden down a gravel road, about five minutes. It's just seven houses in a circle. Can't be more than twenty people living there.'

'And the police? What did they say?'

'Said too many days had passed between the time of death and discovery. If it's more than five days, they drop it. They never spoke to the Kajava people, or those of Björkliden. Those villages protect one another.'

'Do you know Bengt Persson?' Simon asked.

Per-Anders frowned. 'How do you know that name?'

'We saw him watching us when we'd called the police,' Ellen explained. 'The police identified him.'

'He is from Kajava.' Per-Anders rubbed his forehead with a knuckle.

'Does he dislike you?'

'Everyone in Kajava and Björkliden has a reason to hate me.'

'Why?'

'Our families do not agree. There have been disputes, over the reindeer.'

'What kind of disputes?'

'Reindeer intruding on their land. Eating crops. Disturbing the peace. Every day I get phone calls. Angry voices. Threatening to shoot my animals if I don't move them within the hour.'

'I'm sorry,' Ellen said.

'It's how it is.'

'Do you think the Kajava people could have done this?' Simon asked.

'I cannot say.'

'Have you told the police?'

'I have rung the police. I have contacted the National Environment Agency and the Agency for Damage to Wildlife.

I am waiting for the Sami Council to grant me compensation. There is nothing else I can do.'

Ellen nudged a blueberry sprig with her foot. 'I wish we could help. We're just two teenagers asking questions. We don't *know* anything, we haven't really *found* anything.'

'You have helped,' the reindeer herder said.

Ellen looked at him.

'You have come looking for truth. That is more than I can say of most people here.' Per-Anders looked at the ridge. 'Truth angers people, even though they need it. Perhaps it is because they need it.' He rubbed the ridge of his nose. 'There is too little of it here.'

Mark of a Reindeer

Shafts of sunlight slanted through the pines as the three returned to the car. The heat had picked up, the air was hazier, though not oven-thick as it had been on Thursday. It seemed to push them out of the forest, and as Ellen turned to look back the way they'd come, the pine and oak shadows crossed over themselves, forming a dark door. Closing her off.

'Are you interested in seeing the calf marking?' Per-Anders asked. 'My family will be there.'

'I don't want to feel like we're intruding...' Ellen began.

Per-Anders waved her words away. 'No. More people should see it. It's my daughter's favourite part of the year. Besides, I told them you would come.'

'I guess we have no choice then.'

'You always have a choice,' said Simon. 'You can say yes or no.'

'And what do you say, Simon?' Ellen asked. She was aware of Per-Anders watching them.

'Yes, yes, definitely yes. I saw a documentary once about the life of a reindeer herder, and there was a scene when they were calf marking. It will be more interesting to see it in real life.' Simon smiled at the Sami man. 'Thank you, Per-Anders.'

Per-Anders smiled back.

Purnuvaare did not have the feel of a village. Apart from a small local food store called Hanna's Livs, there were no shops. There were no streets as such, either. The country road cut through the neighbourhood, ending at the driveway of the last house. The houses lay scattered on either side, as if they'd been randomly dropped there.

'This road wasn't here fifty years ago,' Per-Anders explained. 'It was all gravel, small roads you could ski and sledge-ride on in winter. Asphalt is no good for that.'

As he said so, they turned off the main road onto a gravel one. It wound its way up to a large red building sitting on a slight crest. Cars and quad bikes crowded the driveway below the rise.

'This is the village hall,' Per-Anders said as he pulled up. 'It's where we have our annual Christmas market. The calf marking is taking place in the large pen on the other side.'

He hadn't parked the car. The engine was still rumbling.

'You aren't coming with us?' Ellen asked.

'I will, when I have left the car at home. I will join you later.' He caught her eye. 'All my family are there, they will welcome you.'

Ellen watched the dust rise as he turned and headed back towards the asphalt road.

'It looks like the village hall in Tyrevik,' Simon said.

Turning, Ellen looked at the red building watching them from the crest. It was made up of two rectangular buildings, and together they formed the letter 'T'. *Purnuvaare*

Bygdegård was inscribed in black on a varnished wooden sign above the porch. The letters had been written with a heated poker pen, burned into the wood. It reminded her of the craft classes she'd had in primary school.

'Do you hear that, Ellen?' Simon said, excitement in his eyes. 'There must be at least a hundred reindeer here!'

Ellen had been aware of the noise as soon they stepped out of the car. Now, she paid proper attention to it.

Beyond the *bygdegård* came a chorus of bleating. Loud, high-pitched, similar to that of sheep or goat. Chiming above the bleats, hollow and metallic, was the sound of bells.

The siblings moved towards the sound.

A large pen lay on the other side of the hall. It was partly amongst the trees, partly out in sunlight. A sea of brown moved inside it.

Reindeer. So many reindeer they were impossible to count. They trotted in circles around the pen, clockwise, forming a massive whirlpool with their bodies. As the siblings watched, one of the animals in the middle made a turn and the whole herd turned with it, causing a ripple effect through the bodies. Dust rose from the ground churned by hooves, bleats and bell chimes clashed against each other in broken rhythms.

People stood lined up against the fence of the pen. They were perfectly still, and it was impossible to hear any talk through the bleating. As Ellen watched, one person stepped through the fence into the pen. Judging by the blonde plaits hanging down over the herder's shoulders from under the cap, Ellen assumed it was a woman. She waded through the animals, arms raised, holding a coiled rope in her right hand. The animals didn't seem to notice her until she made a lunge to the right. Then, the sea of reindeer parted itself. One group swerved to the left, the other to the right, regrouping at the far side of the pen.

The woman approached the left group. Slower this time, drifting rather than walking. Ellen made out smaller animals. Calves, hiding behind their mothers. They tapped their hooves against the ground.

Just as the herd were about to scatter again, the woman sidestepped. She came up close to a calf at the back, held out her arms so he couldn't rejoin the group, sidestepping until he had no more room to move. Then she threw the rope over the head of the animal and pulled tight.

The calf gave a loud bleat. It struggled against the rope, tried to walk away. The woman stumbled along with it at first, vanished from sight as the herd regrouped around her. Then she slipped through a funnel at the side, which led to a smaller pen further down, dragging the calf behind her. In the smaller pen, it tried to get away again, but the woman planted her feet squarely on the ground and leaned back, as if reclining in an invisible armchair.

The calf sank to its knees.

The woman straddled it and took out a knife. She bent down by its head, as if whispering to it, stroking its neck. Then with one swift movement, she made a cut in the animal's ear.

The calf let out a high-pitched, drawn-out bleat.

Ellen drew her breath in. 'That's got to hurt! Is it bleeding?'

The woman made a second cut on the animal's earlobe. Then she patted its neck and stepped off. The calf shook its head, then slowly stood up and returned to the other calves in the pen. Ellen assumed they'd already been marked.

The reindeer herder wiped dust off her face and turned to the people by the fence.

She wasn't quite a woman. A girl, maybe two or three years older than Ellen. A grin crept onto her face. She said something, but her voice was drowned out by the thundering hooves from the big pen.

Another herder stepped through the fence. A boy, Ellen saw, as he turned to the crowd. The girl joined him, and together they moved towards the reindeer.

It became clear that the girl was more experienced. The boy's movements weren't as swift and subtle, he made big efforts to get hold of the reindeer rather than drifting towards them, and he did not have as much control with the rope. He needed several more tries before he finally got a calf. Once he had it on the ground, though, he was as gentle and efficient as the girl. In no time the calf was back on its feet, shaking its head slightly, but otherwise all right.

'Ellen, Simon,' a voice said from behind.

Ellen turned. Per-Anders appeared around the corner of the *bygdegård*. His feet made hardly a sound against the gravel.

'Let me introduce you to my family.' He walked down the slope without looking to see if they would follow.

Ellen caught Simon's eye. His face said nothing. They followed the man without a word.

The people by the pen turned and looked as Per-Anders passed them. They offered no words of greeting, or even smiles. Instead they nodded, faces impassive. When the siblings passed, they stared.

The girl and boy who'd earmarked the calves stood by the big pen together with a tall man. The boy and man had their backs to the siblings, and the girl's face was visible between their shoulders.

'… come autumn, I'll be bringing down bulls,' Ellen heard the girl say.

'Your brother will have a hard time catching up,' said the man.

'It's not fair to compare!' the boy said. 'I bet in two years' time my herd will be twice as large as yours.'

'I'd like to see you try,' the girl said. Then she noticed Per-Anders. 'Dad,' she said, and pushed past her brother and the man. The two of them turned around.

'So you're here at last,' the man said. He looked Per-Anders up and down. He had the same deep, penetrating eyes and pale, flat face. 'You should have come earlier.'

'I am here now,' Per-Anders said. He motioned to the siblings. 'This is Ellen and Simon. Ellen and Simon, this is my brother Mattias.'

The man gave the siblings a long, hard look.

Per-Anders moved on. 'This is my son, Erik.'

'Hi.' The boy's voice was husky, his eyes not as deeply set as the men's, and his face was narrower, more arrow-shaped. He nodded at the siblings and gave them a friendly smile, revealing pointy teeth.

'This is my daughter, Vera.'

The girl had her father's eyes and jawline, the same oval-shaped face. She folded her arms and looked the siblings squarely in the face. Simon fidgeted under her gaze.

'You took them to the hut,' Mattias said quietly.

'Ellen and Simon discovered the heads. They are Lars-Erik Blind's grandchildren.'

Per-Anders's brother turned his gaze back to Ellen. 'How old are you?'

'Seventeen.'

'Why did it take seventeen years for you to get here?'

'I... I don't know, my dad...'

'Let her be, Mattias.' Per-Anders put a hand on his brother's shoulder. He scanned the crowd. 'Where is Maja?'

'At the grill.' Erik jerked his head towards the bottom

of the slope. 'Smells like sausages will be ready soon.' He grinned.

Per-Anders nodded. 'Make sure Ellen and Simon get something to eat.' He turned to his brother. 'A word?'

Mattias grunted and led the way off into the trees.

A heavy silence settled between the youngsters. Ellen shifted her feet. With all the noise from the reindeer it was difficult to focus. Her thoughts scattered around like the animals. She tried catching the other girl's eye, but Vera seemed to pretend she wasn't there, looking everywhere but at Ellen's face. Her own face was like slate.

With the brother, Erik, it was the opposite. When Ellen met his eye he held it. He cleared his throat and leaned in slightly towards Ellen as he spoke. 'Did you get here by train?'

'Yes. With the *Inlandsbana*. And your dad gave us a lift here.'

'Huh.' Erik's expression stiffened slightly. 'Father was quite mysterious about it, you know. Didn't tell us who he was taking to the lake, or why.' He smiled wryly. 'It's like you're a surprise he got for us.' The smile widened into a grin, more playful this time. He held her eye again, to the point where Ellen felt awkward and looked away.

Vera's scowl deepened. She edged back towards the pen. 'Are you coming?' The question was directed at her brother, yet she looked at the ground by his feet rather than at his face.

'But Father said—'

'You're seventeen and only have ten animals marked as your own.'

'We've got guests now, Vera. Don't tell me you're not hungry, you've been rushing around like a wolf in there.'

His sister took a sharp intake of breath. She pursed her

lips, face souring. In one swift move she turned and ducked through the fence.

Erik shook his head. 'Sorry about that.' His cheeks turned red and he rubbed his hands against them as if that would get rid of it. 'She's always a bit cranky, it's nothing personal.' He looked over his shoulder. 'Hungry?'

'Oh yes,' Simon said.

Erik grinned. 'Then let's go grab some food.'

He led the way further back to the left, where women were tending to sausages and smoked reindeer meat on a grill. Smoke curled upwards, past Ellen's nose, making her stomach rumble. She checked her watch. It wasn't quite twelve, yet people were already queuing up along the foothill of the slope. Mostly men, Ellen noticed, although there were women, too. And a surprising number of children. They were all practically dressed in fleeces and hiking trousers, though some of them wore collars or knife belts with traditional Sami knitwear patterns. One little girl wore a leather thong with six tufts of fur round her neck, and she tugged one of them while staring at Ellen.

Looking at the rest of the kids, Ellen noticed all of them wore a thong, but with different numbers of tufts.

The Sami boy ushered them forward to the grill, past the queue. Eyes were drawn to them and one or two people muttered in annoyance. Erik ignored them. He went up to one of the women tending to the grill. 'Maja, I've got visitors.'

The woman looked up. She had a buxom figure, with honey-blonde hair in plaits framing her apple-cheeked face.

Erik motioned to the siblings. 'This is Ellen and Simon. Blind; you know, Lars-Erik's family. They're really starving.'

Maja looked from Erik to the queue. Then without a word she grabbed three bread rolls from a bag and stuck a sizzling sausage in each. Simon was about to take a big bite of his sausage, but Ellen cautioned him, reminding him they were still hot.

Erik led them along the edge of the clearing and sat down by a birch tree beside the smaller reindeer pen.

Ellen nibbled at the sausage. 'Maja isn't your mum, is she?' she said.

'Oh no, she's my aunt. Mattias's wife, my cousins' mum.'

'Your mum's not here?'

'No. Yes.' Erik's voice was short. Tense, as if he were struggling to speak. 'She's everywhere.'

It took a few moments before Ellen realised what he meant. 'Oh goodness, I'm so sorry...'

'It's OK,' he said quickly. Let out a slow breath. 'It's in the past now.' He pressed the last of the sausage into his mouth, cheeks bulging as he chewed.

Simon nudged his sister. 'What does he mean?' His breath smelled of mustard and meat.

'That his mum is dead,' she whispered, as quietly as she could. Erik didn't seem to have heard; he gazed dreamily at the herd as it moved in its constant circle. Or if he had, maybe it didn't matter to him.

The sound of a twig snapping made her look round.

Vera, the sister, was watching them from further away.

'Hi,' Ellen said.

The older girl scowled and walked off.

'Sorry,' her brother said. 'She isn't really all that bad, it's just strangers, people turning up unannounced... She's been like this ever since Mum died.' He fiddled with a leather thong hanging from his neck which Ellen hadn't noticed earlier. There were no fur tufts dangling from it.

'What are those for,' she said, pointing at the thong. 'I've noticed all the kids wear them, with little bits of fur.'

'They're earlobes,' Erik said. 'Kids cut them off each reindeer they mark, as a keepsake. They normally start marking animals at age five or six. When my sister was seven, she had ten. Now, she has over thirty.'

So that's what the second ear cut was for, Ellen thought. 'How many do you have?'

His face soured. 'Not enough. I'm the family's embarrassment.'

'So you don't wear the earlobes because you are ashamed you have too few?'

A high-pitched noise caught their attention. A calf. It skipped up to the youngsters, kicking out with its back legs.

'Looks like someone's come to say hello,' Erik said, relieved to have a distraction. He knelt down to sit on his haunches and held out a hand. The reindeer wandered up to him, sniffed his hand. Then its dewy eyes turned to Ellen, or rather, to the last bit of bread in her hand. It snuffled up to her, hoping to get some.

'Oi,' Erik called, 'that's Ellen's lunch, you've got milk!'

Ellen laughed. 'It's OK.' The calf's pink tongue tickled her palm as it ate the bread out of her hand. A musty scent of earth wafted off its dusty fur, reminding her of stables and horses. 'You're cute,' she whispered, and scratched the animal behind the ears. 'Simon,' she said, 'you want to pat it?'

Her brother, who'd eaten his hot dog in silence, shook his head, but watched the animal closely.

'What does the mark mean?' he said. 'The mark in its ear?'

Ellen pushed the fur on the outside of the ear back to bare the smooth inside. A vertical cut ran along the length of the skin, ending in a downward diagonal to the right.

'It's Vera's mark,' Erik said.

Ellen looked at him.

'Each reindeer herder has their own mark so that the animals can be identified,' the Sami boy explained.

'I thought all reindeer were owned by one herder,' said Simon. He'd taken out his notebook and was copying the earmark onto the page. The calf sniffed at his shoe, and he pulled his leg back.

'Everyone in a Sami village shares ownership,' Erik said. 'Dad and uncle own the biggest numbers, but everyone shares in the responsibility.' His jaw tightened. 'In a Sami village, reindeer herding is the only job you are allowed to have, your only way to make money. If you want another job, you have to leave.'

Granddad, Ellen thought.

'My mark's a diamond. At first I tried to make a circle but with these knives you can only make a straight cut.' Erik grinned, shaking his head.

A deep bleat came from the herd. The calf jerked its head around. It let out a high-pitched cry and scampered back to the other animals.

Erik watched it go. 'That was the mother. They can all recognise their calf's bleat, so they can find them easily.'

A tapping sound made Ellen turn. It was Simon, tapping his pen against his notebook again. 'What earmark did the dead reindeer have?' he asked Erik.

The Sami boy frowned. 'My dad didn't tell you? All the dead reindeer had his mark.'

'Even the heads in the glade?'

'Every single one.'

The reindeer marking lasted for another two hours. Erik went back once into the pen and managed to earmark another calf. Afterwards, he offered to take the siblings on a tour of the village. Ellen asked if his father wouldn't object, whether he'd want his son to help with the work, but Erik waved the protest away. Dad would manage. He had Vera, he didn't need any other help. Besides, he said, it was nice to talk to people his age. Reindeer herding could be lonely. Most of the time it was just you and the animals, you and the forest. The herders worked together sometimes, but people hardly talked. It was as if their work consumed them. And Vera was never any fun.

But of course he loved the animals. They were beautiful, they trusted him. They had always been here, and Erik's people had always been here. It felt right to take care of them.

How could anyone want to harm them?

The name of the village, Purnuvaare, was a mix of the Lule Sami and Southern Sami languages, he told them. *Purnu* (Lule Sami) meant 'a hole covered in stone used for the keeping of meat'. A sort of cellar used by Sami all over the area that was now Svartjokk Sami village, for storing wild reindeer meat back in the day when the Sami were still nomadic. *Vaare* (Southern Sami) was a kind of trading post. The first Sami settler, Lars-Nila Thomasson, came to Purnuvaare in 1786. He'd bought up the land on which the *bygdegård* was now standing from the non-Sami settlers who'd arrived in 1762.

'It was written in the records by the first priest in Svartjokk that he tried to be both a Sami and a settler. It was quite a new thing at the time.' Erik smiled wistfully. 'Things are different now. There's quite a few Sami actors and singers who have two jobs: they're both artists and reindeer herders.'

'Is that what you want to be?' Ellen asked.

'Yeah.' Erik flashed Ellen a lopsided grin. 'I want to be a musician.' He took off his cap and pulled his fingers through his hair. It was stark blond, almost white, like the sunlight glaring down at them. 'I'm in a rock band.'

'You?' Ellen didn't hide her surprise. In his blue fleece, black hiking trousers and heavy hiking boots, Erik didn't look like much of a rocker. 'What do you play?'

'Lead guitar and vocals.' Erik's smile was smug. 'We are quite good, you know. Not bragging. We had a gig in Västerås last year.'

She smiled. 'You must be good, then.' Västerås was one and a half hours west of Stockholm. It hosted some pretty big festivals, with high-profile artists. 'It must take up a lot of time, though. The rehearsals and the travel.'

Erik shrugged. 'It's part of the job.'

'What does your father think?'

That stiff expression returned to Erik's face.

'He doesn't like that you're in a band?'

'Oh, he thinks it's good I play music,' Erik said. 'Teenagers need hobbies, he says, but as a career, it's too much hit and miss. As if he would know.'

'Maybe he just means that reindeer herding is more stable?'

Erik scoffed. 'Maybe it would, if half the herd didn't suddenly die.'

He came to a halt. Ahead of them, a gravel path wound its way between two houses. It ended at a graveyard.

'This is Purnuvaare graveyard. Our public burial ground for two hundred and fifty-five years.'

A stiffness had entered his voice. He avoided meeting the gaze of either sibling. Almost, Ellen thought, as if he knew he'd said too much. She followed as he led the way through the grass overgrowing the path.

If the Old Church graveyard had been small, Purnuvaare's was tiny. It could easily fit into their living room at home. A chapel huddled to the left side, its entrance framed by two sprawling spruces.

'It's not much to shout about, really, but it's an important historical landmark for the Sami. All Purnuvaare people are buried here.'

'Not our great-grandmother,' Simon said.

Erik shifted his feet. 'Marit Blind didn't want to be buried here.'

'Why not?'

The tall boy scratched his neck. 'All of us here are Levinian. Like, a small branch of Protestants, following Luther's style…'

'We know what a Levinian is,' Ellen said. In her mind's eye she saw Stina Hansson, telling them about Marit's faith with that hunger in her eyes. 'I did a research project on the assimilation of the Sami at school, though. No one talks about it, but I wanted to know…'

Erik looked at her with keener interest, almost impressed, it seemed. 'You are right,' he said softly, 'it is overlooked.'

Heat rushed to Ellen's cheeks. She tried to hide it by combing her hair with her hand. 'What about our great-grandfather?' she said, to steer the topic back to their family. 'I assume he was buried here?'

'Nikolaus Blind? Yes, he'll be here somewhere.' Erik led the way through the grass, eyes flitting back and forth across the stones. He stopped behind the church. A granite square lay by his feet, hidden under the thick stalks. He bent down and brushed the vegetation away.

The script was so faded Ellen had to bend down beside the Sami boy to read it.

Nikolaus Blind, 1918–2006. Moss spread out like flower petals over the stone.

'Nikolaus...' Ellen tested the word on her tongue. Was that why her dad's name was Niklas? She looked over her shoulder, beckoning Simon to join her, but her brother held back, clutching his book to his chest.

Ellen turned back to the gravestone. 'My dad told me Marit didn't get along with Nikolaus in their last years together. And then she moved to Svartjokk...'

'She left the Levinian church and became a member of the regular state church instead,' Erik said.

'Why?' Ellen thought for a moment. 'Is it to do with Lars-Erik? Why he left?'

Erik stood up. 'Man, you sure do ask a lot of questions. Even for me, and Vera always calls me a super-annoying chatterbox.' His laughter was shaky, high-pitched. A breeze scuttled through the graveyard and made the grass stalks shiver. 'You'd better ask my dad.'

'Please, Erik...'

A phone signal sounded from Erik's pocket. He pulled out a battered black Nokia, one of those ancient ones with buttons and a tiny screen. 'It's my sister,' he said. 'She wants us back. Dad and Uncle do, I mean. They're clearing up for the day.' He began leading the way back to the *bygdegård*. 'Save your questions for my dad. Maybe then I'll learn something too, who knows.'

It was mid-afternoon when the earmarking finished. The Thomassons led the reindeer across the field, through the trees, and back to their houses. Ellen and Simon took up the rear. Ellen finally grew accustomed to the animals' bleating. The sounds pushed all thoughts about Marit and Lars-Erik out of her mind. For the first time since arriving in Svartjokk she felt calm. When she closed her eyes, reindeer song, snapping twigs and crunching pine needles were the only things left in the world. *I understand why the Sami stick to this lifestyle.* Once you were in nature, you didn't need anything else to keep going. What were computers, phones and fancy clothes compared to sunshine on your face, wind in your hair and the sound of rustling leaves in your ears?

After a few minutes they arrived at a clearing. A large pen stretched out across it, the ground coloured gold by the sun. Beyond it were the back gardens of two houses, one red and one yellow.

Mattias's sons opened the gate to the pen. The reindeer trotted inside, heads lowered, neatly aligned in three lines, three to four animals in each row. The two men closed the gate behind them and wandered amongst the animals, checking the earmarks on the calves. Per-Anders grabbed a hose by the shed belonging to the red house and filled the trough in the pen with water. Vera and Erik disappeared into the shed to drop off their ropes. Mattias went to the shed by the yellow house and came back carrying buckets of fodder. He handed one each to his sons and the three of them began feeding the animals.

After putting the hose away, Per-Anders returned to the pen. He leaned against the fence, watching the animals as they meandered around the area.

'I do not like keeping the animals here,' he said when Ellen and Simon joined him.

The comment took Ellen aback. 'Isn't this where you normally keep them?'

'Gathering doesn't happen until October. In summer, we collect the reindeer for calf marking and then let them roam again. Now we must keep them here for a week.'

'Why?'

'The Natural Environment Agency. They say it would

put the animals at greater risk if they roam freely when there still might be traces of chlorine in the rivers.'

'Isn't that a good thing, though? Won't the animals be safer here?'

'It isn't natural. The reindeer will grow restless.' Per-Anders pulled a hand over his face. Ellen noticed dark rings under his eyes.

One of the reindeer wandered up to them. It was a bull, Ellen reckoned, as she could see no udders. It snuffled at the man's hands, no doubt searching for food. Ellen removed her hands from the fence and put them in her pockets. Up this close, the reindeer's head was large. A thin coat of hairs, or fluff, covered the brown antlers.

To saw off twenty-four of those…

The reindeer stepped to the side, coming face to face with her. It flicked its ears. Ellen glimpsed a knife mark on the pink inside skin.

'Erik told us it was only animals with your mark that had been killed,' she said. 'Was it the same with the other reindeer who disappeared in the past?'

'Yes.'

'Doesn't that suggest all these crimes are targeted at you personally?' Ellen looked at Simon. He checked his notes, nodded to her in confirmation.

'There is a method to these crimes,' her brother said. 'Put together, they appear to be a conspiracy against you.' He edged back as the reindeer sniffed at his notebook. He hugged the book to his chest, not relaxing until the reindeer had wandered away.

Per-Anders let his hands wander over the fence. 'Erik's putting on some coffee. There's cake too, if you want it.'

Ellen pursed her lips to stop herself from sighing in frustration. Now Per-Anders was avoiding her questions. She thought back to Erik's comments as they'd left the graveyard and wondered if there'd been more to his words than just joking. She masked her thoughts behind a smile. 'Thank you.'

'No problem.' The man stepped back from the fence. 'Let's see how they're getting on.'

The Thomassons' kitchen was cramped and cluttered. Pots and pans in various stages of cleanliness lined the kitchen work tables. Glasses and plates stood in stacks by the dishwashing rack, and a glass oven tray stuck up out of the basin.

Erik stood by the stove, spooning coffee into a steel kettle. He turned and smiled as the trio entered, spilling coffee onto the stove as he did so. Vera put mugs and plates on the table. A sponge cake, a bowl of cream and a jar of what looked like cloudberry jam were already laid out.

'Please sit down,' Per-Anders said, indicating a kitchen sofa by the windows.

Ellen and Simon squeezed onto the sofa. They used to have one of these at home, Ellen remembered, before Mum decided it was too much in the way and gave it to charity.

The seat on the sofa sank as they sat down. The stripy pattern was worn, the greens and reds faded.

Per-Anders opened the fridge door. 'Do you take cheese?'

'Dad,' Erik said, 'if not even Vera takes cheese in her coffee, it's pretty certain Ellen and Simon won't.'

'Cheese?' Ellen repeated. 'In coffee?'

'It's a tradition of a sort,' the Sami boy said. 'Only old people do it, though.'

'Calling me old?' Per-Anders said, grinning.

Erik did not return the grin. He filled the pan with water and then returned it to the stove, stirring the coffee granules through. Per-Anders eyed him with concern for a moment before suppressing a sigh and getting a cheese slicer from a drawer.

Ellen looked around the rest of the kitchen. There was a still-life painting on the left wall, showing a pear, a candle and an apple cut in two, the knife lying on the plate beside it, dripping apple juice. In the left corner of the room, close to Ellen, stood a tall, slim bookshelf crammed with what looked like recipe books and magazines. Ellen frowned in surprise. She hadn't expected Per-Anders to be into cooking. The cake was store-bought, the Hägges brand, which her mother got sometimes. The blue package lay scrunched up on the dishwashing rack, sticking out between two plates. And the magazines… Ellen leaned forward past her brother. Yes, that was an issue of *Året Runt*, peeking out behind a recipe folder. Her frown deepened. *Året Runt* was a ladies' magazine; her grandmother was always doing the crosswords and cutting out the odd recipe. Vera didn't seem like the kind…

'You looking for the reindeer pelts and drums?' the girl said.

Ellen opened and closed her mouth. 'I, no…'

'You won't find any here. This is a normal Swedish house.'

'Vera,' her father warned.

'You like Sami culture, Ellen?'

Ellen could feel sweat forming on her brow. She swallowed and tried to look unmoved by Vera's tone. 'Yes, sure, of course. I find it very fascinating.'

'Would you say you support it?'

'Of course.'

'What did you make of the earmarking? What did you think when I made my cut in the calf's ear?'

'Vera, that's enough,' Per-Anders said.

Vera paid no heed. She rested her arms on the chair closest to Ellen and leaned forward until the other girl could make out the zigzag pattern in her irises and the freckles beneath her eyes.

Ellen thought of the high-pitched bleat which had made her flinch and wonder if the calf had been hurt. Rewinding the moment in her mind, she flinched again, internally.

'You know what I say to people who "support indigenous culture"?' Vera continued. 'Who think it's supercool with drums and feathers and stuff, and still call me an animal molester when I earmark a calf? Blah. Just blah.'

The girl leaned back, still gripping the chair, and held Ellen's gaze for a moment. A strange mix of contempt and anger seethed on her face. 'Reindeer herding is a professional job. It's a business. It's sweat and blood and aching legs in the morning. We have to train all our lives to become one. It isn't for the faint-hearted, it isn't a lifestyle you can take for granted.'

'Vera, enough,' Per-Anders said. 'Let's sit down.'

The older girl looked about to give another retort, but then she shrugged and sat down. Erik poured the coffee. There was a faint flush of colour on his cheeks.

Per-Anders asked them about their journey to Svartjokk as they ate. Ellen answered his questions, as Simon was too busy enjoying his cake. The reindeer herder seemed interested enough, nodding and humming in the right places, but neither Erik nor Vera said a word. An awkward tension hovered over the conversation.

Per-Anders started taking cups and plates to the sink when Simon suddenly pointed at a photograph on the fridge, showing the siblings and a blonde woman on a mountainside.

'Is that Erik's and Vera's mum?'

Ellen drew a sharp breath. Per-Anders paused in his movements. His son and daughter tensed.

'What happened to her?' Simon pressed on. 'Erik told us she wasn't with you any more.'

Ellen stared down at the table, hands buried between her knees.

'Erik's and Vera's mother had an accident,' Per-Anders said softly.

There was a loud scoff, followed by the creaking noise of a chair being pushed back. Erik, Ellen saw when she looked up. His hands were shaking.

'Erik,' said Per-Anders, 'what is the matter?'

'I have to go. Rehearsal.'

'I thought you were going in the evening.'

'Double session. We need to practise for the gig.'

'But that is on Wednesday.'

'We don't have any other free days.' Erik stormed out of the room before his father could say another word. He thundered up the stairs and came down a moment later with a guitar strapped on his back. The door slammed shut behind him. There was the distant rumble of a moped coming to life and then the puttering sound as it drove off.

A second silence loomed in the kitchen, broken only by the *tick tock* of the clock.

Vera reached over the table and picked up her brother's plate. After finishing the remnants of the cake slice she licked her fingers and stood up and took the two plates to the sink. 'I'm going out,' she said, heading into the hallway. She fetched her boots, then walked back through the kitchen onto the veranda. Ellen watched as she crossed the garden towards the reindeer pen. Another figure moved out there. Whether it was Mattias or one of his sons, she didn't know.

Ellen looked at Per-Anders. The man tapped his spoon absently against the plate.

She buried her hands in her lap. 'Sorry about that.'

'Why should you be sorry?' the man said.

'We were prying into things that have nothing to do with us.'

'Isn't prying the exact reason you're here?'

Ellen bit her lip and looked down at her hands.

'You want to ask me something. Name it.'

Ellen took a deep breath. 'Our grandfather…'

'Stop,' Simon said suddenly.

Ellen turned to him. 'Stop?'

'We're not here to ask about Grandfather.'

'Simon, Per-Anders is—'

'We are here to continue the investigation,' Simon interrupted. 'We can't be distracted and talk of things that aren't relevant to the investigation.'

'Simon, this is relevant!'

'No, it isn't.'

Ellen cursed inwardly. 'Sorry,' she said to the reindeer herder. 'Will you excuse us?' She began to stand up.

Per-Anders held up a hand. 'No. I will leave. I'll be in the living room.'

The floorboards creaked under his feet as he left.

Ellen sank back on the sofa. 'You really need to explain yourself.'

'I already have. It's you who has to explain.'

'Look, Simon, I'm doing my best just trying to get all our questions answered.'

'You didn't ask about the red car, or for further information about the other killings, or about Bengt and Constable Virtanen and either of them being left-handed…'

Ellen put a hand to her forehead. Simon really couldn't pick any better time to argue, could he? 'Why didn't you just ask Per-Anders about this yourself?' she said.

'You never let me.'

'Oh, come on!'

'You keep telling me to take my own initiative but when I do you hush at me to be quiet and take over. That's called being a hypocrite.'

'Simon, please, I never meant to interrupt...' Her voice dropped. 'Didn't you just ask them about their mum? How relevant is that?'

Simon opened his mouth to speak, but shut it again. He averted his gaze and ran a finger down one of the red stripes in the sofa. 'You're just like Mum,' he muttered.

Ellen took a deep breath. 'Simon, I know this must sound weird to you, but I'm certain that Granddad's leaving Purnuvaare is connected with the reindeer crimes.'

It was the first time she had admitted it even to herself, yet the words felt right as she spoke.

Simon frowned. 'We don't have any proof of that.'

'I know, I know. But I've had this feeling.' She pulled at the hem of her shorts. 'In my gut. And you know that time on the forest track? When you were just about to run off into the glade? I had this prickly feeling in my neck.'

Simon stared at a point just above her hands. He was completely still.

'It was almost as if I knew the reindeer were there, before we saw them. Like the sting was a warning.'

'Like Granddad,' Simon said softly. 'The cherry tree.'

'Exactly like the cherry tree.' Ellen leaned back against the sofa. 'Per-Anders will tell us the truth about Granddad, and then you can ask him as many questions as you want. I won't take over.'

'OK.'

'And I'm not like Mum.'

'OK.' Simon took out his notebook and ran his hand over the blue cover. 'Maybe you aren't a hypocrite.'

Ellen couldn't stop herself from smiling. Then she heard a noise. She turned around.

Per-Anders appeared in the doorway. 'I understand you're looking for truths.'

'Well, yes,' Ellen said. 'We thought you might be able to help us.'

Per-Anders sat down at the table. 'What do you want to know?'

'Why our grandfather left Purnuvaare and why no one in our family ever talks about it.'

'A difficult truth. All the more important that it be known.' Per-Anders placed his hands on the table. 'Your father never told you?'

'No,' Ellen said, unable to keep the bitterness from her voice. 'He never told us a thing. Though he promised he would.'

'And your grandfather? He kept it to himself?'

Both Ellen and Simon nodded.

Per-Anders sighed wistfully. 'It is almost as if he couldn't bear joining these two lives of his together, for fear of what it would do to him and those around him.' He clasped his hands together and leaned forward. 'For the sake of the friendship between my father and Lars-Erik, I will tell you what I know. Just as my father told me, as your grandfather told him. But I warn you, it's not a pleasant tale.'

It was a bitterly cold, snowy day in May, 1960. Lars-Erik stumbled into his home with a girl, Lisbet Persson from Kajava. They'd been seeing each other since October, but had kept their relationship secret due to tension between their families. He was not yet nineteen, she was seventeen. They'd come to speak with Lars-Erik's parents on a matter of urgency.

Lisbet was pregnant, twelve weeks gone. Both she and Lars-Erik knew they wanted to keep the baby. Lisbet said her father would be furious should he find out. He was a man who only spoke through his fists. If any young man laid as much as a hair on his daughter, he'd beat them to a pulp before they could say a word. It was not safe for either of them to stay in Purnuvaare.

Lars-Erik was due to graduate from school the next month. In the autumn he was supposed to enrol at Svartjokk College and begin his studies in agricultural business, the qualification required for a reindeer herder.

But Lars-Erik had a plan for their future. He wanted to give up his place on the Agriculture programme and go try his luck in Stockholm. The city was brimming with opportunities for young men like himself. Factories and building sites needed people. Lisbet would go with him, and together they would raise their family in the capital.

Nikolaus was not convinced. 'The reindeer will be grazing on the sea before that happens,' he said. He would only support the young couple if they married within the fortnight and Lars-Erik started his course in Svartjokk. He could call Sakarias Christiansen, the vicar for the Levinian community in Svartjokk municipality, straight away. Depending on where in the municipality Christiansen was, it could take over a day for him to get to them, but once he'd arrived, the ceremony would be done within fifteen minutes.

As for Marit, she grieved that her son had not let her know of this. A deeply devout woman, she felt shame that her son had given himself over to the temptations of the body, and shame over the disgrace that would spread through their community. She was angry about his irresponsibility for putting Lisbet into this situation. She felt worried for the girl, who would not know how to care for the living thing inside her, this girl who had not yet finished school. But *none of this Marit said aloud. What she did say, was that Lisbet could stay with them until the priest arrived and got the couple married. For now, she would take the girl to Mrs Thomasson, who knew more about pregnancy matters than Marit did.*

Marit and Lisbet had hardly disappeared down the forest track towards the Thomassons', when a car approached from the opposite direction, where the main road lay. Lars-Erik and Nikolaus looked out of the window. Three men got out of the car, iron bars in their hands and hunting rifles strapped over their shoulders.

There was a pounding on the door and angry words were exchanged. Lars-Erik didn't open it at first, but the men threatened to knock the door down.

Gunnar Persson, better known as Gubben, old man, stood on the doorstep, his sons behind him. 'Where is my daughter?' Gubben bellowed. 'I know you've brought her here, I know what you did to her. Where is she?'

Lars-Erik decided to come out with the truth. Nikolaus had brought him up to be honest. 'I am going to marry your daughter. She wants to come with me to Stockholm.'

Gubben Persson lost his temper and hit Lars-Erik in the face. Nikolaus tried to intervene, but the Perssons had no truck with words. The sons came at him with their bars: one blow, two blows, three. Nikolaus sank to the ground.

What happened next isn't exactly clear. It seems that Nikolaus was knocked unconscious. When he came round, the fighting had ceased. A man lay still on the ground beside him. It was Gubben Persson. He was bleeding from a wound in his stomach. Nikolaus put his ear to the man's mouth. There was no sign of breathing.

The sons lay on either side of him. The elder son bled from an arm, groaning. The younger lay on his back, chest rising and falling slowly – unconscious.

And sitting amongst them, his eyes deader than those of the dead man, was Lars-Erik, with Persson's hunting rifle in his hand.

Lars-Erik said afterwards that he knew it was going to happen before it happened. When it did, it was as if someone else were acting through him, and all he could do was watch. He didn't want to kill the old man. When Lisbet, Marit and my parents returned to the Blinds' house, the girl sank down by her father's body and put his hand to her stomach. The police eventually had to drag her away.

Two weeks later, the court found that Lars-Erik had acted in self-defence. He was cleared of all charges. He may have been a free man, but his relationship with Lisbet was over. She never spoke to him again. In November, word reached Lars-Erik that the baby had been stillborn. Lisbet's family, blaming her in part for her father's death, turned her out of the house. She stayed with a friend from school for two months. One night, they went to a dance at the town hall, and Lisbet took a liking to the lead singer of the band. When they moved on to their next gig, Lisbet went with them. She wrote to her mother just once, to say she was moving in with the singer, and that was the last they ever heard of her.

By then, Lars-Erik had already left. He could not bear to stay in the place where he'd killed a man. The city called him, and if he didn't answer its call soon he would lose his chance, forever. One morning in August he took the Inlandsbana south to Kristinehamn, and from there on to Stockholm. He never returned to Purnuvaare.

Lingonberry Glade

Per-Anders lifted his mug and drained the last of his coffee. The coaster stuck to the bottom of the mug and clattered to the table.

'We never heard from any Lisbet when Granddad died,' said Ellen. 'Not at the funeral, not at the wake, not even a condolence card. Granddad never mentioned her when he was alive.'

'Maybe that was why Grandmother separated from him,' said Simon. 'Because she heard about Lisbet and got upset.'

'Is their house still here?' Ellen's voice didn't feel like her own. It was hollow and distant.

'There's a small path leading off from the reindeer pen to the left. It ends at the Blinds' backyard. A ten-minute walk.'

Ellen turned her mug in her hands. The little coffee remaining had gone cold. 'Shall we, Simon?'

She didn't have to look at him to know he had doubts. She imagined his thoughts zigzagging through that brain of his, the word 'investigation' pulsing like an electron. Wandering off to an abandoned house and wasting another hour was probably the last thing he wanted to do.

'We need some time to digest this,' he said.

'You are sure?' asked Per-Anders. 'I can put on some more coffee. There's cake…'

'We'll be fine,' said Ellen.

For a moment, it looked as if Per-Anders wanted to say something more. Then he pressed his lips shut and nodded. It was as if the moment had never happened.

The Blinds' house lay at the fringe of a field. It was a traditional red timber building with white corners, with a wooden shed to its left. The garden lawn, four times the size of their garden at home, was overgrown. Birch and aspen saplings poked their heads up amongst the grass and cow parsley. A grey fence, built out of sticks in traditional round-pole style, ran along the outskirts of the premises. Its gates were open, and lying on its side, toppled over, was an empty water crate.

Once upon a time this would have been a reindeer pen, Ellen thought. She gazed out across the field. Far beyond at the opposite end, she saw a red building amongst the green, and trailing to its left, the metal gleam of cars. Purnuvaare's *bygdegård*. Brown shapes moved in the grass. Reindeer.

How could she have missed Granddad's house from there?

From the driveway, a gravel road wound its way past the house into the trees. The Perssons would have come from there.

Ellen walked up to the front door. There was no porch like at the Thomassons. No *snickarglädje* carved into the wood, no mat by the door to wipe your feet. Not even a doorbell.

She imagined Gubben Persson and his sons, iron bars hefted on shoulders, stomping impatiently with their big feet, yelling at her Granddad to open the door. Why she imagined them to have big feet she wasn't sure. In her mind's eye they were all versions of Bengt Persson.

She placed a hand on the door. The painted wood was smooth under her fingertips. She put her ear against it. First there was only the sound of her own breathing, and then...

Footsteps, creaking against the floorboards. Followed by shouts.

Heart in her mouth, Ellen pulled the door open.

A bird fluttered out above her head.

Swallow. Ellen watched it swerve through the air and land on one of the fence posts of the reindeer pen. It stared back at her with what was probably reproach.

A faint screeching sound made her look back into the house. There, in the top right corner of the hallway, was a swallow's nest. Tiny heads poked up behind its rim, bobbing gently as they cried. Three babies, demanding food.

The footsteps... it must have been the adult swallow, hopping on the floorboards.

'At least the house isn't completely uninhabited,' Simon said.

'Yeah...' Ellen leaned against the wall for support. Sweat beaded on her forehead.

'Do you think they'll pull the house down? No one's lived here since Great-Granny moved out and I can smell mould.'

Ellen sniffed the air. Simon was right. A musty smell reeked from the walls. She stepped away. 'Mould is toxic. We should probably go.'

Yet she lingered. She looked down the hallway to the kitchen. It was narrow. The light spilling in through a window on the right-hand side drew patterns of light that scampered across the left wall. From above the ceiling came the rustling sound of something running. Mice?

'I wonder where Granddad's bedroom was,' Simon said. 'Can we have a look?'

She should say no. Perhaps coming here had been a mistake. What good would it do to wander around Granddad's old home? If he'd never spoken of it since he left, it was because he wanted to put it behind him. Given the true circumstances she could well understand why.

But he wasn't right to have kept it from her. She pictured Dad in front of her on the platform, not wanting to explain why he hadn't gone to visit Lars-Erik's home, or got in touch with the Sami properly. Had he secretly wished they would stumble upon the Thomassons and end up here, at the abandoned house, where all the secrets about Granddad had begun?

'All right, then,' she said.

Floorboards creaked as Simon walked down the hallway and turned left into another corridor. It was narrow, the walls rose high on either side. In the daylight funnelling down from behind, the insides of the house seemed to move. The smell of mould grew stronger.

'I think this must be it.' Simon entered the second room to the right. 'I can see the oak tree!'

'Oak tree?' Ellen quickened her pace.

Despite it not being inside the actual house, the oak tree was the first thing Ellen saw when she entered the bedroom. Standing right in front of the window, thick branches sprawling, it blocked out the sun, veiling the room in shadow.

'The trunk is split in three like the cherry tree,' Simon said. 'Do you reckon this one was struck by lightning, too?'

Ellen walked up to the window and tested the handle. It was stiff, but eventually gave way. Slowly, the window swung open and Ellen perched on the windowsill. She was close enough to reach out and touch the oak tree. Looking down its trunk she noticed an indentation that had probably been used for climbing. She imagined a young Lars-Erik putting a foot on it and swiftly making his way to the higher branches, nimble as a monkey.

'One would think they'd name this place after the tree,' a woman's voice said. It came from outside. Ellen jumped, her gaze darting around the garden. A flash of white from behind the tree. An old woman appeared. Ellen recognised her as the woman she'd seen in the graveyard at the Old Church. The woman's white dress swayed gently around her as she walked, and pine needles stuck to her hair. 'Oak field, Oak glen, Oak place. But it is named after these.' The woman bent down and picked up something from the ground. 'These little ruby drops.'

She walked up to the window and motioned at Ellen to hold out her hand. 'Eat them.'

She dropped three lingonberries into Ellen's palm. Ellen ate one. It was sour, and she grimaced as she swallowed. 'I don't think *lingon* are ripe this early.'

'They've always grown here,' the woman said. 'There's no space for blueberries or mushrooms or cloudberries. The garden becomes a carpet of red every summer. *Puolalaki*. Lingonberry mountain. That's the name.' She smiled to herself. 'When Lars-Erik was young he used to call them blood drops.'

'Wait, what?' Ellen leaned forward. 'You knew my granddad when he was a kid?'

'I told him not to climb the oak tree. It's treacherous. He only took my warnings as challenges. He'd tuck a book under his arm, climb the tree and read until sundown.' The woman reached a knobbly hand towards one of the branches, as if Lars-Erik were sitting there and she wanted to climb up and join him.

Behind her, Simon cleared his throat. 'Ellen, what are you doing?'

'I'm talking to the lady, Simon.'

'Ellen, there is no lady.'

'But she's standing right there, look!'

The woman stared at the trunk, absorbed in thought. 'We all swept it under the carpet, afterwards. The family, the village, the church. I wasn't allowed to keep a single photo of him, not even in my purse. As if you could forget your own son!' She turned towards Ellen and fingered the white paint on the windowsill. 'There is always a lump under the carpet and you feel it move against your foot every day. I could not pretend to ignore it, could not stay amongst people who did…'

The paint peeled off. The woman looked, perplexed, as it drifted down from her fingers. 'There are some people searching for answers,' she whispered, 'but I can't help them.'

'Why not?' Ellen asked.

'They won't let me. I've seen them around the church, looking looking…' The woman fixed her gaze on Ellen. 'You. They would listen to you.'

'Me?'

Simon stamped his foot on the floor. 'Ellen, will you please tell me why you are talking out loud to yourself?'

'Shh,' Ellen hissed. 'Please, go on,' she said to the woman.

The old lady's eyes had grown distant again. From her chest pocket she pulled out a wilted flower. A chrysanthemum. 'We did wrong by you, not trying harder to get in touch,' the woman whispered. Without warning she turned, heading for the forest.

'Wait!' Ellen cried. 'Marit, wait!'

She leaned out too far. The moss-covered ground rushed towards her.

Her brother's voice called from above. 'Ellen, are you hurt?'

Air was knocked out of her lungs. Pain shot through her knees. Her chest ached. She pressed her forehead against the ground, gave a shallow gasp when her lungs could breathe again.

The woman was gone. The only sign she'd been there at all was the chrysanthemum flower lying face down amongst the lingonberries, stalk pointing into the air. A dark shape swooped down. The swallow, tucking its wings in and giving Ellen a quizzical look. It plucked a lingonberry and flew away.

'It was Marit,' Ellen said again. 'I swear it.'

'You don't even know what Marit looks like,' Simon said. He pushed a spruce branch to the side and held it back as Ellen passed. 'She could have been a neighbour.'

'She was talking about Granddad as if she knew him when he was young. She referred to him as her son.'

'Ghosts don't exist, Ellen.'

'You really believe that, after seeing an oak tree struck by lightning like our cherry tree? Wouldn't surprise me if they were both struck at the same time.'

'So are you saying that you now believe in the super-natural?'

'I don't know what to believe any more. But I can tell you what I saw, and that was this.' Ellen held up the flower for her brother to see. 'You of all people can't deny proof when it stares you in the face.'

Everyone had left the reindeer pen when they returned. A few of the animals looked up as they passed. Ellen bent down and looked a calf in the eye. It flicked its ears, revealing a diamond-shaped knife mark. Erik's mark.

Per-Anders wasn't in the kitchen. Their mugs and plates stood drying on the dish rack.

'Per-Anders?' Ellen called. She stepped into the hallway. 'We're back.'

Movement in the corner of her eye. Ellen turned around, coming face to face with Vera. She stood in the doorway to the lounge.

'We have something to show you,' the older girl said, which took Ellen by surprise, as she'd seemed so determined to ignore them until now. Vera led the way through the lounge into a study room.

Per-Anders sat by the desk, staring into an old desktop computer buzzing quietly. Flickering in blue and white was the news feed on a Facebook page.

'Vera thought I should show you this,' he said and eased himself out of the chair. 'Please.'

Ellen nodded to Simon to show he could take the seat. She leaned over his shoulder, resting a hand on the desk, as he enlarged the photo on the screen. It showed Vera, straddling an adult reindeer, for once with a smile on her face. Per-Anders stood behind her. The caption read: *Reindeer owner, not reindeer herder.*

'What does that mean?' Ellen asked.

'They mean that we control the reindeer, rather than looking after them,' Vera said. 'That earmarking the calves and the autumn slaughter is a form of animal abuse.'

Ellen leaned closer to read the name of the person who'd uploaded the photo.

Kimmo Persson. Shared to a Facebook group called *The Real Swedish Norrbotten.* The picture had fifty-five likes.

Persson. Ellen squinted at the screen. On the photo,

the man's facial features were blurred, but they looked just like…

'Is he Bengt Persson's brother?'

There was no shock visible on Simon's face when he spoke. He'd got out his journal after sitting down by the computer, and now his pen hovered above the page, waiting to write down Per-Anders's answer.

The reindeer herder gave it by nodding.

Ellen closed her eyes. First the reindeer carcasses, then the truth about Granddad, then his house, then the woman she now suspected to be their dead great-grandmother, and now this Facebook thing and Bengt Persson's brother…

But Simon sailed through it all as if it was part of their regular schedule. Couldn't he just, for once, show one sign of distress, one sign of emotion?

'How did they get hold of this picture?' she said. Her voice didn't sound like her own.

'I'm certain that idiot downloaded it from my profile,' Vera muttered behind her. 'I posted it last year. I messaged him, asking him how he got hold of it, but of course he never replied. I hate him.'

'Vera,' Per-Anders said.

'But Dad, I do hate him. I hate every one of them.'

Simon clicked on the forward arrow at the edge of the picture. Next up was a video. It showed a man giving chase to a reindeer in the snow. Again and again he leaped onto it, pressing it down on the ground, then stepping off to let the animal stagger back up, only to leap onto it again.

'They keep going until the reindeer can't stand up any more. And then they kill it.'

The man in the video turned to face the camera. He grabbed snow and formed it into a ball, then walked up to the camera and threw the snowball at it. It must have hit the cameraman because a rush of swearwords followed, and the picture wavered.

'Do you know who this is?' Ellen asked.

'Hah,' Vera scoffed. 'We know all of them. I went to school with some of them. They filmed this, knowing we'd see it, knowing we would know them, and report them to the police.' Vera shook her head. 'They have no conscience, any of them.'

Ellen took a sharp breath. Was that Bengt Persson, standing in the background? 'Zoom in,' she told her brother.

'I can't zoom in if it's a video.'

'But look at that man. Isn't that Persson?'

Simon leaned forward, nose almost touching the screen. He hit the pause button. 'Yes, I think it is,' he said. 'And the man attacking the reindeer is his brother, Kimmo.'

'Didn't think stuff like this existed, did you?' Vera said.

Ellen took the mouse from her brother. She clicked on the name of the Facebook group. 'This group is public?' she said, reading the description.

'Half-public,' Vera said. 'Non-members can only see some of the content.'

'How come no one has removed or reported them?'

Vera's face was grim. 'I don't think anyone has the balls to.'

'Not even the police?'

'The police don't care about net hate.' She nodded at the screen. 'Look closer.'

Ellen frowned, but did as the older girl said. The rear of a red car could be seen in the left corner of the video. Sitting on it was a tall man with what looked like sandy hair sticking out from beneath his cap. Was that…

'Virtanen,' Simon said, confirming her thoughts. He turned to her. 'I told you the constable was suspicious.'

'As I told you,' Vera said, 'they can't be bothered. No one here sticks their nose in other people's business. Not even cops.'

'Hover the mouse over the likes,' Ellen told Simon. She scanned the list of names popping up and took another breath of surprise. 'Henrik Andersson? Surely that isn't...'

Yes. It was. Simon clicked on the name and there he was, the hostel owner, grinning at the camera, reclining against a scooter overlooking a forest landscape.

She felt a sudden urge to sit down.

Simon tapped an index finger against his lips. 'Did you show us these pictures because you suspect these men are responsible for the lake poisoning and the reindeer heads?'

'Vera and I think you need to know the truth of things,' Per-Anders said. 'People don't realise that reindeer herders have to put up with this sort of thing every day.'

'Discrimination, Dad, not "thing",' his daughter said.

Ellen frowned. 'Why do they behave like this?'

Vera's expression was tired. 'It's the basic problem. Industry. Profit. Money. When we Sami raise the issue about roads being built across ancient reindeer trails, and grazing areas being deforested to give space for new mines, we get the blame. Nasty comments on Facebook, hate mail, phone calls: all telling us we should stop complaining, thinking that we are "so special", and just adapt to the modern way of life. We get blamed for holding on to our culture, our heritage, our identity. Our presence is an inconvenience to them.'

Her gaze drifted to the computer screen. 'In retaliation, they attack us where we are vulnerable: our reindeer.'

Ellen nodded in understanding. What Vera was describing reminded her of her school project. The enforced assimilation, the race biology studies, the hate crime that was never brought up by the media.

Simon, who'd been studying the pictures on the computer and paid hardly any attention to the conversation, spoke up. 'Virtanen is sitting on a red car. Is it his?'

Vera leaned forward to peer at the screen. 'Yes,' she said. 'That bastard used to drive out with the Perssons all the time. Guess his duty as a cop has forced him to stop, but he's not arrested any of them yet.'

Red… The colour rang a bell. 'The killer who planted the heads in the glade drove a red car,' Ellen said, thinking out loud. 'There was a witness, a Thai woman, she saw him unload the heads from a red car, but she couldn't see his face.'

'There'll be hundreds of red cars around here,' Vera said.

'But this one will have an oil leak,' said Simon. 'And, most likely, bloodstains in the boot.' He thought for a moment. 'It is probably old, too. An old, battered engine is more likely to leak driving on rough terrain. Is it his only car?'

'No, I don't think so.' She snorted. 'He drives that white Peugeot these days, doesn't he?' She looked at her father. Per-Anders nodded.

'So the cars from his village pass through Purnuvaare?' Ellen asked.

Per-Anders sighed. 'They do. Since the new road was built.'

'Dad and Uncle pleaded with the council not to build the road through Purnuvaare,' Vera said. 'Traffic in the morning, traffic in the evening. Stresses the animals. Disturbs the peace. But of course they wouldn't listen. Those men in suits don't care about anything as long as they get money in their pockets.'

'Do either of you remember seeing a red car pass through Purnuvaare on the night of Tuesday 12th or Wednesday 13th?' Simon asked.

'We live off the main road,' Per-Anders said, 'we wouldn't have noticed.'

'Couldn't you ask around?'

Both father and daughter looked to the floor.

Simon cleared his throat. 'I think we need to see the constable's car for ourselves.'

Ellen's eyes widened. 'But what if he's home? Simon, it's a Saturday…'

'I saw him zip past this morning,' Vera said. 'Way past the speed limit, as usual.'

Simon stood up. 'Then this is our chance to find out if it was his car in the woods.'

Ellen tugged at a lock of hair. 'Simon…'

'It would explain his suspicious behaviour, Ellen.'

He was right. It was obvious that he knew he was, by the way he folded his arms and pushed out his chest, daring her to contradict him. She felt Per-Anders and Vera watching her.

She turned to Per-Anders. 'Will you drive us there? Is it far?'

The reindeer herder pulled at an earlobe. 'As long as you're with me, I'm responsible for you. If anything happened, I'd have your father to answer to.'

Ellen resisted the urge to throw her hands in the air. 'What do you mean could happen? That they'd beat us up with iron bars?'

Per-Anders winced at her words. He drew a circle on the floor with his foot. To her right, she noticed to her surprise that Vera smiled to herself. Simon's face was blank.

A voice in the back of Ellen's mind told her she should apologise. Be ashamed. Here she'd told Simon not to be insensitive when talking to Per-Anders and what was she doing?

Per-Anders raised his gaze to Ellen's. 'I cannot put you at such risk. You speak of these men with sarcasm, but their anger, their iron bars... they are real to us.' He glanced at her brother. 'Does Simon not have a caution already?'

Simon lowered his gaze, biting his lip. Ellen let her own gaze hover on the window, through which one could see the back garden, and beyond it a section of the reindeer pen.

'I'm sorry, Ellen. I don't think there is anything more I can do.'

He'd shown them the hut, he'd shown them the lake. He'd shown them – two teenagers from Stockholm – the bloated, beheaded bodies of twelve reindeer.

He'd told them the truth about Lars-Erik.

Perhaps Per-Anders had done more than enough already?

'I should probably drive you home soon. I'll give you a moment.'

Per-Anders left the study. The kitchen back door opened and closed. Vera drummed her fingers against her trousers. Then, with a shrug, she left, too. They heard her footsteps on the stairs, light and muffled. A door closed.

Simon leaned forward. 'We can't let him take us back.'

'He's decided, Simon. Look, he has done a lot for us already, more than anyone else would.'

'If we don't find the owner of the car, no one will.'

She sighed, eyes closing for a moment. Simon was right, again.

'I would like to find out more about their mum, too,' her brother continued. 'Erik was angry with Per-Anders, perhaps he doesn't agree what happened to her was an accident.'

Ellen opened her eyes to look at him. 'I thought that wasn't relevant.'

Simon turned away. 'No, it is not relevant. But they have no mum.'

He left before she could respond. She followed him into the kitchen.

He was gazing at the photograph again.

The woman had to be Erik's and Vera's mother. She had the same whitish blond hair as Erik, the same dimple in her cheek as Vera. Her eyes were large and round and full of laughter. Ellen tried to imagine her father coping on his own, if Mum suddenly… The mere thought made her flinch.

'Everyone we've spoken to has been hiding something,' Simon said quietly.

Ellen nodded. 'It's as if they're chewing the truth between their teeth all the time like a giant piece of gum. Everyone has secrets, Simon.'

'Are there even more secrets about Granddad we don't know?'

Before Ellen could respond, footsteps came down the stairs and Vera appeared in the hallway. She carried a bicycle helmet in each hand.

'You still want to go Björkliden, yes?'

Ellen blinked. 'Erm…'

'Yes,' Simon said, stepping forward. 'Yes, we still want to go.'

'Then bike there.' Vera tossed the helmets at the siblings. 'It won't take more than half an hour.' She opened the front door and started across the driveway before checking to see if they were following.

Ellen and Simon exchanged glances. Looking over her shoulder, Ellen saw Per-Anders standing by the reindeer pen with his brother. Both their backs were turned to the siblings.

'Are you coming?'

They hurried outside, putting their helmets on as they walked. Vera opened the garage and brought two bicycles, one grey and one blue. 'Head off now, before my dad spots you.'

'But if he notices, won't he be angry, won't he try to stop us?'

'Not if you ride like hell, he won't.' The Sami girl motioned to Ellen to take the grey bike, the taller of the two.

'But why are you doing this?'

Vera tapped her fingers against the handlebars and gave an exaggerated sigh. 'What do you think? I want whoever did this locked up behind bars.'

'Won't you come with us, then?'

The older girl's expression grew shifty. 'I'm supposed to stay here.'

'You know these people better than us,' Simon said.

'But if they see me with you, they're sure to be pissed off. Not to mention me.'

'Vera, please…' Ellen reached out a hand towards the older girl.

She pulled her hand back when Per-Anders appeared by the corner of the house.

'What's going on?' the man called. He walked up to them. 'Vera, what have you told them?'

The Sami girl turned to face her father. She planted both feet on the ground and folded her arms. 'I'm giving them the help you weren't willing to.'

'They can't bike to Björkliden, it will be too late.'

'So drive them, then!'

A conflict seemed to take place on Per-Anders's face.

Ellen pulled at her right thumbnail, listening to the bleating of the reindeer, which could still be heard in the distance.

'OK, I will take you there. By car. Put the bikes away, Vera.'

'Thank you,' Ellen said. She attempted a smile.

Per-Anders did not smile back.

Marks of Suspicion

From the outside, Björkliden was a village not unlike Purnu-vaare. The main road passed right through the community. Red and yellow villas lined either side of the road, evenly spaced out between the pines and birches. The blue sign announcing they'd arrived in the village was battered and lop-sided, as if a car had driven into it. There was no sign of life, no people walking on the streets that branched off the road, no cars.

As they took the last left turning, down a bumpy road in great need of resurfacing, something changed. The trees towered on either side, close together, and curtained win-dows glared at them out of houses that had gone years without repainting. A run-down cafe hunched on the right-hand side, the wooden door gaping into an empty seating area. The road was a cul-de-sac, ending by a clump of wizened spruces where a dirty stream trickled through the ditch.

Per-Anders did a U-turn and parked facing the way they'd come. He pointed to his left. 'That's Juha Virtanen's house, over there.'

The house was large, sitting on a slight rise. There was no car on the gravel driveway on the left-hand side, leading up to the garage. Cold clutched Ellen's chest. 'What if his car is in the garage?'

'I remember he used to keep it up at the back.' Per-Anders got out, once again opening Ellen's door. She glanced around her. The neighbourhood was motionless. A cuckoo called in the distance, eerily loud.

Per-Anders led the way across the road up the drive-way. Various clutter lay strewn across the lawn: a petrol-driven lawnmower, a Clas Ohlson hedge trimmer – same as Niklas's – a battered plastic watering can, wilted petunias in clay flower-pots, an opened sack of planting soil.

An overgrown path sneaked its way past the garage on the left, where the birches and aspen leaned in, crowding around the premises.

An old red Volvo estate stood there, headlights peering up through the grass.

'I remember,' Per-Anders said, 'before he joined the police and got that Peugeot, Juha used to tear along in this thing through our village, at least seventy kilometres an hour. They all did. Some still do.'

Simon marched up to the car and looked underneath. 'There's a puddle of oil here.'

Ellen and Per-Anders rounded the car. The oil puddle lay sleek and thick.

Per-Anders bent down and checked under the engine. 'Looks like the car could have got a bump on rough ground. It's the oil filter. It happens.'

He stood up, not bothering to brush off the grass and dirt from his clothes. Then he glanced into the boot and frowned.

'Per-Anders?' Ellen said. She walked to the back of the car and looked in, Simon beside her.

They caught their breaths at the same time. There was

a dark stain, the size of a head, on the grey cover lining the boot.

'Is, is that...'

Per-Anders nodded. 'It is blood. Not fresh, though.'

'It's the proof,' Simon whispered. He fished his phone out of his pocket. 'Ellen, we need photographic evidence. You should take a photo, too.' There was a *click* from his own phone as he used the camera.

'I, yes, of course...' Her fingers fumbled, she nearly dropped the phone, it sat so snug in her pocket. She stared at the stain, blinked, leaned closer towards the grubby glass. She imagined Juha, opening the boot in the middle of the night, not noticing one of the heads had fallen out of the bags until it rolled onto the ground by his feet, leaving unmistakable evidence in his car. She imagined him bending down, his head hidden from view by trees, his seemingly headless shape spotted by Sunan hiding in the shrubbery.

Then came the sound of an engine. A car crunching across the stones. It parked at the bottom of the driveway and a man came out. He looked up at the trio.

'What the hell are you doing here?'

Ellen jumped, heart thumping. For a moment, she thought the man making his way up the driveway was Bengt Persson. He had the same heavyset face, mousy hair and large hands, the same angry-bear gruffness to his voice. Had Virtanen suspected they might snoop around his house, and sent Persson to check them out?

'You,' the man said when he reached them, staring at Per-Anders. 'Why are you here?'

'Kimmo,' Per-Anders said, 'we were taking a look at Juha's car.' He edged away from the Volvo 'We will leave now.' He eyed the toolbox in the man's hand. 'You're here to sort out the oil filter, yes?'

Kimmo... Ellen searched her mind for a moment. Of course. Bengt Persson's brother. That explained the likeness. Now, though, close up, she could also spot the differences. This man wasn't quite as tall as Bengt, not quite so square in the shoulders. His eyes sat closer together, watery pools starkly contrasted against his pale skin, and his face rounder, smoother – childlike. He licked at a half-eaten Magnum ice cream, which she assumed he'd got from the cafe. She tried pairing him up with the man on the Facebook video, heaving himself onto the reindeer.

The man snorted. 'Since when did you become a car mechanic, Mr Reindeer Man?'

If the slighting comment affected Per-Anders, he hid it well. He held up his hands in a sign of peace. 'We'll leave you to it.' He nodded at Ellen and Simon to follow him.

Kimmo bit off a piece of ice cream. 'I know why you're here, Thomasson.'

Per-Anders halted. 'You do?' He stepped back. 'Tell me.'

'You're pointing fingers at innocent people,' Kimmo Persson said. 'Only thing your lot are good for.' He fixed his watery eyes on the siblings. 'It's them what did it, you know. They kill their own reindeer to claim compensation from the council.'

'That would not logically make sense,' Simon said. 'The Thomassons have no motivation for killing their own reindeer.' He swallowed. 'We're conducting an investigation and we are determined to find the culprit.'

Simon, no. Ellen held her breath.

Kimmo stared at him, nonplussed. 'You joking, kid?'

'No.' Simon's cheeks coloured. He took a step back towards his sister. 'Do you know anything about the lake pollution that was discovered on Tuesday?'

Kimmo grunted and shook his head, bit off another chunk of Magnum.

'The lake is not far from Björkliden, did it not affect your water? The council announced on Tuesday that the tap water in villages around Svartjokk would be undrinkable.'

'I don't know.'

'But what about the reindeer heads? Surely you know about that, it was in the news.'

Ellen noticed Per-Anders was perfectly still. Like a tree.

Kimmo Persson wiped his mouth, leaving a white smear on the back of his hand. He tossed the ice-cream stick into the grass. 'I don't know anything. No one here knows anything.' He inhaled sharply through his nose. 'Now clear out of here, before I call Constable Virtanen about trespassers on his premises.' He shoved past them, spitting by Per-Anders's feet. 'Investigation, my arse.'

This time it was Ellen's cheeks that coloured. She almost turned to answer back, when she felt a gentle touch on her arm. Per-Anders's long fingers pressed lightly against her skin.

Leave it, he mouthed.

She looked back towards the car one last time. Kimmo Persson could no longer be seen – he must have bent down behind it.

The cuckoo called again, as if to announce that their time in Björkliden was up.

'Why did you not say anything?' Simon asked when they were in the car. 'I thought you would say something because it's your reindeer.'

'Words don't work with people up here,' Per-Anders said, buckling up. 'For fifty years, the people in this village have been in conflict with the Sami, committed crimes against our reindeer, and they never admit to it.'

'But they could all be working together,' Simon said. 'It could be a con...'

He was interrupted by a phone signal. Per-Anders pulled out an old Samsung from his pocket.

'Erik?' He listened for a moment. Ellen heard Erik's voice, crackling due to the signal. He sounded rushed, which was confirmed when Per-Anders paled, and his grip on the phone tightened. 'We'll be there straight away, don't move.'

He lowered his phone. 'Erik's found a woman unconscious in the forest. One of those blueberry pickers. Barely breathing at all. Police and ambulance are on their way, but they won't be there for another fifteen minutes. We're closest.' His face was grim as he turned on the engine. 'I'm afraid it will be very late before you get back to the hostel.'

It took ten minutes to reach Erik. His moped was parked at the edge of the road, twenty minutes outside Svartjokk. He himself stood amongst the trees, waving both arms as they approached.

'I found her, just lying there, lifeless.' Erik spoke fast, stumbling over his words, his face flushed. 'Police called again, they said they'll be here in five.' He glanced at Ellen and Simon, eyes widening slightly, but said nothing, instead leading the way into the forest.

The woman lay on her side on a bed of moss, half-sheltered by the overhanging branches of a spruce tree.

'When I came she was lying on her stomach, face down, but I turned her to the recovery position so she could breathe.'

Erik knelt down by the woman's head, parting one of the branches to expose her face.

Ellen took a sharp intake of breath. 'Sunan.'

Per-Anders and Erik fixed their eyes on her. 'You know her?' Per-Anders asked.

'We spoke to her, in the cabin at the campsite where they're staying. The blueberry pickers.' She licked her lips. Suddenly her throat had gone dry. 'She saw Juha's car the night the reindeer heads must have been put in the glade, she mistook him for a ghost and ran away. She couldn't identify the man.'

Per-Anders's face was hard as slate. 'Seems he could identify her.' He knelt down and listened to Sunan's breathing. 'Slow but steady.' He stood up. 'You did a good job, son. How did you find her?'

'The other blueberry pickers, they saw me on the road. I'd stopped to...' Erik paused. He glanced at Ellen and blushed. 'I stopped to pee. Had no idea they were there at first. One of them came up from behind, a young woman, said this worker had gone missing. I couldn't refuse her, what with a moped and all, so I said I'd check. I've been driving along, stopping every few minutes, checking the forest both sides of the road. Just pure accident I found her.'

Per-Anders ran a hand over his face, rubbed a thumb over his chin. 'Who is in charge of the blueberry pickers?'

Ellen and Simon exchanged glances. 'Bengt Persson,' they said at the same time.

'It's even stronger evidence that Bengt and Juha are connected to the crime,' Simon said. 'Perhaps they planned it together. Bengt could have found out about Sunan and tried to get rid of her to protect Juha.'

The sound of sirens silenced them. A flash of blue and white appeared through the trees, and then a police car and ambulance parked behind Erik's moped.

Ellen's stomach clenched as she saw Juha Virtanen get

out of the police car. The Sami boy went up to meet him and pointed them out to him.

Was it only her, or did Virtanen's expression darken when he saw the siblings? Simon, specifically?

'How did you find her?' the policeman asked Erik.

The Sami boy told him what he'd told Per–Anders and the siblings.

The paramedic bent down by Sunan and touched her head. 'She's suffered a hard blow to the back of the head. Unconscious, moderate concussion.' He shook Sunan gently by the shoulder. 'Hello? Can you hear me?' He looked at Erik. 'What's her name?'

Erik looked at Ellen.

'Sunan,' she said.

The ambulance driver bent over the woman's ear. 'Sunan, this is the ambulance, we're going to take you to the hospital. Everything will be all right. You're in safe hands.' He looked at Erik. 'You did well, putting her in the recovery position.'

Erik nodded, but the worry didn't leave his face. He edged out of the way as two other paramedics brought a stretcher and lifted Sunan onto it.

Constable Virtanen scanned the scenery, taking notes in his notepad. 'Do you remember the exact location of the other blueberry pickers?' he asked Erik.

The Sami boy shrugged. 'Not ten minutes outside of town. There was a lay-by.'

'And what were you doing out on the road?' He glanced back to the moped, and the black instrument case leaning against it. 'That a guitar?'

'Yes, I play in a band.'

'Were you on your way to or back from rehearsal?'

'On my way. The blueberry pickers called to me...'

Juha eyed him sceptically. 'From the road?'

Erik stared at his feet and explained the more embarrassing reason for why he'd been in the forest.

'Did they say how long she had been missing?'

'I'm not sure... An hour or so.'

Virtanen took notes as Erik spoke, then he strode around the area, scanning the ground, running his hand along the moss.

Ellen cleared her throat. 'What are you thinking, Constable?'

His eyes darted up to her. 'There's no sign of a struggle.'

'So Sunan went with him willingly?'

'We can't jump to conclusions at this stage,' the constable said. He straightened, stretching his back, then returned to the road.

Ellen watched him go. 'I don't understand, I just asked him a question, I just wanted to know.'

'I think maybe we need to ask him more questions,' said Simon.

No. The word was written over Per-Anders's face. His eyes swept over the area Virtanen had just inspected. The piece of cord from the rope that he'd shown them at the railway hut was in his hand; he fiddled with it absently with a thumb. He didn't seem to notice when Simon followed the policeman, striding back to the road. Ellen hurried after her brother, Erik beside her.

It seemed Virtanen had company. A second policeman stood bent over in the ditch, watching a trickle of water struggle through the withered weeds. '...one walked here,' he was saying to Virtanen, pointing at something on the ground. 'Can't be a big foot.'

Simon stepped up to the policeman. He went down

on one knee and inspected the footprint. 'That looks like a size 43.'

'Very precise.'

'The footprint measures 27.6 centimetres from heel to toe. Size 43. A small-footed man or very large-footed woman.'

The policeman raised his eyebrows in surprise, then looked up over his shoulder. 'Well, they certainly don't belong to her.'

The paramedics had lifted Sunan's stretcher into the ambulance. Constable Virtanen spoke to one of them in hushed voices by the open doors. He climbed into the ambulance, the paramedic following.

Ellen rounded the ambulance. She could see Virtanen, standing over Sunan's stretcher, hands on his belt. An oxygen mask covered the woman's face. Already, her chest was lifting and dropping as her breathing became regular again.

Three fingers on Sunan's right hand twitched. Her eyes fluttered open. She stared at the constable.

Then she screamed.

Part II

A Boy's Love for Oranges

He squeezes the oranges, spoons out the bits, pours the juice into a glass. He puts it on the table. Pa stares at it as if it is something the cat brought in. 'Your ma really thinks this will take the bad breath away?'

'Yes. Freshly squeezed fruit is better than store-bought, she says. And healthier.'

Pa scoffs. 'Since when did she become a health guru?' He downs the juice in one and smacks his lips. Picks a piece of orange flesh from between his front teeth. 'I told you, no bits.'

'Sorry.' He makes a mental note to be more thorough next time.

The boy takes the empty glass to the sink and rinses it. He bangs his hand against the tap, right on the wounds beneath his knuckles. He winces and drops the glass in the basin.

'What's that?'

The boy turns and explains.

The man grunts. 'What are we to do with you, eh?' He pulls the circular mint tin out of his chest pocket and pops a mint into his mouth. He sucks long and slowly, like a baby from its mother's breast, pushes the chair back – which scrapes against the floorboards – and stands up.

The boy waits for him to notice the marks on his hand, to ask if it hurts. To say sorry for what he's done, to promise never to do it again.

Of course, Pa says nothing. He lumbers into the lounge and turns on the TV.

In his mind's eye, the boy imagines those lumbering feet against the gravel on the driveway. Crunch crunch, thump thump. Steady footsteps which never slow, never stop. Crunch thump, drag drag. The boy's arms trailing like weeds across the stones. His hands clawing the earth, trying to root themselves and force the man to stop dead in his tracks, to let go of the foot by which he has been sweeping his son across the driveway.

What had the boy done wrong?

The boys in his class call him Klen-Olle, Weakling Olle. Even though his name isn't Olle. 'Mr and Mrs Lahti aren't your real parents,' they say, 'and Torsvägen 17 isn't your real home. We can call you whatever we like.'

They also seem to think they can do to him whatever they like. Once, they showed him a frozen glove they'd picked up from the ice-hockey rink, and said that if he put it on, the most popular boy in school would be best friends with him.

Of course the boy knew it was a joke. Why would anyone want to be friends with him, the skinny loser with no real parents and no real home and who therefore couldn't be real himself? No one ever looked at him, let alone spoke to him. All the boys wanted now was a laugh, a chance to prove to the rest of the school that they were better than him.

And yet the glove beckoned to him. A possibility seemed

to glint there, in the bright diamond ice. What if, for once, the other boys wanted to be nice?

So he put his hand in the glove. Or rather, tried to, because he couldn't get more than the top half of his fingers inside it. The glove was closed to him, its dark inside clogged up with ice.

The boys doubled up with laughter.

What is worse, the boy asked himself that evening. A drunk father who swings you across the driveway, or ten-year-old boys who put you through silly pranks? It wasn't Pa's fault, really. He wasn't himself after vodka, didn't know himself after moonshine. It was as if his drunk self pulled the real Pa out of his mouth and hid him in a box.

The boys weren't drunk when they decided to hand him the glove. They had nothing to excuse themselves by. They had no reason to go telling their fathers about the pathetic kid in their class. Their fathers had no reason for talking behind Pa's back, about how he was unable to have his own sons and adopted a kid who was even less of a man than him. They had no excuse for asking themselves, jokingly, if it was possible to reach a higher level of failure.

So the boy understands why Pa behaves as he does. The driveway is like a mutual understanding between them. The boy isn't supposed to be here. He is a cuckoo, an unwanted, a better-than-nothing.

The boy tries to convince himself that he is like the orange: hard and sour on the outside, juicy and good on the inside. People just need to have patience with him, peel off the ugly surface, and they will find something about him they'll like.

Red is the Colour of Guilt

They were back in the police station, for the second time in two days. Two holidaying teenagers. Ellen could not believe it. It was as if she were living somebody else's life, as if she and Simon had been dropped into one of those *LasseMaja* detective stories. She twirled the coffee Per-Anders had given her round and round on the table, inhaling its earthy smell, but unable to drink it. Her focus was on the police officer's door.

One could hear their voices: the officer's quiet monotone, Erik's higher, stumbling pitch, Malee's birdlike whisper.

Malee. The Thai blueberry picker who'd let them speak to Sunan.

Ellen still couldn't believe the officer had called her in. The woman had arrived ten minutes earlier, escorted by Constable Virtanen and led straight into the office where Sergeant Gunnarson and Erik were waiting. The constable had even joined them in there. Ellen could see the man's silhouette against the window of the door, impossibly large.

He'd almost turned the siblings out of the station when they arrived. 'Only Erik and his immediate family should come,' he'd grunted as the siblings followed Erik and Per-Anders inside.

Per-Anders had put a hand on each of their shoulders. 'They were at the scene of the incident. Surely it would be nicer to let them stay here, after all they've been through already?'

Constable Virtanen had not been able to argue with that. He'd taken Ellen's report and picked them up from the crime scene in the first place, he knew first-hand what they'd been through. That fact seemed to irk him. Then the officer had called him in to his room and five minutes later the constable left the station. To fetch Malee, as it turned out.

Did Gunnarson want her to corroborate Erik's story? Why not then call Bengt Persson, too? Was the officer afraid of repercussions, or was he just going to call the man later when they'd all left?

Would Malee tell the officer that the siblings had been to see her?

Ellen leaned forward and grabbed a sugar packet off the coffee table. She ripped it open, poured the white granules into the cup and grimaced when she took a swig. Too sweet.

The door opened. Erik walked out, followed by Malee, Gunnarson and Virtanen. The boy flashed a smile at his father and the siblings. It was wide, baring all his teeth, but didn't reach his eyes.

'Your son has explained what happened,' the sergeant told Per-Anders, 'and we think the woman had an accident. She walked off from the group, got lost, tripped on a root and banged her head. Malee confirms his story. Hospital called, they will let Sunan go tomorrow.' He shrugged. 'You can all go home.'

'No, we can't.'

Simon. He'd stood up, fists clenched by his sides. 'Sunan did not have an accident. She was abducted and left to die.'

Gunnarson folded his arms. 'Abducted, eh?' Beside him, Malee flinched and stared at her feet. Her right hand tugged at her ponytail.

'Sunan saw the reindeer killer unload the heads from the car. She mistook him for a ghost. The killer must have heard and wanted to get rid of her unless she began talking.'

Constable Virtanen stepped forward. 'Kid, that's quite enough.'

'I'm not a kid, I'm fourteen years, seven months and three days' old.'

'Simon,' Per-Anders warned.

'When Sunan woke up and saw Constable Virtanen she screamed. She pointed a finger at him and said *It's you.* Then the paramedics made her quiet.'

Virtanen scoffed. 'The kid is just rambling, Sergeant.'

'I am not a kid. The car Sunan saw in the forest is identical to Constable Virtanen's car.'

Everyone in the room fixed their eyes on Virtanen.

'How can you claim to know Sunan was in the forest?' Gunnarson asked, looking back to Simon.

Simon looked at the Thai woman. 'Malee told us. We visited the bunkhouse in the campsite where the blueberry pickers stay and she spoke to Sunan on our behalf and trans-lated.'

Now it was Ellen's turn to squirm. Coffee spilled over her hand and she winced in pain, shook her hand as if this would remove the heat. She grabbed a tissue from the coffee table and mopped the mess up.

Sergeant Gunnarson sounded neither shocked nor annoyed when he spoke. 'I thought I told you not to get involved in the case?'

'Yes.'

'But you went to the campsite. Why?'

'Because I did not think you were doing a good job of it. I thought, maybe you knew Virtanen was a suspect and you wanted to protect him because he was a policeman.'

The whole room took a deep breath then. Gunnarson stared at Simon, and Ellen stared at Gunnarson. What if he gave Simon another caution? Why couldn't Simon be a bit more sparing with the truth?

The sergeant surprised them all. He chuckled. 'Is this true?' he asked, turning to Malee.

'Yes.' Malee's gaze flitted from Simon to the constable, as if she was unable to believe what either of them had said.

'When was this?' Gunnarson continued.

'Yesterday, maybe 7.30 p.m.,' the woman said.

'I see.' A smile played on Gunnarson's face. Did this new discovery amuse him? He turned to Virtanen. 'And what do you have to say to this, Constable?'

'I told you, the kid's just rambling.'

'Then it's some pretty well-rehearsed rambling,' the sergeant said. He turned back to Simon. 'Do you have any proof to support your claims?'

'Yes.' Loudly and clearly, his head held high, Simon explained about the oil leak in the forest, the leak on Virtanen's car, the stain in the boot, the man Sunan had mistaken for a headless ghost. Then he produced his phone. 'We have evidence.'

Gunnarson took the phone from him. His thumb flicked across the screen as he swiped through the pictures. Then he scratched his nose. 'I thought we'd come to an agreement about not interfering with the police, Simon.'

'This is not an interference,' Simon said. 'Constable Virtanen's car was at the crime scene, there are traces of what appears to be one of the victims' blood in the boot. Virtanen is a primary suspect and what's more I think he is conspiring with the Persson brothers. Plus, Virtanen is left-handed and the angle of the cuts on the reindeer's horns suggests they were made by a left-handed man.'

Virtanen flexed the fingers of his left hand, then put it behind his back.

'That's quite an accusation, Simon,' said Gunnarson.

'Simon doesn't mean to accuse,' Ellen said hurriedly. 'He's only explaining his theory. Kimmo Persson was probably going to rub the stain off as well as fix the leak.'

The sergeant shifted his gaze to Per-Anders.

'It's true,' the reindeer herder said.

Gunnarson scratched his nose again, then rested his cheek against his knuckles. Fingered the phone in his other hand. Then he turned to Virtanen. 'That's your car, all right,' he said. 'Volvo 260, 2012 model.'

'For God's sake, you can't be serious.'

The sergeant gave a wry smile. 'Can't I?'

'You think I'd massacre some reindeer in the dead of night and put their heads in a circle?'

Gunnarson nodded at Simon. 'Well, this young fellow does. Explain yourself to him, and he won't be asking any more questions.'

'That's not…' Simon began, but a pointed glare from the man silenced him. His gaze wandered to the closed office door, where they had sat just two days earlier, watching the sergeant enter his caution in the register.

'Now,' Gunnarson said, addressing Virtanen. 'Where were you on the night of the 13th?'

'I was with my mother,' the constable said through gritted teeth.

'Why?'

'She was in hospital. I came to drive her home.'

'At half past midnight?'

'Eight. I stayed with her the whole night.'

'At her place?'

'Yes.'

'Remind me where that is again.'

'Ullatti.'

'And you have solid proof you were with her that evening?'

Virtanen dug a battered leather wallet out of his back pocket and produced a slip of paper. Gunnarson took it and peered at it over his glasses. 'Hospital parking ticket, 18.10, valid for two hours. Meaning you left at 8 p.m.' He gave the receipt back. Virtanen virtually ripped it from his fingers.

'But Sunan cried *It's you*,' Simon reminded them. 'She must know him or else she wouldn't say something like that.'

The sergeant bit his lip. 'Do you know this woman, Virtanen?'

'I wouldn't say *know*.'

'But you've met her.'

Virtanen grunted in acknowledgement.

'Where? How?'

The constable bit his lip. He looked at Malee. 'Some of the blueberry pickers sold their berries to me in secret. This older woman, Sunan, did it most times.'

'Is this true, Malee?' Gunnarson asked.

The dark-haired woman nodded. She tugged more firmly at her ponytail.

'And you biked into the forest to do this? Every week, always at the same spot?'

'I not go many time. Sunan, she need money more.'

'Does Bengt Persson not pay you well?'

The woman shook her head. 'No.'

'Can you give me an exact price?'

Malee frowned in thought. 'Thirty krona per litre, maybe a hundred and fifty one day.'

Ellen drew in a sharp breath. A hundred and fifty, that was not much more than she made per hour at the supermarket. And to only pay them by the litre... If it was a bad season, the workers would earn next to nothing. Exactly what Simon had derived from his calculations.

'Constable, hadn't you told Sunan you were busy last Wednesday night?'

'Yes,' Virtanen said quickly, 'I did. But she must have misunderstood. My English is crap and she can't speak Swedish.' His gaze flitted to the officer. 'Selling blueberries isn't a criminal offence.'

'According to their contract, the Thai workers can only sell their berries through Persson's company,' Gunnarson said. 'Sunan breached that contract by selling the berries directly to you.' He took a step towards the taller man. 'Break a contract and you are effectively breaking the law. That isn't something I need to spell out to you, is it, Constable?'

Not a muscle in the man's face moved. 'It was Mother. She used to do it. Before she got unwell.' His lips hardly moved when he spoke; it made his voice drop several notches. 'I told her exactly what you said now. Wouldn't listen.'

His jaw was so tense Ellen thought his teeth would crack. She noticed the man's large hands, clasped in front of him, knuckles bone-white against the pink skin.

'One can't say no to a sick woman.'

'You should have reported this to me ages ago, Virtanen. As soon as it started. You have acted unprofessionally. And if you had indeed told Sunan not to come, why was it your car she saw in the forest?'

The constable shrugged. 'I don't know. Maybe someone tried to frame me.'

'Then they must have borrowed your car at night. They must have known you'd be away with your mother, and that you regularly bought berries from these people. Who have you told about your habits, Virtanen?'

'No one!' The constable was fuming. His cheeks flashed red, the muscles in his face writhed. Then without a word, he marched out of the station.

The sergeant rubbed his nose. 'I think you all need to leave, now. Except you, Per-Anders.' He motioned to the man. 'A word, now.'

Those Who Call Us Devils

Ellen, Simon and Erik waited for Per-Anders by the bicycle rack. It was seven o'clock in the evening now and the sun cast longer shadows over the ground. Malee had left, claiming she had to return to the campsite to work. Ellen wondered if the woman was going to report back to Bengt, or maybe even try to run away. She'd been tempted to call after the woman, but after everything that had happened, felt she couldn't be bothered. Not even Simon said a word.

When Per-Anders finally came out, Ellen emitted a slight sigh of relief. 'Well?' she said.

'The officer thinks it's best you go home. Back to Stockholm.'

'What?'

'Staying here is no good. Several crimes have taken place, you shouldn't get involved.' The man's lips barely moved as he spoke. His hands stirred inside his pockets.

'But we've only got three nights left,' Ellen said. 'We go home on Tuesday! And the train tickets are non-refundable. If we go home tomorrow we'll have to pay for new tickets.'

'I can give you something towards that.'

'Surely us staying just a couple of days longer...' It couldn't be right. Per-Anders must have got it wrong.

'I'm sorry to let you down,' the man said. 'I'll give you a lift to your hostel.'

'No!' she stepped forward, reached out her hand. 'I promise you we can sort this...'

'The officer was firm.'

Ellen cursed silently. What was Per-Anders doing, helping the officer ensure they stayed away from the case? He must have been talked into this, why else would he turn so quickly? Nothing else made sense...

Simon was thinking the same thing. 'But you involved us,' he pointed out. 'You showed us the hut and the lake which were the second and third crime scenes and you showed us that Facebook group with the animal molesters. Plus, you told us the real reason Granddad left Purnuvaare.' He folded his arms. 'I don't understand why you would do all that if you wanted us to stay out of things and go home.'

Per-Anders opened and closed his mouth, taken aback.

'Hang on a minute,' Erik said. 'You showed them the videos? *The* video?'

Per-Anders lowered his gaze.

'You never show that stuff to anyone. You were even reluctant to show it to TV4.' Erik turned to Ellen. 'They did a feature last winter. Less than two weeks after the vid was uploaded. *Lappland Devils.* It was on *Good Morning Sweden.*'

His gaze returned to his father. Per-Anders sighed through his teeth. 'Perhaps showing them the hut was a mistake.'

'Yeah?' his son exclaimed. 'Was inviting them home a mistake, too?'

'Erik, the officer...'

'Really Dad, since when did you care about what some stupid cop said?'

Silence cut the air between them. Ellen held her breath, stole a glance at the swivelling doors.

'We should move,' Per-Anders said. 'This is no place to talk.' He made to leave for the car park. 'Erik?'

The Sami boy backed away.

'You aren't coming?' his father said.

'Go,' Erik told him.

'Erik, Ellen and Simon have to leave tomorrow.'

'Just go, OK?' The boy put his hands in his pockets and clenched them, hard. 'I don't want to talk to you.'

'OK.' Per-Anders backed away. 'Call me when you're coming home.'

His son kicked a pebble so hard it hit the bicycle stand and ricocheted across the lawn, all the way to the road.

Per-Anders pulled up by the wooden wall enclosing the hostel courtyard. 'I'm going to take cash out from the ATM.'

He was out of the car before Ellen could nod. She turned in her seat and watched him cross the road, heading for the cash machine on the pedestrian street leading to the town square.

'The police officer can't force us to leave,' Simon said, shifting his Rubik's cube from one hand to the other. 'We haven't broken the law, and more importantly, our investigation can't be interrupted.'

The reindeer herder had reached the ATM. Ellen envisioned his index finger jabbing the pin onto the keypad, the whizz of the machine as it ejected the money.

'I don't think Per-Anders wants us to leave,' she said.

'Why not?'

They watched him step away from the machine, tuck something into his pocket, a wallet no doubt, then head back to the car.

'It's too sudden.'

She watched the man's features as he drew close. There was an edge to his jaw, as if he was biting down on his teeth very hard, and his eyebrows knitted together into a deep frown.

'He showed us everything, Simon. This morning we were at the lake...' she checked her watch. 'Five hours ago. Whatever the officer said, it really affected him.'

The car door opened. Per-Anders climbed into his seat. He took two 500-kronor notes from his wallet and held them out to Ellen. 'I know this doesn't cover the whole cost for the train ticket, but I think it will help, yes?'

Ellen did not move to take the money. The banknotes were a dividing line: if she accepted them, she accepted the officer's terms – they would have no choice but to go home.

Per-Anders thrust them closer to her. 'I need to see to the animals,' he said.

A warning. He wouldn't wait here forever.

Ellen shifted to the right side of her seat. 'If it was the killer who abducted Sunan, why did he leave her alive? Why let her get away with a mild concussion?' She looked at the banknotes as she spoke: they perched, perfectly still, in the reindeer herder's leathery fingers. 'I was thinking, and I know I could be wrong, perhaps it's because he didn't have the heart to kill her? He kills animals easily but won't harm humans... because that would be murder.'

The banknotes shivered. The fingers holding them flexed, veins writhing beneath the weather-beaten skin.

'You think this?' Per-Anders whispered.

She saw her grandfather in front of her when she spoke. 'Gut feeling, I suppose.'

Per-Anders withdrew his hand. The banknotes brushed against the wheel as he rested his hand in his lap. He stared out the window. 'I remember Juha's mum,' he said. 'She treated everyone as if they were close family. I dropped by now and then, when I'd given Juha a lift from school. She would always ask Juha to take my coat and hat: one should always treat visitors well. There was always something baking in the oven, fruity things of the season. August was blueberry pie, September plum tart. I could tell something ailed her, she would put a hand to her chest sometimes and breathe deeply as if in pain, but she always kept quiet about it and the years went by so I stopped noticing it. Then one day, must have been two years ago, I drove past their house and I noticed the door was open. It was December, minus twenty-three. Shopping bags lay in the hallway and an apple had rolled out onto the porch. She lay on the floor, hair spread out around her head. Heart attack, at forty-five; turned out to be a hereditary condition. Had I driven by five minutes later it would have been too late. Juha felt guilty, angry even, that I was the one who saved her and not him. As if he had let her down. Two months later he joined the police. I think he thought this way, by representing safety in the community, he could compensate for not being there for his mother when she needed him most.'

Per-Anders put his left elbow against the side window and rested his chin against his hand. 'I went to visit her in hospital. She was half-asleep because of medication. She started talking. *Have you bought them?* she kept saying. *She is waiting for you, she has all the berries. She doesn't know I'm in hospital and can't come as normal. You should do right by her.* She must have thought I was Juha.' He lowered his hand, brushed a finger over the banknotes. 'Of course I had no clue then what she was on about, but now... I guess she was referring to the Thai woman.'

'You mean that Juha's mother bought Sunan's berries before she got ill?'

'Mm-hmm,' Per-Anders said.

'I see.' Ellen gazed at her reflection in the side mirror, trying to gather her thoughts. 'He never seemed like that kind of person.'

'He always pretended he was immune to feelings,' Per-Anders said.

'Why?'

'Because he is vulnerable.' Per-Anders snorted gently. He looked down at the money in his hand. 'Anyway. We need to get this over with.'

Ellen grimaced. 'We don't have to leave.'

'You can visit another time. A better time. Your whole family is welcome.' A ghost of a smile touched his lips.

Ellen tried picturing her parents stuck on a stuffy train together for sixteen hours.

The reindeer herder pressed the money into her hand. Then he turned the ignition key.

Five times that evening Ellen typed the home number into the dial screen. Five times she cancelled the dialling and hid the phone under the pillow.

She knew she was acting stupidly. Sooner or later she'd have to make the call, even if it wasn't until halfway back on the train. Why delay any further? She didn't have to give all the details, she could spare herself that trouble until she got home.

Yet every time she got out the phone, Dad's face loomed in front her. The corners of his mouth drooped and disappointment veiled his eyes. She could hear his words: *You have lied to me, Ellen,* followed by her own words: *You have lied to me, Dad.*

She dialled her mum's phone number, but for once – probably the first time in three years – the call went straight to voicemail. Perhaps that was a good thing. If her mum had answered, Ellen wouldn't have had a chance to get a word in. It would all have been about Camilla, how *she* had been kept in the dark, how *she* had been worried. With Ellen's voice on record, Camilla would have no choice but to listen. She would have to make do with her daughter's version of events, and not her own emotional response to them. And so the story spilled out of her, eager to be told, eager to break free.

The banknotes lay in Ellen's wallet. The top corner of one stuck up above the edge, a tiny triangle of red, waving at her.

You can still refuse, a voice within her whispered.

But if the officer saw them in town tomorrow or the day after... Ellen didn't put it beyond the man to put them both in jail. Of course, Simon had been quick to state that, legally, the officer had no grounds to do so unless they'd both committed a criminal offence, and he hadn't officially ordered them to leave the town.

'I don't think people care so much about the law here,' she told her brother as they sat in their room. She reminded him of what Per-Anders said when they'd seen the video. *In the forest, people do what they want.*

'But Kimmo Persson came to fix his car,' Simon said. 'It could have been him who Sunan saw, or Bengt, and they all decided to get rid of her.'

'Were you asleep when Per-Anders was talking? You need to get this idea of him being guilty out of your head.'

The words tasted like bile. She took a deep swig of water, swirled it around her mouth – was almost tempted to spit it out in the basin. 'Besides, if they really conspired together, why would Bengt go to the length of having Juha or his brother abduct Sunan and then kill her, when he could just give her a sharp blow to the head any time? He sees her every day.' And why, she thought to herself, had Bengt not come to the station? Conspiring or not, his employee had been injured. Had he refused? Did the police officer not care whether he came?

Simon bent his head and fiddled with the corner of a page in his notebook. 'Juha is left-handed.'

'He won't be the only left-handed man in Svartjokk.' Ellen frowned. 'How did you figure that out, by the way?'

'When he tried to grab me in the glade, before I hit him, he was leading with his left hand. He used his left hand to open the car door.'

Ellen stared at him. 'You noticed all of that *and* took a picture?'

'Yes.'

'And you didn't think of telling me?'

Simon's look was slightly puzzled. 'I don't know. I think I forgot. I was keeping all the facts in my head.'

Ellen rolled her eyes. 'Any other facts you've been hiding from me?'

Simon squirmed slightly. 'Juha's shoe size,' he said, not looking her in the eye. 'It doesn't match the shoe print in the ditch where the ambulance was. His feet are a size bigger, I saw when we were in the police office. That is more hard proof that Juha wasn't the kidnapper or the killer.' He bit his lip. 'I was wrong about him. And that means: we need to keep investigating.'

Ellen suppressed a sigh. She'd suspected it might come to this.

'We need to check the alibis of everyone tagged on that video,' Simon continued. 'They are all potential suspects and I am convinced they have an idea of who killed the reindeer. We need to speak to Malee again. Perhaps one of the Thai workers saw who abducted Sunan.' He paused in his movements. 'Then I want to find out about the name in the registry.'

'What registry?'

'The one in the Old Church. A name had been crossed out.' He frowned in thought. 'It was on the list of baptised newborns and all the other years on that page said 1960. More specifically, December '60.' He turned the right side of the cube forward towards himself, two turns. 'Grandfather left Purnuvaare in August that year.'

Ellen nodded, remembering Per-Anders's story.

'If Granddad's girlfriend Lisbet was three months pregnant in May 1960,' Simon continued, 'she could have given birth in November and baptised the child in December.' He picked up his Rubik's cube and twisted the upper line three turns clockwise. The upper and far right sides turned red.

'It was a stillbirth,' Ellen said. 'Why would you baptise a dead baby?'

'Perhaps because she was very sad and wanted to give it a name before the funeral.' Simon's frown deepened. 'Or perhaps it wasn't dead.' He twisted the cube: clockwise, backwards, anti-clockwise. Solved.

'That's impossible,' Ellen said.

'No, it isn't.'

'We made a mistake with Juha. We totally misjudged him.' She pulled at her hair. 'I'm not sure that we're capable enough.'

'We are capable.' Simon picked up his notebook. 'I remember something I wrote when we were at Per-Anders's house which I have not had the time to tell you.' He ran a finger down the page. 'Here.' He looked up at her. 'I think Bengt Persson must be related to the Perssons who attacked Granddad. They both come from Kajava, and if that village is as small as Per-Anders claims it to be, the chance of them not being related is minimal.'

Ellen nodded. She hadn't openly voiced the thought, but it had lain dormant in her mind.

'We are capable of solving the case, Ellen, we just have to notice all the details, remember them and piece them together.' He closed the book. 'Besides, Granddad said we should never give up our dreams.'

'Solving the reindeer mystery is your dream?'

'Yes. At the moment it is. Except it is not a mystery.'

Ellen frowned. 'I don't follow.'

'A mystery is something that is not understood, beyond understanding, profound, inexplicable or of secretive character.' Her brother put the cube on the bed, the green side facing her, and pulled his hair out of his eyes. 'The death of the reindeer and the poisoning of Nilajaure is not beyond understanding. It is a whodunnit.' He leaned closer. 'The why will lead to the who.'

She was woken by a pattering sound. Stones, against glass.

Their window.

Ice formed in her belly. She pulled her knees up to her chest, the duvet over her head.

The pattering continued.

Ellen counted ten seconds. Then she flicked the duvet over, cold air prickling her skin, stepped up to the window and peered through the blinds.

Erik stood on the street by the wooden fence, perfectly visible in the peach-coloured light from the sky.

Ellen reached through the blinds and opened the window. 'Erik?'

His eyes found hers. His face split into a grin. 'Knew you would answer!'

'What are you doing here?'

'Let me in and I'll explain!'

Ellen rolled her eyes. 'I'll be down in a sec.'

Erik's grin widened.

'You're a brick,' he said as she opened the door.

Ellen's gaze darted left to right. Svartjokk was deserted. The sun had just dipped beneath the horizon, but a damson hue still tinged the dark blue sky. Standing by the wall was Erik's moped.

'How long have you been here?'

'About ten minutes.'

'Someone could've seen you!'

Erik looked over his shoulder at the street. 'Don't think so.' He looked back at her. 'So, you gonna let me stand out here any longer?'

She rolled her eyes, then stepped back to let him in. 'The stairs creak,' she warned. 'No one can know you're here.'

'Would that get me thrown out?' he whispered, his breath warm in her ear. 'Or, wait, would that get you thrown out?'

She stopped on the step to turn around and glare at him. The stairway window behind her cast a blue shade over his face, giving his green eyes a soft turquoise sheen. Her glare turned into a smile.

Simon sat up in his bed and switched the lamp on when they entered the room.

'You're awake,' she said. Behind her, Erik eased the door shut.

'I heard someone throwing stones at the window,' her brother said.

'Not so loud,' Ellen put a finger to her lips. 'Everyone's sleeping.' She nodded at the window. 'You're closer to the window than me, why didn't you check? Instead of forcing me to get up.'

'It might have been a stranger,' Simon said.

'Well, good thing it wasn't.' She turned to Erik. 'Why are you here?' She folded her arms. 'We didn't think we'd see you again.'

'I'm sorry about that.' Erik crossed the room and put his rucksack on the desk. 'I... there was too much stuff going on. Up here.' He tapped his head.

You're not alone, Ellen thought. She perched on Simon's bed, which earned her a wary, questioning look from her brother. 'Where did you go? After, you know...'

Erik shrugged, avoiding her gaze. 'Various places. Down the river, around the town. Just had to keep moving, so my thoughts wouldn't catch up with me.'

He sat down on the chair by the desk and pulled a laptop out of his rucksack. He wore the same clothes as earlier: the blue fleece and black hiking trousers. She was surprised he didn't take the fleece off; she'd turned the heating up before bed, and the room was hot. 'I got an idea and wanted to show you.' He unzipped the blue case (the same kind Simon had) and dropped it on the desk, but rested the laptop, a MacBook Air, on his lap. 'It's a bit crazy to be honest.' He started typing rapidly, then finished with two left-side clicks on the pad. 'But it might do the trick.' He turned the screen around.

The Real Swedish Norrbotten Facebook group stared back at them.

'Wait a bit...' Ellen leaned forward. 'Is that...'

'It is the group who uploaded the reindeer video,' Simon said, completing her thought.

Ellen folded her arms. 'Why are you showing us this?'

''Cause we should get in touch with them,' said Erik.

'*We?*' Ellen repeated, too loudly. She winced, lowered her voice. 'Get in touch with *them?*'

'Not in person, of course. I mean online. We create a Facebook account and ask to join the group. Ask about the reindeer killing, maybe comment about how messed up it is that the police suspect the Perssons. If we're lucky, one of them will open up and give us insider information. Perhaps even tell us who the killer is.'

Erik made it sound like he was planning a picnic.

'That is a high degree of crazy,' said Simon.

'We'll get caught,' said Ellen. 'Erik, this is dangerous.'

'Dangerous?' The Sami boy scoffed. 'Course it's not dangerous.'

'Your dad and sister don't know, do they?'

'If they did they would have thrown my laptop out the window. Well, Vera would.'

'I get why,' said Ellen.

'Look.' Erik leaned forward, chest touching the edge of the screen. 'I know it's risky. Don't you think I've been toying with the idea all day, unsure whether to go with it or not?'

'The first thing we would need to know is how many of them have alibis for the 12th or 13th,' Simon said.

Ellen stared at her brother, jaw dropping. 'You aren't agreeing with him, are you?'

'This might be our best chance of finding out who the killer is.' Simon looked at her expectantly, as if waiting for her agreement.

'Please, Ellen.' Erik's eyes were pleading, puppy-like.

Ellen's gaze drifted to her wallet on the bedside table, where Per-Anders's money lay.

'Look, I'll show you how it works.' Erik got up and sat himself down between the siblings. He started typing again. 'We'll invent our Swedish Norrbotten lad together.'

Ellen's shoulders tensed. 'What if they figure out it's fake? What if they can trace the profile to us? To your computer?'

'Ellen, the people in these areas… I know them. It will be fine. Don't you worry.' He tapped the mouse button for emphasis. 'Come on, let's create our Norrbottning.' He clicked on the name boxes under the Create a New Account heading. 'Johan? David? Kalle?' He grinned. 'Erik?'

'In 2016,' Simon said, '75,146 men in Sweden were named Johan. It's one of the top ten most common male names in the country.'

'Erik must be up there, too,' the older boy said.

'Yes, but not as many. There were 67,540 Eriks in 2016.'

Erik's jaw dropped. 'Wow.' He returned his gaze to the computer. 'Johan it is, then. Probably safer.' He typed the name into the first box. 'Surname?'

'Gustafsson,' Simon said without hesitation. 'It's ranked tenth of the top ten most common surnames.'

'Ah,' Erik clicked his tongue. 'Common, but not too common. Not the surname you'd pick if you made one up on the spot.' He tapped his index finger to his brow. 'I like how you think, Mr Detective.'

Simon blushed, looking like he would burst with smugness any second.

Erik typed in a phone number and password, leaving the suggested birthday date generated by the website – 16 July 1993 – unchanged.

Ellen put her hand on his wrist. 'Wait. 16th July is today. It's only suggesting today's date. Maybe you should pick another one.'

A smile flickered across his face. 'Good point.' Erik altered the date to 23 November. Then he hit the Sign Up button.

Johan Gustafsson came into being.

'This is like playing the Sims,' Erik said, letting the arrow swoop around the blank profile page. 'Let's bring some life into this guy.'

With just a few clicks and Google searches, Erik and Simon breathed life into their online character. Johan Gustafsson was born in Ullatti in 1993. He'd gone to Hedeby school. After working in Svappavaara as an explosives operator for five years he'd found employment as a mining engineer in Järnberget. His religious belief was atheist, his political view *I don't like politicians.* He was interested in women, his marital status single, his favourite music was Elvis Presley and Eddie Meduza, and his favourite film was *Jaws.* His favourite quote was: *I don't believe in inspirational quotes by fancy celebs or dead philosophers.* The Details About Myself section read: *Facebook, I've already given you enough details.*

Erik grinned from ear to ear. He bent his chin to his chest, took three deep breaths as if to stop himself from bursting into laughter. 'Last but not least, the profile picture.'

'Are you sure that's a good idea?' Ellen muttered.

'Everyone has a profile pic these days. It would look pretty suspicious if Johan just had a blank silhouette. The group would fire questions at him.'

Erik opened a new tab. He typed *Killar från Norr-botten (Guys from Norrbotten)* into the search engine.

'That one,' Simon said, after half a page of scrolling.

He pointed at the photo of a guy in a black T-shirt and cap. Blond stubble covered his chin and jaw. He stood in what seemed to be a car park, in front of a blue Volvo, the car logo visible in the bottom right corner. Snow covered the ground, and yet the guy was biting into what seemed to be a Magnum ice cream.

He was what Ellen's mum would call a 'typical Svensson guy'.

'Weird,' Erik said, his eyes lit up by the screen, 'but perfect.'

'Kimmo Persson was eating an ice cream when we met him,' Simon said.

Erik made the photo Johan Gustafsson's profile picture and chose an image of a Volvo on a field, pine forest in the background, as the cover photo. 'All ready to go,' he whispered, and typed *The Real Swedish Norrbotten* into the Facebook search engine. It appeared at the top of the hit list.

'Join group,' Erik said and clicked the button. A pop-up box appeared on the screen: *Answer these questions to explain to the admins why you want to join the group. 1. Why do you want to join The Real Swedish Norrbotten? 2. Were you born in Norrbotten?*

Erik's fingers hovered above the keyboard. He began typing, then deleted what he'd written, and smacked his lips in thought.

'May I?' Ellen said.

Erik handed the laptop over to her.

Ellen took a deep breath. All her instincts screamed at her to shut the computer down. She flexed her fingers, allowed the white box to fill her vision, forcing the real world out of her mind. Her fingers clicked against the keys.

On the lookout for real, Swedish brothers to share a beer

and hunt with. Fed up with the state of this country. One neighbour is an Arab, the other an Asian, and the third a Lapp woman. What happened to Swedish culture? What happened to patriotism? It's sickening.

I am a Norrbotten son born and bred from the humble village of Ullatti.

'Wait,' Erik said. 'Change the name of the town. Ullatti is too close, they would know if a Johan Gustafsson lived there.' He reached past Ellen to type a different name, his arm and shoulder brushing against hers. *Vettasjärvi.* 'That's on the western border of Norrbotten, far enough that they wouldn't know anyone there.'

Done. The three youngsters held their breath, not daring even to look at each other.

The request was accepted. Seconds later, a post materialised on the group feed.

Please give our latest member Johan Gustafsson a hearty welcome! The member who'd posted was a Markus Ringqvist.

Statistics appeared in blue writing on the right-hand side of the post. *Seen by One, Seen by Two.* Three. Five. Ten. Then came the comments.

Welcome, Johan.
Welcome home brother.
Damn good of you to join.
Where are your friends?

Ellen froze. She stared at the fourth question as if it had come alive and crawled out of the screen. She dragged the mouse over to the name of the writer: Freddie Arvidsson. The profile picture showed a bulldog terrier sitting by a tractor.

She clicked onto Johan's profile page, moved the mouse over to the Friends section on the menu.

The page was blank, save for the two words *Zero Friends.*

She returned to the Facebook group. *Got rid of FB a year ago but decided to make a comeback. For realz.* She hit Reply.

Freddie Arvidsson wrote back within the minute. *FB needs ppl like u.* Three likes. One of them by Kimmo Persson.

Ellen let her hands glide down on the duvet. She leaned back, closed her eyes for a moment. Became aware of her heart pounding against her chest.

'That was a close one.' Erik's voice sounded out of breath, as if he'd been holding it for a long time. 'Good thinking, Ellen.'

She pulled herself back up. Both boys stared at her. Simon's mouth was slightly open.

'The big challenge comes now,' she said. 'How to make them give information.'

'Erik, can you click onto the list of members?' Simon said. His notebook was in his hand. When did he get that out? Ellen hadn't noticed.

There were fifty-four names on the list. Ellen recognised Kimmo's, Bengt's, Henrik's and Juha Virtanen's names. There were a couple of other Perssons on there too, but Persson was such a common surname it was actually more likely they weren't related. Erik randomly clicked onto names, doing a quick scan of their posts and the About section on their profile.

Simon wrote down every single name, including hometown when this was given. When he was done he said: 'Can we look at the videos now?'

Ellen tensed. 'I'm not sure.' She glanced at Erik. 'Maybe it will be too much for you.'

The boy shrugged. 'I've seen stuff like this so many

times they've stopped having an effect on me.' He leaned forward over the screen as he clicked on the Photo and Video section on the menu. The video Per-Anders had shown the siblings was third on the list.

'Bloody hell.' Erik leaned even closer, so his forehead nearly touched the screen. 'There's nametags and comments here. Dad got the video sent to him via a fake email, so we didn't get all this information. The camera jolts a lot as well so it was hard to identify everyone before. Now we can.'

Bengt and Kimmo Persson's names were on the list of tagged people, along with Henrik Andersson and Markus Ringqvist.

'Juha isn't on there,' Ellen noticed. 'But that is him on the left, isn't it?' She pointed at the tall figure to the far left, his head and shoulders cut out of the video. He seemed to have the same heavy build as the police constable, but without a face to identify him it was impossible to draw conclusions.

Simon leaned in past Erik's arm. 'The video was edited two hours ago,' he said, pointing at the tiny writing beneath the video title: *Håll koll på renjäveln* (Keep an eye on the damn reindeer). 'Juha might have had his name removed after today's events.'

It was true, Ellen admitted. Maybe the man wanted to forget he'd been involved in all this, to go clean, so to speak. But why, then, hadn't he left the group?

'Five of these people live in Kajava,' Erik said. 'The other two in Björkliden.' His eyes darkened. 'It's embarrassing that they went to the same school as me.'

He pulled out a pair of headphones from his pocket, and they played through the video again. Ellen's chest contracted as she listened to the reindeer's bleats. The older boy scrolled through the Comment section.

Bloody good film, he wrote, which immediately

received a like by Freddie Arvidsson. *You done any more of this stuff recently?*

Not since winter, came Freddie's reply. *Hard to get to the animals in spring and summer, they move around more and they get so aggressive when they have their young ones.*

He referred them to the two latest uploads on the video menu. The first dated back to March that year and showed three men laying traps in the forest.

'Fox traps,' Erik said. 'Doesn't matter how many sanctions the Hunting Agency introduces, people here just keep on doing their own thing. They shoot anything on four legs.' He smiled cynically. 'You'd think we lived in anarchy.'

The second video was of a dogfight, uploaded in May. It was filmed indoors in what looked like an old barn. A ring of men cheered the dogs on – an Alsatian and a pit bull terrier. Henrik could be seen on the right, and behind him, a man Simon suspected was Kimmo Persson. The harsh growling and yapping of the dogs stung Ellen's ears. She tensed each time the dogs bit into one another, drawing blood. In the end, the Alsatian limped away, dragging its left hindleg behind it. Then the men ambled up to a table with a cashbox on it – presumably where they'd placed their bets. Henrik, they noticed, got no money back.

'I think you should write a post asking about the reindeer heads, if anyone knows who could have done it,' Simon said afterwards. 'That is the main reason we created this account.'

'Maybe it's better to ask one of them personally, in a message,' Ellen said. 'We can't risk them getting suspicious and removing us from the group.'

'You never know,' Erik said, 'this Freddie here might

add me as a friend. He's acted friendly enough.' As if the computer heard him, a notification flashed in blue on the screen.

Freddie Arvidsson sent you a friend request.

Erik, who'd taken the computer back, looked from Ellen to Simon and back at Ellen again. She nodded. Erik hit Accept.

You and Freddie are now friends.

This was followed only seconds later by: **Freddie sent you a message.**

It was an FB conversation like any other. How-you-doings followed by where-you-froms, what's-your-job followed by how-did-you-find-the-group. Freddie fired them one after the other. Erik struggled to keep up at times. Ellen and Simon watched one chat bubble pop on the screen, multiplying itself by the dozen, as Freddie sent one message after the next. Erik's jaw worked as he wrote, as if he chewed through every response before sending it out through his fingers. The tap and click of the keyboard were the only sounds in the room.

After about ten minutes, Erik typed the question hovering in all their minds. *You heard about that circle of reindeer heads in the forest?*

Seen 01.26 appeared in tiny writing beneath Erik's message, indicating Freddie had read it. No bobbing chat dots suggesting he was typing a response appeared.

'Perhaps we scared him off,' said Ellen.

Erik and Simon said nothing.

Two minutes passed. Then, without warning, a grey chat bubble appeared.

I need to sleep. Up at 6 in the morning.

The youngsters sighed at the same time.

OK, Erik replied. *Cu bro.*

The green chat light next to Freddie's name vanished.

Ellen folded her hands together. 'Well, that was that.'

'Intense.' Erik placed the laptop on the duvet and rolled onto his back, pulling knees to chest. 'So tired now.'

Ellen ran her hand over the computer. Freddie Arvidsson's profile picture hovered in her mind's eye. She wondered if he really had gone to sleep. 'Guess you need to go back,' she said to Erik.

'I'd rather not, to be honest.'

Ellen looked over her shoulder at him. 'Won't your family wonder where you are?'

'I doubt it.' Erik blew at a lock of hair that had slid over his eyes. It lifted a fraction, the yellow hair tip waving through the air, before landing at exactly the same spot. He tutted and pushed it away with the back of his hand. 'Dad's probably at my uncle's, getting a telling off for bringing you two over.'

'But you can't stay here! There's nowhere to sleep.'

'Actually, I've thought about that already.' He nodded towards his rucksack leaning against the leg of the chair.

For the first time Ellen noticed what else was inside it. 'You brought a sleeping bag?'

Silence met her from the bed. When she turned back to him, Erik looked at her sheepishly.

'You invited yourself here without asking us?'

'It was a snap decision. Didn't have time to tell you in advance. Besides, I don't have your numbers.'

'076-349210 and 073-088532,' Simon said promptly.

'You'll have to repeat that later. I haven't got a super-memory like you.'

Ellen, now standing up, began to pace up and down the room. 'What if the owners notice?'

'Do they knock on your doors for morning inspections?'

'No.'

'Then it shouldn't be a problem, should it?'

Ellen rolled her eyes. 'Try not to use the bathroom.'

'All right, boss.'

'I mean it. We can't allow you to be seen, not even by other guests. We're in enough trouble as it is.' She turned towards him. 'What did you do all day, after leaving the police station?'

Erik frowned. 'I told you, I drove around. I hung around at my friend's place in the evening. My friend in the band. We're working on a new song.'

'You didn't go home at all?'

Erik's tone grew short. 'Why do you ask?'

Ellen looked towards Simon. He was fiddling with the Rubik's cube again, but she could tell he was listening. She thought of how Erik had stormed out when Simon mentioned his mother. She had to phrase this carefully.

'I just couldn't help noticing things seemed tense between you and your Dad, and that maybe it had to do with your mother.'

At first, she thought she'd gone too far. Erik sat stock still, staring into nothing. Then he shifted position slightly and let out a slow sigh.

'My Dad and I have been estranged since Mum died.'

'Why?'

'We have different opinions on what's best for me.' Erik drummed his long, slender fingers against his laptop. 'Mum was very supportive of my music. Told me, if I found music was my true calling, I should go for it. All in. What with her... gone, Dad thinks it's more important I prioritise the family business. Says my support is more important now so we can keep it all going. He means for me and Vera to take

over after him, and that it would be too much for her alone.'
He smiled drily. 'She'd disagree, though.'

Ellen pictured his sister's stubborn face. 'I can imagine.
What about your cousins, though, couldn't they...'

Erik shook his head. 'They will have my uncle's herd.
It's like two reindeer herds in one, the Thomasson business,
managed by the two Thomasson families. One person isn't a
whole family.' He sighed. 'I think Dad thinks I'm being selfish,
but I'm not... I just don't know how to make him see that.'

Ellen curled the end of the duvet around her finger. 'I
know it isn't the same, but we haven't got on so well with our
Dad this past year either.'

Erik looked at her. 'You haven't?'

'He had a quarrel of some sort with Lars-Erik before
he died but has never told us what it was about. He's been
oddly tense about it. Then he and Mum have been arguing...'

Erik's face was grim. 'It sucks,' he muttered.

'But between you and your dad, things weren't always
bad, right?'

'Guess not.' There was a shrug in Erik's voice. 'He's
just pissed me off ten times too many.' Erik sat up properly,
resting elbows on knees. 'Not all young Sami want to be reindeer herders, you know. I'm not some kind of black sheep.
That's what you thought, wasn't it?' An edge crept into his
voice. It reminded Ellen of his sister, Vera, when she'd con-
fronted Ellen in the kitchen.

'Your dad,' she began, 'would you say he's one who
always tells the truth? Even at times when it's better to stay
quiet?'

Erik cocked his head to the side. 'You want my honest
opinion?'

Ellen held his gaze. There was no need for her to say
yes, or even to nod.

'He's just a shadow of himself. Something broke within him after Mum's death. Since then, he's been ignoring the truth rather than dealing with it.'

Ellen noticed Simon's expression change. Apprehension, perhaps? She bet they were thinking of the same thing: the picture of Erik's mother on the fridge.

'Do you want to talk about it?' she asked.

'Not now. I'm exhausted.' He made a wry grimace. 'Gonna do like our new friend Freddie.' He stepped over to his rucksack and pulled out the sleeping bag. It was a bright orange thing, glowing in the dimly lit room. He climbed inside, but poked his head up one last time. 'Don't you dare go home tomorrow.'

'Absolute zero chance of that,' Simon said. He looked at his sister.

'Yes,' she said. She caught Erik's eye. 'Couldn't leave you all alone with the fake Facebook profile, right?'

They exchanged knowing grins and turned the lights out. It did not make the room much darker, though, as the light seeping through the gaps in the curtains grew brighter – the sun must have risen from its one-hour nap. Anxiety crept back into Ellen's thoughts. They'd been given the opportunity to go home, but instead they'd put themselves at an even greater risk than before. By creating the Facebook page, they'd exposed themselves to more people. If something went wrong now, it wasn't only one or two people who could retaliate, but two communities – Kajava and Björkliden. What would Sergeant Gunnarson do, if he found out they'd disobeyed him a second time? If Henrik found out about Johan Gustafsson's true identity, would he kick them out of the hostel?

When Mum heard the voicemail, would she fly over and pick them up in person and lock them up in their rooms for the rest of the summer? Would they come home only to discover their parents were divorced?

Ellen shut her eyes tighter to push the thoughts away. She did not know what she feared more: the visions that would haunt her through her dreams, or the reality she'd wake up to in the morning. Her worries pulsed inside her, like that pulse in her neck when they'd discovered the reindeer. Except this time, the sensation was far worse.

Deliverance

Pa steps on the boy's Lego fortress. He howls and clutches his foot, jumps on the spot a few times, before staggering back to the sofa. He sits down and massages his foot. 'Apologise,' he growls, spittle flying from his lips.

The boy can smell it from where he is sitting. A sour mixture of vodka, sweat and unbrushed teeth. He looks over to the fruit bowl on the kitchen table. It is empty. It has been empty for two days. Ma has been gone for about an hour now. She should be home soon, with oranges in bags.

'Apologise,' Pa says again. The boy shuts his eyes and his mouth and clutches a piece of Lego to his chest.

'Right, that's it.' The sofa creaks as the man stands up. 'You're coming with me.'

He grabs the boy by the collar and drags him outside. Gravel scrapes against the boy's legs, cuts through his jeans and draws blood. He pleads with his father to stop.

Pa will have none of it.

Afterwards, the man kneels down beside the boy's head. 'You forced my hand,' he whispers. 'You didn't say sorry.'

He's waiting for it now. The 'sorry'. The boy can tell, by the slight tremble in the man's fat lower lip and the widening of his eyes.

'What is a father to do with a boy who shows no respect?' he continues. 'What is a man to do, when words have no effect?' Pa's beady eyes are watery. Spittle dribbles down the corner of his mouth. 'You force me to hit you, boy. You've given yourself these scars, not me.' He strokes the boy's head, lets his fingers tangle in the soft, blond hair. 'I do not want to punish you, son.' He pops a mint into his mouth.

He is only drunk, the boy tries to tell himself. He is pissed out of his mind. He will sober up soon, he will forget all about this. Soon, they will be a normal family again, soon Pa will help him build his fortress.

Soon, Pa will hit the bottle and it will start all over again. Pa is like that. He loves it, even though he won't say it.

'Do you wish I was dead, Pa?' The words slip out. The boy wants to reel them in, but they're there now, they're out. They've slithered out of his mind and set themselves free.

'Yes,' his pa says. 'Yes, I wish that.' Then he rises and lumbers back to the house.

A little later, the Saab pulls up on the driveway. Ma gets out and opens the boot. The boy can see them from where he lies: oranges in red net bags, peering up at him from inside plastic carrier bags.

'Get up and wash your clothes,' Ma says as she passes him. 'And take a shower, you smell bad.'

How can she even smell him from here? It's Pa who needs showering, Pa the one who smells...

Then something wanders up his nose. A scent, a bad scent, no – a stink.

The boy's collar reeks. Pa's breath seems to have stuck to the fabric.

He rests his forehead on his hands. Tears creep out of his closed eyes.

He rushes out of the driveway.

There are no sounds in the forest. Winter puts the trees and the ground to sleep, winter freezes the tears on his cheeks. Snow crunches under his boots – it is the only noise in the world.

A tingling feeling creeps into his crotch as he stands there. He glances over his shoulder at the outdoor lavatory. The utedass peers at him from between the trees, too far away.

The boy crosses his left leg over his right. If he legs it he could make it, but Lord forbid Pa or Ma should walk in on him with his trousers down.

He fumbles with his trouser button. Only ten minutes outside and his fingers are already frozen stiff. Pressure builds up, he can't hold it any more… Warm wetness enters his underwear, seeps down his trousers and creates golden pools at his feet. Rather that than freeze his willy off. The urine creates a strange comfort in the cold, a second skin draped over the inside of his trouser legs. He closes his eyes and begins to wander, aimlessly, matching his footsteps with the beating of his heart.

He doesn't realise two hours have gone by until suddenly a voice calls him through the cold.

'Boy, boy! Stop hiding and come the hell over here!'

Pa. Pa has noticed the boy is missing. If he does not come soon, Pa will get angry again. He probably already is.

The boy hurries back to the house. The lights from the windows appear between the trees, he is almost there when he stops dead in his tracks.

Something lies there in the snow. Dark and massive, like a hibernating bear.

Pa.

Has he passed out? Was he really that drunk?

The boy reaches the body and peers down at it. He notices the pink neck peeking out between the mousy hair and chequered shirt. How soft must that be, with its folds of flesh overlapping one another, merging with the sagging skin of his face, making him seem a creature of flabby meat and no bone.

Would it be hard to break that neck? One stamp of the boot, one twist? Would Pa twitch like a marionette, a strangled noise escaping his lips?

The boy's eyes distinguish every grain of snow on the ground; his nose picks up the sharp reek of moonshine from his father's mouth. His ears pick up the sound of the void that fills this hibernating world, the absence as the forest holds its breath.

Pa stirs.

The boy bolts. Branches rip at his clothes as he sprints through the forest with a speed he did not know he had. He has no idea where he's going, all he knows is he needs to get away. He passes neighbours, he passes the ice–hockey rink. It's not far enough. He needs to go somewhere no one knows him, where no one could decide to send him back to Pa.

He collapses outside a house three hours later. The windows are dark; checking his wristwatch, he sees it's twenty past ten in the evening. He hammers his fists and screams at the top of his voice.

When the door opens, he loses his balance and is about to fall when a pair of slender arms catches him.

'Jesus Maria, what are you doing here?'

A woman's face swims in front of him. Her face is framed by a halo of blonde hair, and her orb-shaped eyes are pools of sum-

mer sky, a shade of blue he hasn't seen for months. She smells of saffron and hearth fires.

'I ran away.' The boy can't recognise his voice when he speaks.

'But,' she stammers, 'your family...'

'They weren't my real family.' His voice breaks as he speaks; he shuts his eyes to avoid seeing the woman's reaction. 'I've never had a family...'

He slumps down on the woman's threshold and cries out all the tears that have built up in his eyes all evening, all day – all his life.

'Let's get you inside,' the woman whispers. 'Lucky for you we have a spare bed.'

He dries his eyes then and lets her lead him inside. He doesn't know if he should feel joy, shame or disbelief that it's all over. He doesn't want to know.

Separation

Rain pattered against the windows the next morning. It woke Ellen up at 6.25. Her sleep up here in the north was a lot lighter than at home; the slightest sound or movement was enough to stir her. Even with clouds in the sky, it was light enough to be mid-morning, or midday.

A change is coming. That's what Granddad would have said about the weather. Ellen pictured his face in front of her, the way it had looked at her that time in the cherry tree so many years ago. Would he still have looked at her the same way, knowing that she knew about his past? Would he have looked away?

Erik and Simon were up not long after her. They got dressed, Erik packed his sleeping bag, and at seven, when breakfast started, Ellen snuck down to the canteen and grabbed some bread, ham and cheese, which they had in their room.

Simon explained the plan he'd gone through with Ellen the previous night. First, they would go to the campsite and speak to Malee, to find out if any of the blueberry pickers had witnessed Sunan's abduction. Should that fail, should Malee be too afraid to speak, or even worse Bengt Persson turn them away, they would go to the Old Church parish house to find out if the name crossed out in the ledger was that of Lisbet's stillborn child. After that, they would go to the hospital to speak to Sunan. Visiting hours began at eleven.

'She might remember more about her attacker now. And Malee might know something, too.'

'Malee?' Ellen repeated.

'She will translate.'

'But if we're turned away from the campsite, which actually is quite possible, how will we get hold of her?'

Simon's smile was smug. 'I got her phone number when we visited them, have you forgotten?' He flicked back a few pages and showed his sister the number scrawled on the top. 'I will call her and ask if she will come with us.'

'But still, she might not want to speak.'

'Then I will use Google Translate.'

Ellen bit her lip. She'd sighed in exasperation at Simon's stubbornness too many times, and it felt wrong to do it in front of Erik.

'It actually isn't too bad,' Erik chipped in. 'Works in emergency cases.' He gave her an upbeat smile.

Ellen wondered how real it was, whether it functioned as a mask to hide his uncertainties. 'You're all good with our plan, then?'

'Yeah, of course, why not?'

'You don't think it sounds crazy?' She glanced at her brother. 'Two teenagers playing detective?'

Erik looked at her in astonishment. 'Course not! It's supercool! It's like, what's that book…' he clicked his fingers, 'the one about the kids with the detective agency.'

'*LasseMaja*?'

He clicked his fingers again. 'That's the one.'

Simon grinned from ear to ear.

The older boy's face grew thoughtful. 'One thing,

though.' He nodded at his laptop, which he'd turned on and put on the floor. 'The Facebook group.'

Ellen tensed.

'Shouldn't we try to press them for more information? It's probably one of them who did it.'

'We already said yesterday we couldn't be too forward,' Ellen said carefully. 'We can't risk rousing suspicion or scaring Freddie off.' They'd checked Johan Gustafsson's Facebook profile, and there were no new messages from Freddie Arvidsson.

'What about your hostel owner? Hampus?'

'Henrik.'

'He was in one of the photos, no?'

'But Henrik wouldn't...'

The distant sound of a door opening and closing cut Ellen off. Footsteps came down the corridor, past their door, and then another door opened and closed. The bathroom, Ellen reckoned. It was right beside their room.

She checked her watch: 7.41. 'People are waking up. We should get a move on before everyone comes down for breakfast.'

Erik was about to object. His lips were slightly parted and he kept opening and closing his hand, as if wondering whether to speak out or not. Then he turned his back to Ellen to put away his laptop, his good humour all gone. It was like his sudden outburst during their *fika* with the Thomassons after the calf marking. Again, Ellen wondered whether it was a mask to help him cope. The reindeer killing, the tension between him and Per-Anders, the reindeer herding and the music, the loss of his mother, which clearly still haunted him...

She looked out of the window at the pitter-patter rain. If change was coming, it didn't seem to be a good one.

The gentle tinkle of cutlery drifted up from the canteen as they started down the stairs. They should have left earlier, Ellen knew, before the other guests were up and about. They should have made their plans yesterday evening and been ready to get up and away this morning. The wooden steps creaked beneath their feet, as if the house knew what they were up to and wanted them to be discovered. At the bottom of the steps she paused a moment to take in her surroundings. Ahead was the corridor with the ground-floor rooms, a little wooden table with a glass vase standing by the left-hand wall, just in front of them. Crossing their corridor was another, which led all the way down to the kitchen. Just around the corner from where the teenagers stood was the entrance to the canteen, and opposite that, the entry to the lobby and the front door.

Ellen crept past the vase and peeked around the corner. The kitchen door was slightly open. There were the faint sounds of a dishwasher. There was no one around.

'Let's go,' she whispered, stepping forward.

Then the kitchen door opened wide to reveal Laila, pushing a trolley with more food for the breakfast buffet.

Ellen stepped back, reaching out a hand to guide her brother, but Simon reacted too late. Ellen's rucksack pushed against his chest and he stumbled back, right into Erik, who backed into the table and sent the glass vase crashing to the floor.

The rolling sound of the trolley stopped. 'Hello?' came Laila's voice, followed by heavy footsteps.

Ellen cursed under her breath. She glanced back up the stairs, wondering if they could dash to their room in time, but before she could act Laila appeared. 'Ellen, Simon,' she said, surprised. 'What happened?' Then she noticed Erik. 'Who is this?'

'Laila, I'm sorry, it's not what you think…'

'I'm Erik,' the Sami boy said, his voice steady.

Laila pointed at the sleeping bag in his hand. 'And that?'

'I had to stay for the night. Had nowhere else to go.'

Laila put her hands on her hips. Her steely gaze moved between Ellen and Erik. 'I don't suppose either of you know the first rule of staying in a hotel, hostel or any kind of paid accommodation? No guests.'

'Look, Laila, I can explain, please, just don't throw us out...'

'Erik came to help us with the investigation.'

Ellen froze. She looked at her brother in shock.

Simon continued, unfazed. He stepped up to the woman, a piece of glass crunching under his shoe. 'He's helped us get in touch with a group of people that maltreat reindeer. They're called *The Real Swedish Norrbotten.*' He took out his phone. 'Your husband is a part of that group.' He opened the Facebook app and showed Laila the group page. 'Henrik is in one of their videos.'

Ellen stepped in front of him, trying to block his hand with her arm. 'It's nothing serious, Laila. We were just gonna leave, we won't bother you...'

'Laila needs an explanation for our behaviour, Ellen. And Henrik's. Especially if Henrik has kept this a secret.'

Laila stared at the teenagers. 'You'd better explain yourselves.'

'We will, we promi—'

'Without him.' Laila nodded at Erik. 'He has to leave.'

'But Erik is part of the investigation, it was his...'

Ellen put her hands on her brother's shoulders. 'I'll deal with it, Simon.'

She felt his shoulders tense. No Touch, his golden rule, had just been violated.

'I'll explain things to Laila; you and Erik go to the campsite.' She lifted her hands. 'That's the best option.'

Simon's expression when he turned around surprised her. His eyes were wide, pupils dashing back and forth. He breathed heavily through his nose.

'You'll manage without me, I know!'

He met her eyes. She saw a 'but' forming on his lips.

'You heard your sister,' Laila said. Her voice was calmer now, but the steel had not left.

Erik touched Simon on the arm. 'Come on, bud, let's go.' He picked up the journal which Simon had dropped on the floor when Ellen backed into him, and headed for the lobby. That finally got the younger boy moving.

'I'll catch up with you soon, I promise!' Ellen called after them. There was no response apart from the front door opening and closing.

Laila turned to her, folding her arms. 'Now then, young lady, in the kitchen. You have some explaining to do.'

'Give me one good reason why I shouldn't send you and your brother packing this instant.'

They were in the kitchen. Laila leaning against the worktop beside the sink, Ellen sitting on a stool by the long metal table in the centre of the room. The woman was lit up behind from the light seeping through the windows. The rain had stopped and sunshine was breaking up the clouds.

'We didn't know Erik was coming. He just showed up without warning, throwing stones at the window. I swear, I would never have invited him or thought of sneaking someone into a hotel room, ever. But he was just standing there, out in the dark, and it felt mean not to, and we had this…' Her words petered out. How much dared she tell Laila about the investigation? Wouldn't that give the woman another reason to throw them out?

Laila frowned. 'I didn't think you knew anyone in this town.'

'We don't.' Heat rushed to Ellen's cheeks. 'We met him yesterday.'

The woman raised a pencilled eyebrow. Ellen felt more stupid by the second. She pulled at a thumbnail. 'Erik is Per-Anders Thomasson's son. The reindeer herder whose reindeer were killed, the ones we discovered. Erik had an idea about how we could get closer to the people who might know who'd done it. They'd... the Thomassons, that is, had shown us footage of the hate crime that keeps happening, and we were... looking at it again, for clues. The thing is, Simon just happened to see Henrik in one of the videos.' She forced herself to meet the woman's gaze. 'Simon has Asperger's. He can't tell when something he says is rude or... inappropriate. He can't assess situations, doesn't adapt. He didn't mean to put you on the spot. In his mind he was just explaining things to you.'

Laila's expression was stony. 'What were you going to do with the footage?'

'Nothing. It was just for reference... for what we were gonna do next.'

'And what was that?'

Ellen clasped her hands together and pressed them against the table, the steel surface cool and hard against her skin. She was silent.

Laila folded her arms. 'I'm a patient woman, you know. I can wait here all day, there's plenty to be doing in the kitchen. It would be a waste of your time, however.'

Ellen closed her eyes. She could not lie now. Laila would see through it. What was stopping her from telling the woman about the investigation? That Laila would tell Henrik and Henrik would tell the killer, if he even knew who that was?

Then she remembered how Laila had approached them the morning after the accident, asking them how they were feeling, whether they didn't want to go home.

'I can't get the reindeer out of my mind,' she whispered. 'They're there, all their heads, circling around me, grinning. I can't sleep. If I help Simon solve this, maybe it will all go away.'

'It won't.'

Laila's voice was softer, quieter. When Ellen opened her eyes, she saw the woman's shoulders were stiff, her grip on the edge of the worktop tighter. 'I know you think your mind might be put at rest, figuring out who did it, but believe me, it won't. Horrid things like that, they stay with you. Justice won't make them go away. Denying that only makes you naive.'

For the first time, Ellen properly took in the woman's olive-hued skin, her lustrous black hair, that slight Middle Eastern accent. She wondered why Laila had come to Sweden, what horrors she had escaped from. Were those horrors keeping her up at night, too?

The woman seemed aware of it, because she gave a wry smile.

'If Henrik was actively involved in a group called *The Real Swedish Norrbotten*, he wouldn't have chosen to be with me, would he?'

Ellen blushed and looked down at her hands. 'So you knew about the group?'

'I found out.'

'Do you know Bengt and Kimmo Persson?'

'No, I'm glad I don't. But Henrik had the bad luck of going to school with them. It was all peer pressure.'

'Why didn't he leave?'

'Some of the people round here, in the little villages, they're capable of things. Things you don't want happening to you.'

Ellen thought of Gubben Persson and his sons, advancing on her grandfather with their iron rods.

'But you said he's not active any more?'

'Apparently one of the guys was attacked by his own dog, and Henrik had to drive him to hospital. He used that as an excuse for not coming any more.'

'Did he say who the man was?'

'No.'

'It couldn't be someone you know?'

'Goodness girl, does it look like I have the time to play detective?' She stepped back and grabbed a cloth hanging over the tap by the sink. 'I can see talking sense isn't going to make you any less foolish. Go back to your room.' She began wiping the worktop with broad sweeping motions.

'You mean we can stay? You won't kick us out?'

Laila paused in her movements. She looked over her shoulder at the girl. 'I don't kick people out for being naive and distressed.'

Ellen flinched internally at the woman's words, but she sat up straight and tried to hold her head high. 'But reindeer have been slaughtered,' she said. 'A woman almost died. Trying to find out why doesn't make you naive.'

'I'll bet you this kitchen that the police have known all along who did it. Or have a good idea who did, at least.' Her hands squeezed the cloth, forcing water drops out of the fabric. 'They turn a blind eye to most things.'

Juha Virtanen's headless figure in the corner of the video loomed into Ellen's inner vision. She pushed it away, tried to focus on the drops, perfectly aligned under Laila's hands. 'I can't believe *everyone* in Svartjokk is like that.'

Laila gave a sardonic laugh. 'Then you'd better change your beliefs.'

Pupa

The young man remembers a time when he liked oranges. When he imagined that the peel was his own skin and that the sweet fruit inside was the real him, the better him, the him that hid from the world, waiting for the right moment to emerge.

He still likes oranges. He eats one before or between shifts. He's just had one now, in his bedroom, his fingernails tainted orange by peeling.

Ma says all those vitamins will make his skin glow.

'That's how you'll get rid of that acne. Nature's care. Those chemicals in the pharmacy prescriptions do more damage than good.'

The young man plucks at a pimple. It turns an angry red between his fingernails and won't budge as he tries to pull it off his skin. There's a whole herd of them scattered along the edges of his face, preventing stubble from growing, determined to keep his body shackled in adolescence.

His gaze drifts to the calendar hanging on the wall beside the mirror. My 20th is written in spindly lettering on Saturday 11th. He counts the empty squares from today till then. Five days to go. Ma has already stacked the presents in the lounge. He touches them every day, stroking the wrapping paper, pulling the shiny string through his fingers, just to remind himself they're real.

His fingers wander back along the calendar to today's date. Freedom Anniversary is written in red ink.

Seven years since he ran away.

His finger retreats another seven squares. Monday 30th. A red cross is nestled in the date, inside the zero, barely visible unless you squint. Old Pa's grave must be even more barren now, the writing faded more than ever, bleached by years of exposure to the sun and elements. Moss would be extending its gnarled fingers over the granite.

The man's death had been announced in the newspaper a week after the young man, then a boy, ran away. The boy wrote a letter to Old Ma, offering condolences and everything else he assumed you had to write to the family of someone who'd died. He'd asked his New Ma, Kerstin, to check it for him and yet it still took three weeks before Old Ma replied.

When she did reply, she only wrote three lines. In pencil, on a torn-out page from a notebook. Nils drank himself to death. He fell unconscious in the snow and twisted his neck when he fell. Don't come to the funeral. He had a feeling she blamed him for the old man's death, even though the boy hadn't seen him since that time in the back garden. The boy had had his chance to kill his first foster father, but he'd left him behind in the snow.

The young man pulls out the note from his back pocket. The writing is smudged, the paper has turned blue from living in his jeans for so long. He turns the paper over and over in his hands, without unfolding it.

A buzzing noise makes him jump.

A fly on the mirror.

The young man's hands curl into fists. He snatches the fly swat from its perch on the wall and smacks the insect down.

It lands on the bureau, kicks its legs sluggishly.

He pulls the legs off, one after the other. He removes the wings. He prods the limbless body with the needle from Ma's sewing set.

Each jab becomes a boot stamp in his mind: his boot, on Old Pa's neck, again and again.

His face writhes and contracts, not sure whether to smile or twist in disgust at what he's doing.

Afterwards, he flushes the thing down the toilet. He cleans the needle and wipes the fly swat.

Sunlight pierces the tips of the trees as he leaves the house. His watch tells him it's a minute to seven. A minute to being late.

'You're up with the birds, I see.'

The boy almost jumps again. His gaze darts over to the man in uniform standing on the porch of the neighbouring house.

'I'm always this early.'

Constable Gunnarson holds the boy's gaze a heartbeat longer. His eyes wander to the boy's hands.

The boy shoves his hands down in his pockets, feels the paper against his skin. He walks over to the van and reverses out of the drive. As he heads down the road, he glimpses the constable in the side mirror, watching him.

'Completely normal,' the boy mutters to himself. 'I am completely normal.'

A red car he doesn't recognise stands in the Laponia Tours car park. A green Övningskör sign (Practise Driving) sits on the back window.

'Are you the electrician?' a voice calls as he steps out of the van. It's a girl, a tall blonde girl in her mid-teens, with hair curling down to her waist and plump cheeks the hue of Ingrid Marie apples.

'Yes, you said there was a problem with the RCCB?'

'The what, sorry?'

'The residual current circuit breaker.'

She shrugs. 'I've no clue. Per-Anders is out, he just told me to let you in and you'd know what to do.'

'It's my job to know.' He sniffs the air as she reaches past him to close the door. 'Do you use Garnier shampoo?'

She blinks. 'How did you know?'

'Your hair smells of green apples. Golden Delicious, to be precise. Garnier do a shampoo with that scent.'

She gives him a curious smile. 'You seem to know a lot of things.'

'I don't know your name.'

'Oh, how silly of me!' She holds out her hand. 'I'm Sofie. New summer worker here.'

When he tells her his, she smiles. 'That's always been my favourite boy's name, I used to say if I ever had a son that's what I'd call him.' She repeats it to herself. On her lips it sounds like a blessing.

A feeling he hasn't felt since that night he stumbled into New Ma's house floods over him. The feeling of coming home.

Storyhunter

Ellen closed the door to their room, leaned back against it and let out a deep breath. They could stay. Her gaze wandered over the beds, the desk, the floor, which now looked oddly bare without Erik's sleeping bag. Laila's expression as she'd left, a mixture of empathy and disapproval, hovered in her mind's eye.

A vibration from her pocket interrupted her thoughts. She got out her phone. Two new messages flashed on the screen, both of them from Simon. *The staff at the campsite turned us away. We think Persson must have told them not to let us in.* The message was sent at 8.53, fifteen minutes ago. The second message had come at 9.02. *I called Malee to ask if she could meet us at the hospital at 11 and speak to Sunan. She said she would try to come.*

The green chat symbol next to Simon's name glowed, showing he was still active. *What are you doing now?* Ellen typed.

The response came within seconds. *We are going to the parish house to speak to the priest of the Old Church. When are you coming, Ellen?*

Ellen's heart went out to him. *Soon,* she typed, *I promise. Good news: Laila will let us stay.*

Of course, Simon responded. *She understood that she couldn't stop our investigation by kicking us out.*

Ellen let out a tired laugh. 'Oh, Simon,' she said to herself. *I'll be at the parish house as soon as I can. It's beside the Old Church, yes?*

It is three minutes down the road from the church. The chat bubbles bobbed up and down as Simon typed. *I want to ask Erik about the photo of their mum.*

Are you sure?

Yes.

Can't you wait until I reach you?

It will take you twenty minutes to walk here.

Why can't you wait such a short time?

I think our mission here will take a long time. I don't want to waste time, so I want to ask him now.

Ellen drummed her fingers against the phone case. The digital clock on the screen switched from 9.18 to 9.19.

She should go. Not to monitor her brother's behaviour, she could not do that forever. Asperger's or not, he would soon be fifteen. But the way he'd looked at her when she told him to leave... Did her presence give him a sense of security? An affirmation that he was doing OK? Was he less confident without her?

Movement through the window by Simon's bed. She stepped forward, gazing out at the street.

Was that a woman, disappearing around the corner? A wisp of white hair, the hem of a white dress?

She opened the messenger app, but Simon's chat symbol had turned grey. She left the phone on the pillow and settled down by the desk.

Then a Facebook message popped up on her screen. *So where do you live, Johan? I haven't seen or heard of anyone with that name here before. Are you new to Svartjokk?*

Freddie Arvidsson. Ellen and Simon had entered his log-on details onto their Facebook apps in the morning, so they wouldn't have to rely on Erik's laptop to keep in touch with the man.

Tension curled into a fist in her gut. She traced the outline of the pit bull on his profile picture with her thumb. *I heard one of you guys got badly bitten by one of the dogs.* She began a second sentence, then deleted it and clicked send.

She scanned the group's pictures again. Thoughts spiralled through her mind.

I can't see you in any of the pics, she wrote, *yet your name's been tagged on almost every single one. How is that?*

Freddie's chat symbol turned from green to grey. Inactive. He was probably working.

The screen showed 9.21. Ellen drummed her fingers against the bedpost of Simon's bed. She did not know what to do. Perhaps she needed him, as much as he needed her. Yet the photo on the Thomassons' fridge hovered in her mind's eye. *Things happened,* Erik's voice echoed. *Really dreadful things. And he never recovered.*

Ellen sat down on Simon's bed and opened up Google. She typed in: *reindeer herding accident.*

A number of articles popped up on the results list. *Maret's Magical Discovery – A Unicorn*, an article from *Aftonbladet* about a Norwegian reindeer herder, was the first result. Next was a feature on Afghan migrants who'd got work as reindeer herders, and several links about reindeer killed in traffic. Ellen scrolled past them all and stopped at the seventh hit.

It was an article from the Sami Radio website: *Reindeer herding the most dangerous job shows new research.*

She made a new search. *Woman killed in reindeer herding accident.*

She struck lucky on hit number one. *Reindeer Herder Froze to Death in Blizzard | Svartjokk Kuriren.*

Ellen caught her breath. She tapped the link to the article.

04. Febr. 2015. On Saturday morning, the day after the blizzard that ravaged many parts of Norrbotten, reindeer herder Per-Anders Thomasson set out in search of his wife, Sofie, who had been missing since 20.30 Friday eve…

Ellen's pulse quickened as she read. She leaned forward over the desk, hair brushing the keyboard. When she'd finished, she typed *Sofie Reindeer Herder Svartjokk* into the search engine. Again, an article from *Svartjokk Kuriren* was first up on the results list.

Jokkmokk born Sofie Abrahamsson takes up reindeer herding in Svartjokk. The article was dated 1996. Ellen clicked on the link and skimmed through the article. *Sofie Abrahamsson, 30, has always had an outdoor spirit. She grew up on her parents' farm for sled dogs and has always helped out rearing and training the animals, from puppy age to adulthood. At age 15 she moved to Svartjokk…* The rest of the article talked about Sofie's work at Laponia Tours, how this had got her in touch with the Svartjokk Sami Village, and eventually Per-Anders Thomasson.

Ellen scrolled down to the bottom of the page. The journalist's name was Bertil Hansson.

Ellen returned to Google and typed the name into the search engine.

A long list of articles from *Svartjokk Kuriren* appeared

on the results page. She spent the next ten minutes leafing through them.

At article eight she hit bingo.

It was a short text, more of a stub than a real article, and half of it was headline. *Man in Purnuvaare Shot to Death in Argument.*

There was no mention of names, nor of the circumstances behind the shooting, no indication of who had started the fight. The stub didn't even clarify that the conflict had been between Sami and non-Sami.

Again, Ellen's gaze settled on the journalist's name. 'Hansson,' she whispered to herself. She fetched her wallet from the bedside table and dug up Stina Hansson's business card. She rubbed her thumb over the logo, a decision forming in her mind. She grabbed her phone.

Change of plan, she wrote to her brother. *Going to the newspaper office. Maybe c u at church.*

Five minutes later she was walking out of the hostel, headed for the office of *Svartjokk Kuriren.*

'You're back,' Stina Hansson said as Ellen burst through the door. The brown-haired woman sat at the secretary desk, coffee in hand. She eyed Ellen up and down, clicking the nails of her right hand against the mug. 'I knew you would be.'

'I found an article your dad wrote,' Ellen said. 'That is, I assume it's your dad.' She handed over her phone to the woman.

A little smile stretched across the journalist's lips as she scrolled down the screen.

'That's my old man all right.' Stina Hansson gave Ellen an appraising look. 'You must have done quite a deal of digging to find this.'

'I want to know more about the woman. Sofie Abra-hamsson.'

'Abrahamsson, yes. A tragic tale.' Hansson handed back the phone to her. 'The number of *Kuriren* readers must have spiked during that time.'

'She actually froze to death?'

'Well, it was probably hypothermia that dealt the killing blow. Her foot was stuck between the rocks and there was no way for her to take shelter.' Her gaze softened. 'Thomasson blamed himself. He got a whole bunch of hate mail, full of accusations and insults and empty threats.'

'Death threats?'

'No. More like cryptic messages, about Sofie being all alone in the afterlife and how her spirit would haunt the lands where she died. Weird stuff, if you ask me.'

'What did Per-Anders make of it?'

'Hard to say. He was always hard to read. But he explained that in Sami religion, there exist three different worlds, or dimensions. Ours, the living one; Rotaimo, the realm of the dead; and Saivo, an in-between realm where dead spirits stay before gaining passage to Rotaimo. But Sofie wasn't Sami.'

'Was the person who wrote the strange message Sami, d'you think? I can't see a non-Sami knowing so much about their religion.'

Stina Hansson shrugged and sipped her coffee. 'All this information can be found in books or on the internet. Ten minutes on Wikipedia and you know it all.'

'What did Per-Anders think?'

'As I said, he's a hard one to read.' Stina Hansson placed her mug down. 'There was something lost about him, though, after the accident. Like a sheep without its flock. Or, I guess, a reindeer without its herder.'

'This person who sent the hate mail, did they know Sofie and Per-Anders personally?'

Hansson shook her head. 'The letters were unsigned. He showed me a couple to see if I recognised the handwriting.'

'But he did seem disturbed by them?'

'Wouldn't you get disturbed if you got hate mail?' Hansson finished her coffee. 'I am a journalist, he wasn't telling me the whole story. I was already writing a feature on the daily harassments – angry phone calls and text messages – that many reindeer herders have to put up with, and he agreed I could mention the letters… but I guess he didn't want me to go into the details. Not that I'm one of those sensation leeches at all.' She walked over to the sink and rinsed the mug out. 'There was one line, though, that stood out from the rest.' She put the washed-out mug on the rack and let her gaze drift to the ceiling. *'You've betrayed moral decency itself.* Don't know why or how I still remember it…'

'It sounds very formal,' Ellen said. 'Well written. As if the writer were well read.'

'Well read and Svartjokk don't exactly go hand in hand. Unless you are Levinian, of course. Then you'd be steeped in formal writing.' Hansson grabbed a tea towel hanging from one of the drawers and wiped the mug dry. 'But that wouldn't fit with the Sami afterlife stuff, unless this person was a mix of the two.' She made a sardonic smile. 'With some of these so-called religious people, it's hard to believe they have any faith at all.'

'What do you mean?'

'They don't exactly practise as they preach.'

Ellen leaned against the booth by the sink. She remembered Per-Anders's story about Lars-Erik. She saw her father again, returning from his northern journey with nothing but a squat little bible in his hands.

A message from Simon interrupted her thoughts. *Erik has told me about their mum. She died in a blizzard two years ago. We've spoken to a priest in the parish house. They're helping us look through their records to see who wrote down the baptisms in 1960 but it could take a while still.*

'Tell them they can stop their search.'

Ellen looked in surprise. She registered Stina Hansson standing beside her, peering over her shoulder. 'The priest's name was Sakarias Christiansen,' the journalist said. 'They won't find him, though. He died some time ago. What are they trying to get hold of him for?'

Ellen tried to relax her grip on her phone. 'There was a name crossed out, in the ledger in the Old Church,' she told Stina. 'Simon wanted to find out who'd done it and whose name it was.' A beep from her phone made her look down. Simon had sent her a sad smiley. *Ask if they have any info on Sakarias Christiansen*, she wrote back.

'Ah yes, that old chestnut of a mystery,' Stina Hansson said. 'My pa inquired about it, too. When he found out that Lisbet Persson had lost her love child, he paid her a visit. She was staying in her school friend's flat here in town. I think he wanted to write a little feature about her experience: young-woman-overcomes-tragedy kind of thing. But Lisbet wouldn't tell him anything about the stillbirth itself. And she seemed surprisingly well, considering. Pa said she was bustling around the flat, making him coffee, being generally high-spirited. There were baby-feeding bottles in the sink, and a baptism dress in the wardrobe. Lisbet said it all belonged to her friend's sister's baby.'

The journalist gave a small, satisfied smile. 'My theory is, her baby never died. Lisbet had it in secret, probably so it wouldn't have the same unforgiving Levinian upbringing. Then she gave it away to social services.'

'Did your father find any concrete proof?'

'He chased up the hospital about it. Got hold of the midwife in charge of Lisbet's birth but she was as close-lipped as ten clams. Wouldn't disclose any personal information to someone outside of the family.'

'And your dad never found out what happened to the child, where it was placed?'

'As good as vanished into thin air.'

'And then she ran off,' Ellen said. 'With this musician…'

'December '60. The year rock 'n' roll came to Svartjokk. Fresh start for both Lisbet and baby.' Stina Hansson cocked her head to the side. 'Who told you all this, Per-Anders?'

Ellen nodded. 'He said she broke all contact with Lars-Erik and ran away with Ronny.'

'Ronny Arvidsson, of Ronnyz' with a "z". I remember my pa playing that at home.' Hansson shook her head. 'Silly music really, never my thing.' She checked her watch. 'I'd let you stay, but I do actually have stuff to do – two telephone interviews, an article to write, a feature to edit! It may be Sunday, but as you can see,' she motioned to the empty desks around her, 'we aren't exactly well staffed, and the work doesn't do itself.' She wandered into the booth and sat down at her desk. 'Did you get an answer to all your questions?'

'I… yes, I think so,' Ellen said. *No*, she thought. New questions were popping into her brain by the second. On her phone, a message flashed and glowed.

Freddie Arvidsson: *I do the filming.*

Glancing up, she noticed Stina Hansson was watching her. Waiting for her to go.

'Actually, I did wonder... How do you know all this? About Lisbet?'

'Pa confided in me about everything. I grew up without a mother, so there was no one else to talk to. All his speculations were safe with me. And I have a sharp memory.'

'And your father had a sharp eye, noticing all those things in the flat.'

'It's all about observing details. Journalists and detectives have that in common.' The journalist cocked her head to the side. 'You would make a good apprentice, you know. You have the mindset.' The sound of typing punctured the air, announcing that Ellen's visit was over.

Johan, want to meet for a drink at the bar sometime? Freddie Arvidsson wrote.

Ellen stopped dead. She was halfway down the stairs.

A new message came from Simon. *We can't find any more information on Christiansen, but he was Purnuvaare's priest in the 60s. And I just remembered that Per-Anders mentioned him in Granddad's story. What are you doing now?*

Then from Freddie: *Any day this week?*

Ellen swiped the man's message away and called her brother.

She didn't know whether to feel relief or anxiety. The call had ended a minute ago. She was sitting on one of the benches at the town square, beside the fountain. The sun beat upon her head. It was getting hot. One could never have thought it had rained that morning.

Having learned nothing more at the parish, Simon and Erik had set off for the hospital. They'd found out on its website that the patients had their lunch at midday, and wanted to catch Sunan before that, along with Malee. When she'd called, they were already in the waiting room, with the young Thai woman. Simon said little, as he was trying to get more information from Malee about Sunan's abduction and didn't want to be interrupted. Erik congratulated Ellen on her findings. After the hospital, he would call Purnuvaare's current priest and ask if she knew whether Christiansen had been in charge of the ledgers of the Old Church between 1960 and '61.

Ellen looked down the pedestrian walk. From the town square it was about fifteen minutes to the hospital. She'd make it just as the boys were admitted to see Sunan, hopefully. It was 10.21.

Freddie Arvidsson's chat symbol still glowed green.

Say you can't meet him, Erik had said. *You're busy, you've got work, you've got a gym session.*

What if he knows? she'd said. *Maybe I've asked too many questions and now he's suspicious.*

She turned the phone on silent and replayed the videos again. Was it her, or did the camera tip to the left? She tried picturing Freddie Arvidsson behind it, hefting it through the woods across moss and snow and hidden roots.

Holding it in his left hand.

Did you get badly bitten by a dog once? she wrote. Freddie was still active, but hadn't seen the message.

Freddie Arvidsson. Ronny Arvidsson. Lisbet Persson. Granddad. Twelve reindeer heads in a circle.

Her gaze rose to the clock on the town hall, to the number twelve staring down at her in Roman numerals.

Damn it, why hadn't she asked Erik about reindeer sacrifices?

A flutter made her look down. A crow stood there, not one metre away from her feet. It trod on the spot, pecked at the ground.

'I haven't got any food for you,' Ellen said.

The bird opened and closed its beak. Uttered a guttural squawk. Then it flew off, right across the square, in the direction of the hospital.

Ellen followed.

Passing the hostel, she noticed a white van in the courtyard. A toolbox stood on the ground. Daniel the electrician was back, it seemed.

A buzz from her phone made her stop. *I did, a few years ago*, Freddie had written. *Nearly had my hand off.*

Is it the dog on your profile pic?

Yes. A moment's pause. *Why did you ask about the dog, Johan?*

Ellen frowned. Her gaze darted around the street. And settled on the electrician, now in full view by the toolbox, looking at his phone. Typing.

Hej, Ellen.

The girl looked from the man by the hostel to her phone and back again.

Daniel Johansson crossed the street towards her. This time there was no kindness in his eyes.

Confrontation

'It's never too late to get in touch.'

She kicks her feet, heels brushing the water. Her head is tilted back, face to the sky, her yellow locks almost touching the jetty.

'I'm sure your parents would love to hear from you.'

'You don't know them.'

'Nor do you.'

'Ma abandoned me.'

'Your pa, then.'

'He is dead.'

Her bright eyes widen. 'Daniel, you never…'

'I mean he is as good as dead to me.' The young man runs a finger along the spring between the wooden boards. They are ingrained with bird shit.

'What about their families?' she says. 'They still live here, yes?'

A fly lands right next to his hand. He hits at it, but the insect evades him. Its buzzing sounds like a taunt in his ears.

'Then it's decided.' Sofie draws her feet back. Even though they are wet, she puts on her sandals. 'You're meeting them.'

'Sofie, please…'

'You don't have to be so anxious, Daniel. Let someone help you, for once.'

'You have helped me.'

'How?'

'You're kind.'

She heaves a long sigh. 'Daniel, you're twenty-five years old. It's about time you found your roots.' She stands up and wipes her shorts, which are spotlessly clean and outline the shape of her buttocks and hips. 'I'll speak to Per-Anders. If there's anyone able to trace your pa, it's him.' She walks back to the shore where they have left their bikes, hair swaying behind her. He knows the matter is settled, whether he wants it to be or not.

'You speak of Per-Anders quite a lot.'

She shrugs. 'He's a friend at work. He's nice.'

'Nice.' The word is salty in his mouth.

'Yes, nice.' She tosses a lock of hair over her shoulder. 'There's loads of nice people out there, Daniel, you'll see if you start mingling with them.'

How is the young man to tell her? He isn't anxious. She should know, shouldn't she? For five years, they've been friends.

Five years, and he's never kissed her.

What kind of a man goes five years without kissing the girl he loves?

For he does love her. He wants to stand up and tell her so now, at the top of his voice, loud enough for all of Svartjokk to hear. He. Loves. Her.

Instead, he lumbers back to shore. She waits for him at the crown of the hill, tapping her delicate white fingers against the handlebars of her bike. 'Will you come to my place for fika?' She reaches out to touch his hand.

What is that pity doing in her voice? That care in her eyes?

Does she think him weak? A coward, in need of looking after? Is that what she's been insinuating all this time? Is that why she keeps spending time with him?

    He snatches his hand back. 'No, I don't think I will.'

    He avoids looking her in the eyes but he can see her whole face drop, lips turning downwards. 'Fine.' Her tone is curt.

    Immediately he regrets it. He reaches out a hand. 'Sofie...' but she's already set off – how fast her legs go, turning turning, blurring as she gets further away.

    I'm not afraid to make contact, he wants to tell her. *I'm not afraid of trying.* But he is afraid of what he might find, what he most probably will find, should he try to contact his biological parents: another man and woman turning their backs on him, another two stares of indifference, of petty annoyance telling him that he is intruding, that he is the one who doesn't belong.

    That is one disappointment more than he can bear.

The Watcher

'Where are we?'

Daniel answered by pushing the screwdriver further into her back. She imagined the metal pushing against her skin, threatening to pierce the cloth and hurt her.

'Do we have far to walk?'

'No talking.' The electrician prodded her again. 'Faster.'

Ellen increased her pace. Bracken tore at her legs and mosquitoes filled the air with high-pitched buzzing. She didn't hit them away as they settled on her limbs to eat, lest Daniel prod her harder with the screwdriver, or the drill, or the pliers, or...

There were so many things in that toolbox. Her phone, he'd prised it out of her fingers after buckling her up in the van.

But he did not have a gun.

After a while, the forest thinned out. Light trickled down through the pines.

Ellen's pace wavered.

'No slacking,' Daniel said.

'You're taking me to the glade.'

'And you aren't stopping till you're there.' He pushed the screwdriver harder against her spine, making her hiss in pain. Their footsteps fell heavy against the blueberry sprigs until the ground evened out, and the shadows of the trees were replaced by the glare of sunlight.

The reindeer heads were gone. Nothing but dead grass met Ellen's eyes. Here and there were dark marks where the heads had lain.

Daniel placed his toolbox by the rock. He kept the screwdriver in his hand – the left hand. The right, he brushed across the rock.

Ellen paced back and forth, keeping within the faded stains, the boundaries of the old circle. 'Why have you brought me here?' She gazed into the trees. Could that spot by the fern be where she and Simon had come from, three days earlier? Or was it there, by the two young birches, bending towards one another, forming a gate into the thicket?

How long would it take to sprint to the road?

She took one step, two. Green, murky shadows leered at her behind the birches, but beyond them – that yellow sliver running through the trees, could that be the track?

'It is thirty-five kilometres from here to the town,' Daniel said from behind. 'I'm sure you're a good runner, but in the van I'll overtake you in minutes. Anyway, I don't think you want to leave.'

'Why is that?'

'Because you want answers. I can give them to you.'

'My brother will notice I'm missing. Laila will notice you've mysteriously disappeared. The police will be here any moment. They'll arrest you.'

'There will be no police. No one wants to suspect me.'

Ellen turned around. A thin smile played on the man's

lips. 'People pity me.' His gaze wandered back to the rock. 'Do you know what they call this glade, Ellen?'

'Which "they"?' she muttered, although she knew the answer. Daniel must have known she did, for he remained silent, and stock still, not even twitching a finger. Waiting.

'It's called a *seit*,' she said.

'Do you know what the Sami used the *seits* for? Before Christianity?'

'Weren't they holy places?'

Daniel brushed his hand down the rock. 'They were reminders of the godly powers ruling the earth. People left parts of their catch as offerings. And there were sacrifices.' His gaze drifted across the glade. 'Each winter a white reindeer cow was offered to the sun goddess Beaivi so she would return to the world and put an end to the long darkness. People smeared butter on their doors to give her the strength to rise back into the sky.'

Ellen remembered his shiny hands that time in the kitchen, how he'd wiped them on his trousers when he spotted her. Had that been butter on his hands, rather than sweat? She turned to him. 'But now is summer. And why twelve animals instead of one?' She swallowed. 'Why their heads? Their antlers?'

'In the bones of an animal some of the soul still remains, and through those the animal can live on.'

It sounded like a quote from a book.

'She needs them,' he continued, 'to keep her company.'

'Who?'

'Sofie.'

'Sofie Abrahamsson?'

Daniel sank to the ground. He leaned back against the rock, held the screwdriver in his left hand and turned its metal point against the palm of his right, as if trying to wriggle a hole through the flesh. 'I loved her.'

'But... she married Per-Anders.'

'Per-Anders never loved her as I did.'

Ellen walked up to the rock, until her shadow stretched over the man's legs. She tried to look into his eyes but he kept his head down, so that all she saw of them were his lashes.

Ellen knelt down on one knee so their heads were at the same level. 'Were you sacrificing the heads to Sofie?'

Only Daniel's left hand moved as he spoke. 'She spoke to me in a dream. She said: *I'm lonely, Daniel. This world is full of shadows and I'm one of them. Please Daniel, send me animals to care for. Or this solitude might kill me again.* Never denied her a wish, I have. She outshone the sun.'

The sun. Twelve heads in a circle, marking the sun's journey across the sky. Ellen's mouth fell open. 'You're telling me you wanted to raise Sofie from the dead?'

'The dead never leave us. Even when we want them to.'

She looked him up and down. Noted the grey hairs visible on the sides of his head like little bird wings, the fine wrinkles by his eyes. A middle-aged man, believing in resurrection? Surely not...

Ellen remembered the picture Simon had shown her. 'That's why you placed the horns in a cross. You were using them to draw the Sami sun symbol.'

'In all my fifty-six years, the sun has never shone on me. The world would have me a creature of the dark. Of winter.'

'You did it out of grief. To honour her.' Ellen spoke to convince herself. No one could believe in resurrection. 'You thought it would make you feel better.' She tried, and failed, to come to grips with that idea.

Daniel made no attempt to correct her. 'I imagine her beside me when I'm up at Dundret. Teasing me, correcting me, saying I'd got the facts wrong.'

'She also led the tours?'

'No. But she knew so much more about the midnight sun. The reindeer, nature... She grew up at a sled dog farm, helped her parents run tours... She knew the national parks like the palm of her hand.'

Ellen nodded, remembering the article she'd read on the internet.

'Rotaimo is depicted as a hill or mound,' Daniel said. 'I hoped doing the tours would bring me closer to her. Rotaimo is...'

'The world of the dead. I know.'

Ellen sat down beside him. The rock bit into her back no matter how she shifted her position or twisted and turned. 'Why did you try to frame Juha?' she asked. 'You used his car.'

The electrician pressed the screwdriver harder against his palm. 'I didn't like him.'

'That's not reason enough.'

'The van is the only vehicle I own,' the man said. 'If anyone had seen me, seen the logo, they'd have known who it was.' He ran a finger along the screwdriver. 'Besides, I knew Juha was off to his Ma that night. I knew he bought berries off this Thai woman, pretty much in the exact area where I wanted to drop the heads. It was a no-brainer.'

'Did Juha tell you about the berries?'

'No.'

'Then how did you know?'

'Rumours.'

Ellen waited for him to elaborate, but the man

remained silent. She tugged at a fingernail. 'Why attack her? The Thai woman.'

'I thought she would talk.'

'She can't even speak Swedish, or English!'

'Even if she spread the word in Thai, there would be a risk of someone finding out.' He glanced at the girl. 'You did.'

'How did you know?'

'Bengt told me.'

'How did he find out?'

'One of his workers must have told him, no?'

Ellen picked at a fingernail. Malee couldn't have betrayed them, could she? Why else, after everything that had happened, would she agree to meet Simon in the hospital and act as Sunan's translator again? Ellen revisited the bunkhouse in her mind. That other woman who'd opened the door, or one of the people in the kitchen… How could Ellen know that some-one hadn't been listening in on them by the door? She cursed herself. Reckless, reckless, she should never have got herself and Simon involved…

Was Malee at the hospital now, talking to the boys? Was it a trap, would Bengt confront them?

Had Erik and Simon realised she'd gone missing?

'How many people knew what you'd done?' she asked the electrician.

Daniel twisted the screwdriver deeper, until it drew blood. 'Not many.' He licked the blood up, baring a pale tongue. 'Far more suspected.'

'Bengt and Kimmo? Juha? Henrik? Everyone on that Facebook group?'

Daniel said nothing. He didn't need to.

'What about the police officer?'

'Sergeant Gunnarson was my neighbour for eight years. My parents told him about my… habits, when the first reindeer disappeared.' His voice lowered. 'It started with flies. Picking them apart, legs and wings. Then it moved on to butterflies, and other insects. Rats that had already been caught in the mousetraps at home. Evidently that fact remained behind closed doors.'

Ellen's hands curled into fists. She banged them against the ground. 'Why are you telling me all these things?'

'Because you wanted answers.' Daniel rested the pricked hand on his knee, flexing and curling the fingers. The scar was clearly visible now, the white square with its pine-like tail. Aware of her gaze, Daniel lowered the injured hand to the ground. 'The dog's bite snagged a tendon. Damaged the nerves. My left hand is the strong one now.' His voice softened. 'You remind me of her.'

Ellen shifted further away from him. In her mind's eye she saw Daniel's left arm descending on a reindeer's head, the metal teeth of his saw catching the sun, leering wickedly. She imagined what Simon and Erik would think if they saw her, sitting side by side with the reindeer killer as if they were friends just enjoying the sunshine. *You need to get out of here*, a part of her said.

Could she talk Daniel into taking her back?

'How did you figure out it was us?'

A thin smile flickered across his lips. 'You underestimated the power of small communities. You put your hometown down as Vettasjärvi. Yes, it is far from here, but the Norrbotten villages keep in touch with each other. Seventy people live in Vettasjärvi and those seventy haven't changed since... well, for at least fifteen years. There has never been a Johan Gustafsson in that village.'

Despite herself, Ellen blushed. 'Everyone else fell for it.'

'Pretended to,' the electrician corrected her. 'Bengt smelled a rat right away.'

The girl considered telling him that the Facebook profile was Erik's idea, that she'd actually doubted the plan from the start.

Daniel seemed to have heard her thoughts. 'That moped in the courtyard belongs to Per-Anders's boy. He struck me as the type who can never stop himself from getting involved in something. Always has to come up with suggestions and solutions. Just like his mother.' His voice hardened. 'I would never have let my kid take off like that in the night.'

'Do you have kids…?'

'Sofie would have been the mother of my children.'

'You'd never have been a good father.'

His eyes grew tender. 'I'm not a bad person.'

'You sawed those reindeer's heads off! You abducted Sunan intending to harm her. You are a criminal.'

'And what is a criminal? Someone who makes bad choices. Nine times out of ten because their childhood got fucked up.'

'Do you regret it?'

'I make a habit of not regretting things.'

Ellen pulled her knees to her chest. 'Take me back to the hostel, Daniel.'

'Ellen…'

'Talk through this properly, with Per-Anders.'

'Per-Anders betrayed me. He must suffer the consequences.'

'He's suffered enough.'

'Has he really?' Daniel pointed the screwdriver at her. 'You don't know what he's done.'

Ellen edged away from him. 'Please, please, put that away.'

'It's not a gun, Ellen.'

He held it like a gun, though. In his left hand, aiming at her face. Her gaze darted down to his right hand. A single blood drop oozed from the wound in his palm.

He could take out her eyes with that thing if he wanted.

'You don't want to hurt me.'

'No,' he agreed, 'I don't. Hurting people puts you into all sorts of trouble.' His mouth twisted. 'But no one gives a shit about some animals.'

'You sawed their heads off,' she said, struggling to keep the tremors out of her voice. 'You left their bodies in the hut to rot. You poisoned—'

She was cut off by a buzzing noise.

Ellen and Daniel stared at the toolbox.

'Someone's calling you,' the electrician said.

Simon. Oh, he'd discovered something was up after all…

Before she could get it, Daniel stepped in her way. 'Uh-uh.' He picked up the toolbox. The phone still rang; she imagined Simon's name in white and the phone symbol flashing underneath…

Daniel waved the screwdriver in front of her. 'Don't think you can try anything.' He reached out and grabbed her by the wrist, the shaft of the screwdriver pressing against the underside of her arm. 'You must stay with me.'

He yanked her towards him, causing her to stumble, and began to walk before she'd fully regained her balance.

'Please, Daniel, where are we going?'

The electrician did not answer.

Choose a Side

Her phone rang two more times in the car. Long calls, lasting ten ringtones each. She twisted in her seat towards the back, tried to reach out, but the toolbox was on the floor under the driver's seat, way out of her reach. Daniel didn't snap at her or hit her hand. He kept tapping his fingers against the steering wheel and glancing at the rear-view mirror. The speedometer tipped over 120 at times, and when the wheels skidded over the white midline the road roared.

He almost crashed into a tree when he jerked the car off the road down a forest track.

Ellen stiffened. It wasn't the same track Per-Anders had led them down. The trees did not stand as thick here, and far ahead the wood seemed to slope downwards. Just to their left was an aspen, ashen and barren, its crown missing – as if someone had chopped its head off.

When Daniel wrenched her door open, a prickly feeling entered her neck.

'You're taking me to the lake, aren't you?'

He yanked her out of the car and pressed the screwdriver against her spine. 'Walk.'

He marched her down to the lake. They stopped at the

metre-long strip of pebbly shore she'd seen from the hill. He made her sit down on the stones, and then paced up and down, thrashing the screwdriver through the bushes.

Ellen glanced back behind her. Green, yellow-tinged shadows stared back at her from between the fir, spruce and pine. A gentle breeze drifting in off the lake stirred the leaves – the only movement in a landscape that seemed to hold its breath.

'They will find us,' she said.

Another thrashing sound from behind her.

'You can't keep me here forever.' She looked over her shoulder at the electrician. Sweat dripped down his face and he worked his jaw as if chewing. He pulled a black iPhone from his pocket.

Had someone tried to call him? Bengt, Kimmo, Henrik? The police?

'Freddie Arvidsson,' she said. 'Why do you have that name for your Facebook?'

Daniel's pace quickened. His footfalls grew heavier. 'Didn't feel comfortable with my own name.'

'Why?'

Daniel said nothing.

'Did the others on the group know? Did they ask why you had a different FB name?'

'They knew, and they didn't ask. We're all local to one another.'

'So you didn't want to hide your identity from them?'

'No.'

'But you did want to hide it from someone else?'

Daniel's jaw tightened.

'Was it Sofie? Were you afraid of what she would say if she found out about the group? Were you afraid she would tell Per-Anders and you would all get caught?'

'The Sami already had a good idea who most of us were. It wouldn't have made a difference if Sofie had told him.'

'Then what other reason was there?'

Daniel raised his gaze to the sky. 'I've wished all my life I was someone else.'

'Like Ronny Arvidsson's son?'

Again, the electrician said nothing, but he lowered his gaze, and gradually slowed down to a standstill.

'Ronny Arvidsson was bandleader for Ronnyz',' Ellen said. 'The dance band who were big in the sixties. Are you his son?'

Daniel's face darkened. 'No.'

'Ronny married Lisbet Persson in April 1961,' Ellen said. 'He'd met her in Svartjokk in December 1960, on one of his Christmas gigs. When the band were due to set off to the next town, Lisbet went with him, and never returned to Svartjokk. It seemed there were things in her past she wanted to leave behind. She'd had a stillbirth in November 1960, after a love affair with my grandfather. She ran away with Ronny when his band came touring to Svartjokk, only two months after the stillbirth. In the registry of baptisms in the Old Church, a child was baptised around the time of her miscarriage, but the name had been crossed out, and there was evidence suggesting the presence of a baby in Lisbet's flat before she left.'

Daniel's fingers flexed and curled. He knelt down on his haunches, so that his face was at the same level as Ellen's.

'How old are you, Daniel?'

'Fifty-six and a half.'

'You were born in November 1960?'

He nodded.

'Did you know your parents?'

'I did not have real foster parents until the Johanssons

took me in, when I was twelve. Kerstin and Fredrik. Good people. I didn't deserve them.'

'And before that?'

'All sorts. I was taken to a Levinian family up in Salmijärvi. They did not treat me well. My foster father would drag me along the driveway to our house and beat me almost to unconsciousness. Until I ran away.' Daniel took off his cap. 'You can say his name, Ellen.'

'Whose name?'

'My biological father's.' A sad smile flitted across his lips. 'You've more or less said the full truth already. There's no point pretending now.'

Ellen looked at his grey-streaked sandy hair. It slanted across his forehead at a diagonal, much like Simon's did. A dimple sat at the left corner of his mouth, which deepened as he smiled. Dad had a dimple on that exact spot.

Ellen closed her eyes. The image of Niklas waving her off at the Kristinehamn platform floated in her mind's eye, then Lars-Erik in the cherry tree; the smell of him, the way he'd squinted down at her as if to see whether she could decipher his thoughts.

Ellen opened her eyes. Daniel looked at her in exactly the same way now.

'Lars-Erik Blind,' she said, her tongue numb as she spoke. 'Your father is Lars-Erik Blind. You are my half-uncle, and my dad's half-brother.'

Daniel surprised her by letting out a slow, deep sigh. He sat down and leaned against a blueberry-shrouded stone. 'I've been waiting all my life for someone to say that.' He looked at her. 'You never guessed it?'

'I never thought...'

'Family resemblance not strong enough?' Daniel narrowed his eyes. Eyes, she realised now, that were the same turquoise as Lars-Erik's and Niklas's.

Ellen folded her arms. 'You have nothing in common with us.'

'Nothing? Genetics get no say in the matter?' When Ellen didn't answer, he continued to speak. 'I was twenty-five when I decided to make contact with my biological parents. Per-Anders gave me their addresses, introduced me to my grandparents, and I posted my letters. Two months, it took, before Lisbet wrote back to me. *Visit me on Thursday 16th, 17.00.* Six words. Plus an address. I made the ten-hour journey down to Gävle: five o'clock on the dot, rang the bell for so long a neighbour opened her door to glare at me. When Lisbet finally opened she looked me up and down once and said: *You had to be as tall as him, didn't you?* I never had to ask which "him" she was referring to. No hellos, no hugs, no acknowledgement that I was her son.' Daniel held Ellen's gaze as he spoke, perhaps searching for signs of sympathy, empathy or pity. 'This Ronny turned up after an hour and only wanted to know when I was leaving.

'That went so badly, I was stupid enough to think at least meeting number two couldn't be any worse. What a naive kid I was. Lars-Erik wouldn't even let me within a thousand miles of his home. He took me to this dodgy coffee-shop on the outskirts of Tyrevik only to explain why he couldn't let me see his family and how it was fundamental they didn't know of my existence. *My son is starting university and is looking for a flat, things between me and my wife aren't so good right now…* Turned out his wife had got sour with him after finding out about his little teenage romance and the illegitimate son due to come visit the next week. A bloody good job he did of dodging the truth. I wasn't his son, or Lisbet's, at all. I was an inconvenience.' Daniel rubbed his nose with a knuckle. 'Getting turned away by not only one but two parents... Christ, it ignites some feelings, Ellen. Pretty damn furious ones.'

He let his hands hang limp between his knees, fingertips brushing the turf. 'Only my grandmother, Marit, accepted me. After moving to Svartjokk she'd invite me for *fika* on a Saturday, in a gap between my shifts. To be honest, I think she mainly did it out of charity, to make up for how Lars-Erik had turned me away. Every time I tried to bring the matter up, or as little as say his name, she bit down on her lip so hard I thought she'd bite through it. I think she even broke off the little contact with him she had.' His gaze drifted to the lake. 'It's as if I'm a pair of scissors, cutting people's lives into pieces wherever I go.'

Ellen opened her mouth, but the retort she'd planned to spit back at him evaporated. She closed it quickly, dug her heel into the ground.

Daniel did not seem to have noticed. He wiped sweat off his forehead with the back of his hand and sat up straighter, pulled up his knees and rested his hands on them. 'Then along came Bengt and Kimmo Persson.'

He seemed to have forgotten Ellen was there. His gaze had shifted again, to a fallen pine trunk some ten metres ahead of him.

'They came late one evening, along with Juha Virtanen and Henrik Andersson. Somehow, word had reached them I was visiting Marit. They insisted I stop. *Lars-Erik fucked your ma over. Don't mess with his kind.* They invited me – no, ordered me. They made it pretty clear there was no other option.' Daniel wiped his face again. His left heel bounced: up down up down, forcing a sapling blueberry sprig to the ground. 'It was old instincts kicking in. See a threat coming, tuck your tail between your legs and walk where you're told to walk. I went with Bengt and Kimmo to this communal garage, scrapyard kind of place in the woods, outside Kajava. That's where they kept the dogs. Locked up in this old barn that they'd converted into a dogfighting stadium.'

'Why?'

'Guess they must have been bored. People shoot, yes, but there's not really much stuff going on up here. People look for entertainment the illegal way.' Daniel twisted a twig of the sapling and twiddled it between his fingers. 'I told myself as we went in: I'll only stay a few minutes. Have a look, say thanks for taking me, then leave and never come back. Sofie would hate me if she found out. She was in my mind all the time.

'But then the dogs were taken out of their cages. Those brutes had been fed nothing but water and mangled reindeer bones during the last week. They were baying for blood, bets were made and before I knew it I'd put down two hundred kronor on a pit bull bitch with a dodgy eye and was shouting at her to rip the other dog's throat out. She was the underdog of the pack.

'You must understand, I'd always learned that silence gave rewards. Let your food quiet your mouth, and Pa won't hit you with the buckle of his belt. Never in my life before had I been urged to *make* noise...'

Daniel looked to the sky. 'I felt closer to the real me that afternoon. Daniel Johansson has never really existed. I was named Daniel by a woman who'd abandoned me at two months old and tried to forget I existed. I was named Johansson after two people who only took me in because I collapsed at their door as a runaway child in foster care. I loved those people, but their names fitted me like clothes a size too small – not at all. I had to leave it all behind, I had to find something that fitted me better. So I moved to Björkliden...'

The man swatted at a mosquito hovering by his face.

'You know, I lied earlier, about not regretting anything.' He turned to face her. 'I turned Sofie away when I needed her the most. Probably because of pride. Spent so much time coping on my own, I didn't want to appear weak in front of her. We always want to seem strong to the people we love, no?'

Simon walked into Ellen's thoughts.

'All that time being ignored meant I didn't recognise kindness even when it stood right in front of me. If I had, if I'd been taught how to love, if I hadn't been abandoned, perhaps Sofie would have chosen me instead of Per-Anders, she would never have gone off into that blizzard…'

The man's gaze grew empty. Somehow, it made him seem younger than his actual fifty-six years.

'You trying to make me believe you did nothing wrong?' Ellen said.

'I think you're the only one who will listen.' Daniel turned to her. 'I saw you with your brother, on the mountain. Asperger's, right?'

Ellen was about to look away, but then she bit her lip and held the man's gaze. 'Yes.'

'I bet you listen to him even when you'd rather do anything but. You stay with him in the wet and dry because no one else will, because he needs to know that he is cared for, that he matters. If you don't listen, he will be invisible.'

'That's not true. There's loads of people who care for Simon. We're not like you.'

'We're more alike than you want to think.'

Ellen rose. She pivoted on her foot and paced through the blueberry sprigs. A symphony of snapping erupted from beneath her feet. She paused. 'You abandoned your grandmother for some racist animal abusers and a pit bull terrier. You went to live with them, when your grandmother had no other family in the area?'

From the corner of her eye, she saw Daniel grimace. 'I kept meaning to speak to her, give her a quick call to explain.'

'But you were afraid you'd lose your new friends if you did?' Spittle flew from Ellen's lips. She wiped her mouth. 'I guess Sofie found out as well?'

Daniel's hands curled into fists.

'That's why she stopped speaking to you, wasn't it?'

The electrician lowered his head. 'No matter what I do, I betray someone.' His hands grew limp. 'It's as if I'm cursed.'

'You could have chosen to stay away.'

'I needed something to make me forget.'

Ellen wasn't sure if he meant his past, or his break-up with Sofie. 'What happened to the dog? After it bit you?'

'I took Bengt's rifle and shot her. Buried her in the garden.'

Ellen felt her insides turn cold. Her gaze wandered up towards the hill. Please, please, she thought to herself, let someone appear. She half-rose as a snapping sound came from amidst the pines, but it was just a bird.

'You know, I'd never felt in control before I killed the first reindeer. As a kid, I was always the one being beaten. Being the beater, exercising power over another living being, I couldn't get enough of it. It was like alcohol, but ten times better.

'I knew that what I was doing was wrong. But I had to forget. I had to get rid of my anger before it burned me up from the inside.' The man closed his eyes. For a moment, he seemed to be sleeping.

Then he stood up. 'Now it's gone, I feel empty. The reindeer are dead, the lake is polluted, Per-Anders's grazing land is ruined, but I have no peace. If anything, I'm more restless.'

His gaze drifted across the lake. 'My foster mother, Kerstin, once said to me that the ghosts of our past only bother us if we fear them. It took me till… this week, on the morning after making the circle, to realise she was wrong. There are no ghosts of our past, only our actions and regrets. They fester in our brain during the day and inside our eyelids when we want to sleep. Embers, never burning out.' He sighed. 'They never will, as long as I'm alive.'

His shadow fell over Ellen as he drew near. 'Stand up.' His voice was barely more than a whisper. 'Hold out your hands.'

She saw the rope too late. The man whipped it out of his pocket and had it lashed around her wrists before she could even gasp in surprise.

'Stay still, Ellen, I'm not going to hurt you.' He tightened the knot, locking her wrists together. 'I need you to stay.'

He led her to a pine tree by the water's edge and tied her hands to the trunk, looping the rope twice around it and securing the bind with another knot over her wrists. He placed his phone in her hands. 'You can hold it there, yes?'

The black iPhone 7 was heavy in her palms. The video-camera was up on the screen, showing a close-up vision of her fingers.

'When I give you the signal, you start recording. Whatever you do, don't stop. You must continue through to the end.'

The end of what? Ellen thought, though she kept it to herself. Daniel was so close she felt his breath, strong and minty, on her cheek.

As if hearing her thoughts, he stepped back. Took a deep breath and closed his eyes, putting a hand against the tree for support, resting his forehead on his bicep.

Ellen bit her lip, counting the seconds.

Daniel's eyes were calm when he opened them. There was knowledge in those irises, as if he knew some vital secret unknown to everyone else. Then they hardened and focused on her. He knelt down so his eyes were in line with the camera. Nodded at Ellen.

Ellen pressed the record button.

'I am not a villain,' Daniel began. 'I know that from your end, Per-Anders, that's probably hard to believe right now. From your end, Ma… well I guess you've never given a shit about what I am. If you had the power to decide I wouldn't be anything at all. And you, half-brother, I mean I have zero hopes for you, I'll be honest. Travelling all those hundreds of kilometres from Stockholm without seeing one of your closest relations?' Daniel tutted and shook his head. 'This is the last time I'm trying to show you I exist. You'd better stick with me to the end.

'I am a victim. I was never brought up in the right way and it means I can't do the right things. I can't recognise goodness when it stands in front of me. I tried to tell you, Ma, but you didn't want to listen. I tried telling Pa, and he pretended to listen even though he tried to end our conversation every minute. Then he had the nerve to die on me. I tried to tell you, Per-Anders, but you only saw the Persson in me and ignored the Blind. What can a man do, eh? You had me cornered in a cul-de-sac. It creates some pretty serious anger issues, and you have to channel all those feelings somewhere, yes?

'I'm not saying I defend my actions. I'm saying you can't define me by them. If I am a villain it's because you all made me one. You've all killed me at some point. That's why I'm signing off for good.'

Daniel turned and stepped down into the water. He waded out till it reached his knees, then looked over his shoulder into the phone.

Through the phone, into Ellen's eyes.

'Daniel, what are you doing?'

A muscle in the man's face twitched.

A prickly feeling entered Ellen's neck. *No*, she thought. He wouldn't.

Daniel walked further out, until the water lapped at his chest.

'Daniel, no…' she tugged at the rope, tried to tear it by pulling her hands in opposite directions, by scraping it against the bark.

He was up to his neck in water now. The iPhone captured every millimetre the lake gained on him.

She only had to move her thumb a millimetre across the screen to press Stop.

The prickly feeling became a heartbeat pulse in her neck.

He was underwater now, a few bubbles on the surface the only sign he still existed.

Then she heard the footfalls. Many of them, moving fast. Thrash, thrash, thrash. A figure darted past her.

Stopped.

'Per-Anders?' Ellen tried to wave her hands, which resulted in an awkward jerk that nearly made her drop the phone.

The reindeer herder almost looked at her. His gaze landed on the black iPhone, hovered there for a moment.

'Ellen!'

The other footfalls drew nearer, one set small and light, the other heavier, slower.

A pair of hands moved into her vision. Pale, long-fingered hands with rounded nails.

Her father. Behind him, watching closely, was Simon.

'Did he hurt you?' Niklas's eyes rushed up and down

the length of her. When they spotted the phone, they darkened. 'What did he make you do?'

'He's drowning.' Ellen motioned with her hands
towards the lake. 'He did nothing, but he's drowning.'

Her father followed her gaze. He locked eyes with
Per-Anders.

'The chlorine is still in there?'

The man nodded.

'If he's submerged for more than two minutes he will
die of chlorine poisoning,' Simon said.

Niklas bit his lip. He stood up, pulled off his shirt and
stepped out of his shorts.

'What are you doing?'

Niklas walked past his son down to the shore. 'No,'
he said, waving away the hand Per-Anders extended to him. 'I
owe him this.'

Then he entered the lake.

'No, Dad!' Ellen and Simon cried as one.

Too late. A new set of bubbles grew on the surface,
marking the spot where their father had gone underwater.

Water to Cleanse

A prickly feeling in his neck wakes him up. He's bathing in sweat, he can feel it pooling between his shoulder blades, making his nightshirt stick to his skin.

Something has happened to Sofie.

Daniel, you silly, she would say, bad things don't happen just because your neck hurts. Telepathy wouldn't work like that, even if it existed.

As she speaks, though, her imaginary face clouds over in doubt. This isn't the first time he's had this feeling.

He makes it down to the hallway where he leaves his phone each night. If he keeps it by the bedside table he always wakes up and immediately opens his Facebook to check what she's doing, what she's thinking, what she's feeling, and that almost always makes him late for work. Sofie is dangerous to his mind, he needs to keep her at bay, even if it is only as far as the stairs.

He hardly feels the stairs under his feet. His body is light, as if some invisible hand is dangling it from a string. It's another person's thumb dialling Sofie's home number, another voice asking for her. A sense of foreboding has taken over his body and he can do nothing but wait and watch it unfold.

'Yes.' A man's voice, dry and curt.

Per-Anders.

'What's happened to Sofie?'

'She's not come back.'

His voice is too even, Daniel thinks. Polished, smooth, like ice.

'From what?'

'The reindeer gathering.'

'You had a gathering in this blizzard?'

'It took us by surprise. The skies were blue. You must have seen.'

Daniel had seen. It had been a classic February day, crisp and bright; he'd stopped for twenty minutes along the road to admire the view while working. 'Didn't you check the forecast?' As he speaks, the wind outside grows stronger, shaking the bones of the house. Through the living room window he sees snow, turning the night stripy.

'The herd scattered,' Per-Anders says. 'She wouldn't leave until they were united again.'

Daniel bites his lip. 'How many hours?'

'Five.'

'She's been gone five hours and you haven't searched for her?'

'Visibility is too poor for scooter driving.'

'What about the police?'

'They won't head out in this weather.'

'Bullshit.'

'Yes,' Per-Anders says. 'It is.'

Daniel holds the phone in his hand for two hours afterwards. His thumb tap tap taps against the screen, composing one *message after the other. It does not ring, it does not beep. If Per-Anders has seen the messages, he pretends that he hasn't.*

Until 5.16 a.m.

We've found her.

Daniel knows he should be relaxed but instead his worry increases. He responds with **How is she?** *but Per-Anders does not get back to him. Perhaps he's turned his phone off.*

Daniel throws his own phone at the wall. The prickling sensation becomes a heartbeat in his neck.

Per-Anders's message stares up at him from its green chat bubble. **We've found her.** *Not* **She's OK**, *or* **She will survive.**

The article appears on Kuriren *at 7.42. A minute before his next client in Nattavaara calls and asks why he hasn't arrived to fix the fuse box yet. He blames it on the winter flu, all the while looking at the article picture and stroking Sofie's printed face with his eyes.*

Froze to death, did she?

Tears sting his eyes.

He shifts his gaze to the snow standing in massive blocks on the driveway, the lawn, the porch. Trapping him as it trapped her. Kimmo will have to clear the lawn again.

He squeezes his eyes shut. He sees her pain, throbbing in the red inside of his eyelids. Did she scream, when her foot got trapped between the rocks? Was she hurt? Did she finally regret turning her back on him?

You could have been here, he thinks. He can almost see her, in the corner of his eye, cradling his blue coffee mug in her hands. Puckering her lips as she always does when in thought, probably mulling over the new activity she's been organising with Laponia Tours.

'Was he really worth it, Sofie?'

He sees the man's thin-lipped smile again, his slight frame leaning against the open door. Inviting Daniel inside, while keeping his hand on the door handle and his right foot on the threshold. Sofie hovers inside, that tray of raspberry shortbreads that was never offered to him in her hands.

Never before in the world could five metres have felt like five thousand miles.

Per-Anders's smile returns again. A copy of itself, fifteen years younger, another moment in which Per-Anders leans against an open door with a hand on the handle and a foot on the threshold.

You are welcome, his body language says, but not welcome.

In his mind's eye, Daniel walks past the reindeer again, Per-Anders's voice pouring over him. 'Calf marking starts tomorrow,' he says. 'If you want, you can come and watch.' The man stops and turns to face him. 'Come any time.'

Come and see my animals, but don't make yourself at home. It was so clear now, in retrospect. All Per-Anders wanted was to keep Daniel and Sofie on opposite sides of his threshold.

Daniel opens his eyes, opens Facebook. The adjustments to Sofie's profile have already been made. In memory of sits in white letters, font-size fourteen or sixteen, above her name.

Above her profile picture, where she smiles like a model for a toothpaste ad, right hand holding the rope, left hand resting on the bull reindeer's neck.

His fingers begin to tremble. It takes three attempts to save the picture onto his photo gallery and send it to his email. Five minutes later he holds it in his hand, the paper warm from the printer.

He takes out the scissors from their drawer and cuts the paper in two, saving the side with Sofie's face. Then he cuts the reindeer into shreds.

He repeats the process again, again and again.

Conversations

The waiting room smelled of cleaning detergent and leather. Henna-red chairs were lined up in eight rows, facing a wide TV perched on the wall. Hiding in the far left corner was a coffee machine.

Niklas headed straight for it. He jabbed at the buttons and tapped his foot on the floor while his Americano was prepared.

'How are you feeling, Dad?' Ellen asked. The doctor had already taken a blood test to check for any chlorine, and asked him to wait for the results.

Niklas lifted the mug and took a sip, back still turned to her. Steam rose up past his head.

'Do you feel sick? Like you're going to throw up any minute?'

He turned, a weak smile on his pale lips. 'I feel OK.' His voice was faint and he stared emptily into his mug.

'Are you sure?' The image of Daniel on the stretcher flashed through her mind again. He'd been coughing violently when Niklas and Per-Anders carried him back to the road. When the nurses lifted him out of the ambulance he wasn't moving a finger, and his face was hidden behind an oxygen mask. They'd taken him straight to the operating theatre. All Ellen had seen of him before the doors closed were his sandy tufts of hair, waxy in the sun.

So similar to the tufts her father was now pushing out of his face.

Could there be any chlorine hiding in her dad's system? According to Simon, he'd been in the water for forty-nine seconds. Would that be long enough for the doctors to have to pump his stomach?

Niklas's face was pallid, his eyes bloodshot. But he had no cough, no nausea, no stomach pains.

Before she could ask him again, the door to the examination room opened and a male nurse called his name, announcing they'd got the test results and the doctor wanted to talk them through with him.

Niklas put his cup back down on the coffee machine, under the nozzle. 'Can you keep an eye on Simon? Make sure he doesn't wander off again?'

She gave a slight nod. 'Yes.'

The gentle thud as the door closed behind him echoed like a gunshot in Ellen's ears.

She looked over to Simon, who was sitting on the floor in the far left corner of the room, half-hidden from view behind an armchair, Rubik's cube in hand. *Click, snap, click*, it said as he twisted and turned it. He'd been fiddling incessantly with it during the car ride, too. When they'd arrived at the hospital he'd headed straight for the toilets. Ellen had stood outside while Niklas went to the reception to give his personal details. Simon never locked doors in case they jammed and he got trapped. A few minutes passed, during which she heard no sign of the toilet flushing or a tap being run. Frowning, she put an ear against the door.

A low, monotone sound emanated from the other side.

'Simon?' Gently, she opened the door.

Her brother sat slumped on the white-tiled floor. His head was between his knees and he rocked gently back and forth.

Simon's In Distress mode. He hadn't done that since he was ten.

'Simon,' she whispered softly. Knocked on the door, using one knuckle. 'Simon.'

The monotone grew in volume.

Ellen had eased the door shut just as Niklas reappeared. Still leaning against it with an ear against the wood, she explained the situation.

Her father ran a hand through his hair. 'I told him Daniel was my half-brother when we were in Per-Anders's car, on the way to the lake.'

'He didn't say anything then?'

'No, we were focused on finding you... and I guess he was suppressing his emotions.' He'd looked at her carefully. 'Daniel told you, didn't he?'

Ellen barely managed a nod. The truth still lay in a tangled heap in her brain. She could not muster the strength to make sense of it. She felt drained, wrung dry, all emotions squeezed out of her.

'Per-Anders told us about Granddad's past,' she'd said numbly. 'We never talked about whether you knew or not... Simon was so focused on the investigation.'

Her dad had smiled weakly then. 'Once Simon is on track to solving something, nothing will stop him.' The smile faded. 'If not for him, then...'

Tears filled Niklas's eyes. He blinked, and two of them, one from each eye, ran down his cheeks.

Ellen reached out a hand to him. 'It's OK, Dad, don't think about it any more...'

Her father's gaze flitted to the toilet door, then to his watch. He sighed exasperatedly and knocked on the door. 'Simon, I need to go to the waiting room, I have my appointment soon.' He pressed his ear against the door, assuming the same stance as his daughter.

The monotone grew even louder. People passing by turned their heads round to stare.

Niklas took a hissing intake of breath and pressed his eyes shut, one finger on each eyelid. Ellen leaned forward to touch his arm. 'Go to the waiting room, Dad. I'll try to speak to Simon. We'll meet you there.'

First, Niklas shook his head, eyes still closed. A moment later the muscles in his face relaxed and he pulled his fingers down, opening his eyes, settling his gaze on her hand. 'Yes,' he said through a sigh, 'you're probably right.' He hugged her hand in both of his before he left.

Ellen leaned back against the door. 'Simon,' she called softly, 'Dad has gone. Please, talk to me. Let me know how you're feeling.' She wetted her lips. 'Dad said it's thanks to you I'm safe, and that Daniel's alive. Won't you tell me what happened? I was thinking about you the whole time…'

The monotone ceased. A shuffling sound from the other side. Then came the metallic click of the handle being pushed down, and the door opened a fraction. A strip of sandy hair and storm-grey eyes became visible through the gap.

'I knew as soon as Sunan described her attacker that he was Daniel,' he said in a hushed voice. 'She said that the man who kidnapped her had a long scar on his arm, and that she'd suffered a blow to the left side of her head. I remember seeing his scar on Mount Dundret, that it was on his right hand. I copied it down in my notebook because it looked interesting.'

'You never told me that,' his sister said.

'Ellen, you know I only say things if I'm a hundred per

cent sure they're relevant. My suspects then were Virtanen and Bengt Persson.'

Ellen let slip a small smile in acknowledgement. 'Of course,' she said. No words were wasted with Simon. Every single thing he said carried relevance to that particular moment.

'Then Erik saw Freddie Arvidsson's PMs on Johan Gustafsson's profile and realised something must have happened to you. We scanned through Freddie's footage on the group and I saw that all the pictures tipped slightly to the left. Then I saw his right forearm in one picture and noticed the tennis ball scar. I deduced the scar must have made Daniel favour his left arm.'

'And what happened then?'

'We drove to the hostel on Erik's moped. The driveway was all muddy from the morning rain so all the footprints had settled. The prints beside those of the wheels were identical to those I saw in the ditch in the forest. Erik spoke to Laila and she confirmed that Daniel had been there and then taken off without warning, so it was obvious Daniel was the culprit. I called Dad then but he was already on the way to the airport.'

'Already?'

The strip of hair moved as Simon shifted his position. 'He said he had a gut feeling. I didn't understand.'

Something twisted in Ellen's own gut, but she pushed the feeling down. 'And Per-Anders? Did Erik call him?'

'Yes. Erik called Per-Anders and Per-Anders called the police.'

Simon explained they'd first headed towards the forest glade where the heads had lain. Upon seeing no van on the track, they continued down to the turn-off leading to the lake, and found Daniel's van parked just off the track, half-hidden by the trees. Per-Anders led the way to the lake.

In Ellen's mind's eye, Daniel crossed the road towards her again. They drove through the forest, walked down the path, his screwdriver pressing into her spine. His head vanished under the water.

If Dad and Simon had come just a minute later…

'You saved us both,' Ellen whispered. 'You're the hero, Simon.'

Something stirred in her brother's iris. The door opened up another centimetre so she could see his lips.

'I was scared.' The pupils, half-hidden from view under the hair, shifted back and forth as he spoke. 'I was scared I would lose you, like Erik lost his mum.'

'Simon, it's OK to be scared or worried sometimes.' She thought of the black iPhone, now in the hands of the police, on which she'd caught it all on film. 'I often worry what other people think of me.'

Was the officer watching the video now? Was he frowning in suspicion as he heard her voice on the clip? Would he notice the jolts of the video as her hand shook?

'Why?' her brother whispered.

'I don't know, I… I guess I just don't want to be misunderstood.' She pictured the policeman in her thoughts. He'd been so kind to them during the ride into the hospital, talking about Tyrevik, about the women's football team and what a shame it was the club had gone bust. And about Simon's deductions, of course.

You were right and I was wrong, Gunnarson had admitted. *Perhaps I should offer you my hat and badge.*

Even now, Simon's response brought her close to a smile. *Your hat is the wrong size for my head, I don't have a safety-pin for sticking the badge onto my shirt, and you said it was a crime to impersonate a police officer.* He stayed quiet the rest of the trip;

all three of them had. They'd sat together in the back, Niklas in the middle, his arm around Ellen's shoulders, his other hand resting palm up on his lap, in case Simon wanted to hold it. He never did.

'Ellen,' her brother said, pulling her out of her thoughts. 'I don't misunderstand you.'

'No?'

'We are siblings. We share 50 per cent of the same DNA, so we are each other's closest relations. If there is any person we can understand, it's each other.'

'Is that why you were scared to lose me?'

The pupils turned away then, and her brother seemed to hold his breath. Three, four, five seconds. On the sixth, a nod.

She ran a finger along the door frame. 'Does that mean that from now on, you will tell me if you feel upset at any point, or just want to talk?'

Simon followed the movement of her finger. 'Maybe.'

'No more whispering through closed doors?'

The door opened to reveal Simon's face. A tentative smile hovered on his lips as he spoke. 'No more closed doors.'

The sound of a door opening almost made Ellen jump out of her seat. Niklas, returning from the doctor's consulting room. She cast a look around, noting the waiting room, Simon in the corner...

Her conversation with Simon still looped round and round in her head. Looking at him now, deliberately ignoring their Dad with his lips glued together, it seemed like little more than a daydream.

'They cleared me,' her father said. 'No chlorine found.'

'That's great, Dad.'

He passed the chairs towards the coffee machine, as if not hearing her. Ellen watched as he lifted the cup and gazed at the faint wisps of steam still rising from it. He ran a hand over his face.

'Is something wrong?'

Niklas's jaw tensed.

'Dad?'

He let out a slow sigh. 'It all feels wrong now,' he said softly, 'looking back. I went into a polluted lake, to save a crazed half-brother I'd never met. At the expense of my own children.'

Ellen stared down at her hands resting in her lap. 'What you did was brave.'

'There'd have been no need for bravery if that man hadn't abducted you and…' …*planned killing himself on video as vengeance on the relatives who'd ignored him all his life*. Niklas didn't have to speak the words for Ellen to know that he thought them. It was written on the deep lines in his forehead and the drooping of his lips. His grip on his coffee cup tightened, the knuckles and veins highlighted under the pale skin.

'Surely you must be angry at me?'

Ellen opened and closed her mouth, unsure what was appropriate to say, when she noticed Simon glaring at their father over the rim of his cube. She turned to him. 'Simon, what's the matter?'

'I am angry at Dad.'

'Why?'

Simon addressed their father. 'If you had told us who Daniel was before we left home, then we wouldn't have been tricked by him and Ellen wouldn't have been kidnapped.'

Niklas's eyes filled with tears. He straightened his back, paced up and down the room, as if to rein the tears in. 'Granddad loved you,' he said. 'He was afraid you'd be scared of him if you found out he'd killed a man, that you wouldn't want to see him again. He couldn't bear losing your love. He made me swear not to tell you.'

'But after he died you could have told us.'

Niklas came to a halt. 'Your mother didn't want me to. She was still afraid it would upset you – you particularly, Simon.'

'I am more upset that you didn't tell me.'

Niklas winced. A single tear rolled down his cheek. 'When you'd turned thirteen, Simon, I told Granddad it was time to break the silence. You were old enough. He refused and then... not long before he died, he told me he'd included Daniel in his will. It felt like a second betrayal, almost, though on a smaller scale, and upset your mum greatly, too.'

'Is that why you had so many quarrels with him at the end?' Ellen asked.

'Yes.' Niklas turned his coffee cup around in his hands. 'She didn't want him to get any money from a family he'd never belonged to. She didn't want you to know about him. I could tell you about Granddad's past, after your trip here, but only if it went well and we'd sorted things at home.'

Simon narrowed his eyes. 'Then you'd be telling part of the truth, but not all of it. You would be telling us a white lie.'

'Simon...'

'I think Sergeant Gunnarson should make parents telling white lies to their children a criminal offence.'

Niklas sat down on a chair in the row in front of Ellen. He motioned with his hand. 'Come here, Simon. Sit down with us.'

He had to repeat the request three times before Simon budged. He sat down next to Ellen, on the right, so that she was between him and Niklas.

'How did you get here?' Ellen asked, to change the subject.

Simon fidgeted. 'We've already talked about this.'

'I want to hear it in Dad's words.'

Niklas tapped his long fingers against the rim of his cup. 'I came by plane, from Bromma airport. Three hours ago.'

Simon pursed his lips and stared down at the floor. He twitched his right foot up and down.

'Per-Anders picked me up,' Dad continued. 'We stopped at your hostel to fetch the boys and then went to the forest. That's where I explained to Simon about Daniel.'

He took another sip. A single drop ran down his chin. He didn't wipe it off. Ellen watched it tuck in under his chin, trickle down his Adam's apple and disappear under the shirt collar. A shirt still sodden with lake water.

'What did Mum say when she heard?'

'I don't know.' Her father bit his lip. 'I haven't told her yet. I left her a voicemail.'

'A voicemail,' Ellen repeated.

'There was no time to have a proper talk.'

'Has she tried calling you back?'

'No.' Niklas pulled at an earlobe. 'Well, I haven't actually checked.'

Ellen swallowed. 'She'll be absolutely livid.'

'I know, I…' Niklas ran his hand over his face again. 'I'm sorry.' He breathed out, slowly. 'I will call Mum as soon as we're out of this building.'

He drained his cup. One long draught, three more drops spilling down his throat as he swallowed. He smacked his lips and wiped them with the back of his hand.

'There is a reason why I didn't tell her. Why I was already on the road when Simon called.' The plastic chair squeaked as Niklas twisted around to face his children, leaning over it. 'A strange feeling came over me, like a sting, or… a pulse. A second heartbeat. Hitting and beating, beating and hitting. A certainty came over me, that you and Simon were in danger. That's why I set off. I had to be ready: on the road, all set to jump on the first plane should one of you, or Per-Anders, or anyone from Svartjokk, try to contact me.'

The warmth that had grown in Ellen's chest during her talk with Simon seeped away. Internally, she winced at every word. She could just imagine her mother, pacing up and down the house the same way Dad had paced around the waiting room. Pulling at her hair, perhaps shouting out some curses that would make their neighbours peek over the hedge to see what was going on.

So much for sending me and Simon away so they could talk, she thought. At this rate, things could be even worse between her parents when they got back.

Then the image of her grandfather rose to her mind. The smell of him as they sat together in the cherry tree – lavender and boat varnish. The way his voice tickled her ear as he whispered to her about the cherry tree's shadow.

'Have you had this… feeling… before?' she asked her father. In the corner of her eye, she noticed Simon fold his arms over his chest and lean back against his chair, hair covering his eyes. She could almost hear his denials like a mantra in her mind: *The gift of foresight does not exist, there is no scientific evidence to prove it.*

'No,' said Niklas.

'So Granddad might never have known that you had the ability.'

'I'll bet you anything he did,' Niklas said. He fingered the coffee cup, as if surprised to see it was now empty. 'He had this way of knowing things, even when there seemed to be no evidence that there was anything to know.' He pressed the cup between his hands. 'The night before he died, he called me. *A feeling's been creeping on me, Niklas,* he said. *I can feel it in my bones. Something is going to happen to me soon. I just want you to be prepared when it does.*' Niklas flicked the scrunched-up cup onto the chair beside him. 'He hung up on me before I could respond. And the next day...'

He went out for his eight-kilometre run, and never came back, Ellen thought, completing her father's sentence. Heart attack, age seventy-five. *No age for a modern man,* Mum had said. Niklas never uttered a word.

Ellen waited for him to do so now. To admit what he should have admitted thirteen months ago.

Granddad's foretelling wasn't just small talk. Those pulses Niklas and Ellen had felt, that was Sapmi, warning them. Sapmi was alive. Sapmi was real.

Instead, her father picked up the cup, crossed the room and tossed it in the rubbish.

Perhaps it was too much to ask of him right now. He'd just risked his life to save a half-brother he'd pretended didn't exist. A man he must have hated. He'd confessed to his children about the secrets he'd kept from them their entire lives.

Her dad's life had flipped upside down in a matter of minutes.

'When did Granddad tell you about Daniel?'

'He didn't.'

She frowned at him.

Niklas took a deep breath. 'It was Lisbet Arvidsson.'

'What?'

'She called, on the home telephone, wanted to speak to my father. I told her he was out on the boat and wouldn't be back until evening. *Oh never mind,* she said, *you can just pass on the message to him. Tell him his son Daniel has just paid me a visit and would very much like to see him.* I swear she chortled under her breath as she hung up.'

'When was this?' Ellen's voice was dry as she spoke.

'1987, '88, can't remember exactly. I'd just started my teacher training but was still living at home. I do remember watching him, though, when he set off in the car towards Tyrevik, to meet this first son I had no idea existed.' Niklas pulled a hand over his face. 'I moved out three months later. Your grandmother another four after that.'

'You were angry.'

'I was furious.'

'How could Granddad not...'

'Simple. Fifty-six years isn't the kind of silence you break so easily.'

'It shouldn't matter how many years it is,' Simon muttered. 'It is not an excuse.'

'He must have meant to tell you,' said Ellen.

'I don't think so.'

'He wouldn't keep something like that from you.'

'Enough!'

Niklas stood up. His hands clenched at his sides. 'It gets to a point where the silence can't be broken. It's... it's like stitching, or needlework. Ignoring that you've made a mistake at the beginning but deciding to unravel it all when you're nearly at the end, and have someone else do it for you, to save yourself the trouble.' He closed his eyes for a moment, breathing in through his teeth. 'I know you want to think of your granddad in the best possible light, and he was a great granddad in many ways.' Niklas locked eyes with his daughter. 'But we all have flaws, things we don't want others to know.'

'You are our dad. You can't keep things from us,' Simon said.

'I will try not to, from now on.'

'You have to swear.'

Niklas put a hand to his heart. 'I swear.'

'You will never keep anything from us and tell any white lies?'

'I will never keep things from either of you again. I will always be honest. No more white lies.'

Simon held his dad's gaze for a few seconds, his expression intense and unflinching. Then he gave a curt nod and returned his attention to the cube again, twisting and turning it.

Niklas put his hands on his knees. 'I don't know about you, but I'm feeling pretty hungry. Haven't eaten anything since breakfast.' He stood up. 'How about we eat something at the cafe and continue our talk afterwards? I need the bathroom, too.'

Ellen picked at a fingernail. She still felt the metal point of Daniel's screwdriver drilling into her back. A shudder ran down her spine. 'You go ahead,' she said weakly. 'I'll come.' Eating, conversing... as if the world was back to normal. The kidnapping still pulsed, fresh and vivid, in her mind. It had split her in two: the Ellen before and the Ellen after. She felt out of touch with herself.

Her dad hovered, chewing his lip as if wondering whether to speak, ask if she was OK. Then he nodded and left the room.

Ellen looked at the way her index fingers and thumbs met, forming a heart-shaped circle.

'It was them,' she thought. 'It was the reindeer who broke the silence.'

She didn't realise she'd spoken out loud until she noticed Simon watching her with narrowed eyes. He was still fiddling with his cube.

'What?' she said.

His gaze wavered. 'It was Daniel's violence that broke the silence. That's what happens when people don't tell the truth.'

'Then, if we're ever going to function as a normal family, we must the break the silence between us.' Ellen stood up. 'Once and for all.'

Solstice

It happened the following morning over coffee and cinnamon buns. It took place in the hostel canteen.

Niklas perched on the chair facing the train station. No trains passed at this time, yet his eyes flicked back and forth over the rails as if expecting one to appear. Ellen and Simon sat on the brown leather sofa opposite him. On the table lay their phones, Simon's showing the pictures from the glade, Ellen's showing the fake Facebook page. In between the phones lay Simon's notebook.

Ellen told Niklas about their journey from start to finish, beginning with their train journey, their arrival in Svartjokk, all the way to the moment Daniel had tied her to the tree. Simon filled in on the detective details.

'Daniel tried to befriend us at Mount Dundret,' he said, 'but he was lying.'

'It wasn't all lies,' Ellen interjected.

'But his behaviour was suspicious and you didn't notice.'

She bit her lip. That was true.

'In retrospect,' her brother continued, 'I think it was

because he is Dad's half-brother. Maybe that's how it is with a blood relation.'

Ellen's and Niklas's eyes met. 'It's more than just that,' she said, and she told them about the pulse in the neck, which both she and Daniel had felt.

She told them about seeing Marit.

The silence that answered her didn't make her fiddle with her fingernails or tense her shoulders. It allowed her to lean back, rest her head on the sofa, and bring the last bit of bun to her mouth. Sweet cinnamon melted on her tongue.

'Granddad used to say people and nature are connected,' Niklas said. 'Like the tree and its roots. Modern life makes people forget, but those who remember... he said they might see or feel things that would be impossible to explain in scientific terms.'

'So you mean Marit's ghost was real?'

'If you saw her, she must have been real to you, no?'

Ellen looked at her hands. Three of her fingernails were ripped but the rest had started to regrow. 'It's as if Sapmi never really left Granddad. When he died, he passed it on to us.' She looked up at her dad. 'Perhaps we were meant to come here.'

The corner of Niklas's mouth twitched, but a smile never came. He leaned back on the stool and drummed his fingers slowly against the table.

'What's wrong?' his daughter asked.

'I am wondering how to explain all this to your mother.'

He did it with the calm and care with which Ellen had told her own story. He hid nothing, asked the siblings to fill in on details he'd forgotten. Ellen and Simon had taken a shower and dressed in their least sweaty clothes. They sat close together to fit into the camera screen. Mum needed to see they were well. Though Ellen still expected her mother to scream and tell the siblings to leave so she could have a word with their father, alone.

But her mother said nothing. Ellen didn't know what to do with her silence. She searched her mother's face for a sign; a twitching muscle by her eyes, a frown on the forehead, a pursing of the lips. Nothing. Camilla's face, for once without make-up, was naked, childlike and unknowable.

So Ellen smiled. A tentative smile, lips parted just enough to show her front teeth. Camilla would know if her daughter overdid it, put on a show just to lay her mother's mind at rest. And she would know if Ellen underdid it.

If Niklas had been honest with Ellen earlier, he would have told her that this was the first time he'd made direct contact with Camilla since he'd left for Svartjokk. He had not told his daughter yet how things had fared at home.

When she heard about Henrik's involvement in the dogfighting, Camilla asked if Niklas had checked the siblings out of the hostel and booked them in at the Laponia Hotel instead. When he said they hadn't, her nostrils flared and her eyes widened. 'They can't stay under the same roof as a man like that!'

'Henrik wasn't involved, Mum,' Ellen explained. 'He had no idea about the killing.' In fact, the hostel owner had come knocking on their door on their return. Laila had told him about her conversation with Ellen and their investigation, and Henrik felt guilty for not having taken greater measures to keep the electrician away from the siblings. *I knew what he was like*, he'd said, *what all of them were like, Bengt and Kimmo.*

I didn't want to snitch on him, or tell the police about the Facebook group, in case they found out… I was a coward.

Camilla didn't seem comforted by this. 'Must you stay another night?'

'Mum…'

'You need to come home, Ellen. The horrors you've been through! And Simon…'

'I am quite all right,' Simon said. Ellen pointedly avoided her mother's gaze.

Their dad intervened. 'Things won't be settled until we've spoken to Daniel.'

'You cannot forgive him, Niklas. He kidnapped our daughter!'

'I'm not going to. What he's done can never be forgiven. I think he knows that.'

'There's no knowing what such a horrible man can think.'

'You can trust me on this, Camilla.'

'Really?'

'I promise.'

'Then you'd better keep your promise.'

One hour after speaking to Camilla, Ellen, Niklas and Simon entered Daniel's room at the hospital. Soft, lemony light filtered in between the sandy curtains, casting a stripe of light on the bed.

Daniel lay with his eyes closed, head to the side. His hair had been combed back over his head, making him look even more like his half-brother. There was a tube in his arm, attached to a drip standing to the left of the bed. There was a wet patch on the pillow beside his mouth, probably from saliva.

Niklas pulled a chair forward and sat down. Ellen and

Simon stood on either side of him, hands resting on the back of the chair.

Niklas cleared his throat. 'Daniel? Are you awake? It's me, Niklas, and Ellen and Simon.'

Daniel's eyelids fluttered. 'I knew you were coming.'

'The nurse told you?'

Daniel's eyes opened. His blue eyes were pale, as if they'd been diluted by the lake water. 'No, Per-Anders did. You missed him by twenty minutes. I'm told I owe you my life. Brother.'

A line appeared on the electrician's forehead. 'I would have thought he'd tell you. Then again, knowing him, I'm not surprised he didn't.'

'We're not here to forgive you,' Niklas said.

'Forgiveness is not what I'm looking for.' With a groan, Daniel propped himself up on his elbows, edging back to use the pillow as a backrest. 'I just don't want to be forgotten.'

Niklas snorted. 'You think slaughtering twelve reindeer and forcing a teenage girl to record your suicide is a good way to be remembered?'

'I hoped when you all saw the video, you would feel regret. That you would finally remember the brother and uncle you could have had, but never wanted.'

His gaze settled on Ellen. A knowing gaze that made her avert her eyes, and think back to those words he'd said by the lake. *I think you're the only one who will listen.*

'How difficult was it to write a simple letter directly to my father?' Niklas said. 'Or to me?'

'What do you think I did? How else would I have got in touch with my mother in the first place? My parents refused me.'

'I can't apologise for my father's behaviour. Yes, perhaps he was wrong not to acknowledge you, but nothing can justify what you did to my daughter and to Per-Anders. And that poor Thai woman. It's too late for any kind of pardon.'

'Then why did you save my life?'

Niklas's jaw tightened, and his fingers, resting between his knees, curled slightly.

'When my head went beneath the surface I opened my mouth straight away,' Daniel continued, his gaze rising to the ceiling. 'It was as if someone had covered my mouth with a cloth and poured lava down my lungs. I remember seeing arms flail above me and wonder whose they could be. Then everything blacked out. Next I knew, your face was there. It blocked out the sun and the sky and the trees.' His head turned to face them again. 'Then I cursed you, to myself. I had one wish left in the world and again, a relative messed it up.' He sat up straighter. 'So, why did you save my life?'

Even though Ellen, from where she was standing, only saw the left side of her father's face, she could see the emotions contort inside it. Niklas uttered the words he'd told his children in the hostel lobby. 'Because you are my brother.'

Daniel gave a wan smile. 'Blood is thicker than water.'

The water looked cold. It nibbled at Simon's toes, causing him to pull his feet back and inhale sharply through his nose. After wiggling his toes for a few seconds, he lowered them back in, and repeated the process, again and again.

If Ellen had brought her sketchbook, she'd have copied the scene down in pencil within minutes. Remade it at home with charcoal and colour pastels. Now, she made the drawing with her eye, outlining Simon's figure, the creases in his shirt and the strands of his hair.

'Simon,' she called when he was done.

As she'd expected, he didn't look up.

'Simon, if you're upset about something, you should talk to me.' She stepped onto the jetty. It squeaked under her feet as she walked out to her brother.

'I suck at detecting.'

The words, or rather, *the* word, glued Ellen's feet to the wooden boards. 'What do you mean?'

'I mean what I say. If I had been a good detective, I would have known from the start that Daniel was guilty. It was obvious, in retrospect. It is always the person you suspect the least who is guilty and instead I made the big mistake that many detectives do, suspecting the first suspect, who is almost always innocent in books.' Simon stabbed his heel at the water. 'In *LasseMaja and the Circus Mystery*, their main suspect is Ali Pasha, the wrestler who is big and strong and has a moustache. In fact, it was the balloon girl who was guilty, but they never suspect her because she befriends them at the beginning.'

Ellen chuckled. 'Are you saying men with moustaches look like criminals?'

'No.' Simon pulled his feet back and crossed his legs. 'I am saying that Ali Pasha looked dangerous.' Then he twisted to look up at his sister. 'Daniel isn't how a villain is supposed to be.'

Ellen knelt down beside him. 'Villains don't just behave one way, Simon. There isn't a set model, like in books or movies. Villains are just people, with both good and bad. The bad just took over.'

'But will Daniel get the good back now?'

'I don't know,' she admitted. 'I hope so.'

Simon dipped his big toe into the water. 'Daniel said blood was thicker than water.'

'He didn't mean that literally, it's just a saying.'

'I know what it means. It's a fact that blood is thicker

than water, it coagulates and acts as a binder, like egg, but water just washes things away.' He lifted his foot up and they watched the water dripping from his toe. 'Maybe that is why Granddad and Dad and you and Daniel got visions. And me, as I dreamed about the oak tree. Sapmi was bound to our blood and wouldn't let us go even though we wanted to ignore it.'

At Ellen's silence, he looked up at her. 'Why aren't you saying anything?'

'That's the first time I've ever heard you speak in metaphors.'

Simon shrugged. 'That particular metaphor is based on a biological fact so it's OK to use it.'

Ellen shook her head in wonder. 'You're a damn genius, Simon.'

Her brother smiled. It was the most peaceful smile he'd made in a long time.

Epilogue

BEFORE THE ASHES

The fir trees wore thick braids of snow on their branches that winter. Snow crowded Tyrevik's streets and Niklas had to plough the driveway free every morning. For the second year in a row, a white Christmas seemed likely.

Ellen brushed snowflakes off the parcel as she approached the house. She held it tucked under her arm, sheltering it with her duffel coat, but somehow the flakes still curled their way around the coat, sticking to the white cardboard and her knitted sweater. A little smile crept onto her face as she imagined her parents' reaction. They'd been waiting a whole month for the arrival of the graduation cap. Ellen wouldn't wear it until June, when the senior year celebrated finishing school, but preparations for the ceremony always began at the start of the school year. Now, with the cap here, the countdown had really started.

As Ellen was always home first on Fridays, she checked the letterbox before heading inside. It was the same kind of Christmas advertising they'd had the past two weeks. She leafed through the brochures so quickly she didn't notice the postcard slip out of the pile until she almost stepped on it.

Ellen picked it up. The card showed a reindeer on a mountaintop. Behind it, framing it with its molten glow, was the midnight sun. A single snowflake fell on it and melted, running down past the reindeer's leg until it dripped into Ellen's palm. *Merry Christmas and a Happy New Year* was written in red ink on the back. The handwriting was compressed, as if the writer didn't want to take up too much space on the card, and the letters leaned slightly to the left. The words *Best Wishes, Daniel* nestled in the bottom right corner.

When she got inside, Ellen placed the card on the piano amongst the others. She pulled out one of the cards at the back. It had the same reindeer motif, the same writing, the same red ink. The only difference was one number in the dates: 12/12/17 and 12/12/18.

Had he got their card by now? It was Simon who'd chosen this time: a bullfinch perching on a frost-covered branch, the bare outlines of birch trees in the background. She wondered if there was much snow in Halland, down by the west coast, and if Daniel missed the winters in Norrland.

Her hand pulled away. Thinking of Daniel Johansson still conjured visions of his eyes before they sank underwater, daring her to throw the phone away.

Her fingers wandered on to the next card in the row. On the front was a photo in black and white of a reindeer herder with two of his animals on a barren moor, mountain peaks distant on the horizon. *A photo of my father, Olaf Thomasson, Arravare 1968* was written inside on the left, in handwriting that spaced all the letters out.

The herd had grown back to the size it was before the incident of summer '17. Nilajaure lake had healed and the running water in the area was clean again.

Glued onto the right side was a colour picture of Erik and Vera, a young reindeer standing between them.

Ellen smiled to herself. She hadn't seen Erik since summer last year and now, finally, she would see his band live. They had their first gig in Stockholm in a fortnight and the Blinds had invited Erik to stay with them.

Everyone in the Thomasson family had signed the card. Erik had written *I look forward to seeing you soon!* on the bottom, and Vera had written *Sending warm hugs and kisses.*

Reading the older girl's message made Ellen smile. When the Thomassons had seen them off at the station as they were about to go home, Vera had leaned in and muttered in Ellen's ear: 'I'm sorry I was rude earlier. It was wrong. You seem really nice.' Then she'd given Ellen a hug. It was possible that Vera would join Erik when he came down to Stockholm, but she hadn't confirmed it yet.

Ellen's gaze slid back to the first card. From what Ellen knew, Daniel had no contact with the Thomassons. The Blinds had no contact with him either, save that one card that turned up in the letterbox last December and now this other one.

They could never be friends or family, but they could be known to each other. They could be remembered by the greetings they exchanged each Christmas.

Everything could be remembered.

Ellen could not help herself. She drifted into the study room, as she had last Christmas after staring at Daniel's card. The article lay on top of the pile of pens, rulers and rubber bands that littered the top drawer.

56-Year-Old Arrested for Beheading Reindeer.

There was the glade, veiled in sunlight. Two broken lines of greenish grass forming a cross in the middle marked out where the horns had lain.

Flies buzzed in Ellen's ears. Rot lingered under her

nostrils. Her gaze dived down to the last two paragraphs. *The accused pleaded guilty and was on Thursday last week sentenced to four months of psychiatric care... The Sami Council criticised the punishment for not being harsh enough...*

Due to the 56-year-old's attempted suicide the court judged him to be unstable of mind...

The accused claimed his motive was vengeance but refuses to disclose any further information to the press.

During the police investigation it was discovered he was the grandson of Gunnar Persson and the son of Lars-Erik Blind, who were involved in a fatal dispute between Sami and Kajava Levinians in 1960, originally reported in the Svartjokk Kuriren *by its founder, Bertil Hansson. Following up on Hansson's investigation, the police found proof of the 56-year-old's family ties to Persson, in a ledger of baptisms from the Old Church. A name in the ledger had been crossed out, and while Hansson failed to find the priest or parents responsible, police officer Göran Gunnarson successfully gained access to the archives from the town hall and the parish office in Purnuvaare, and retrieved the names of the priest (now deceased) and the parents. We can now confirm that it was indeed the 56-year-old's name that had been crossed out.*

'The motive isn't quite clear,' Gunnarson says. 'It could be shame, regret or a wish to protect the child.'

Svartjokk Kuriren *has attempted to get in touch with the man's mother without success. The family of his deceased father visited him in Svartjokk hospital the day after his suicide attempt.*

Police Officer Gunnarson acknowledges that without the witness accounts from the two teenagers who discovered the reindeer circle, the crime would have taken longer to solve. The teenagers wish to remain anonymous.

Simon had threatened to write a letter of complaint to

Stina Hansson about how she had twisted the facts. 'She is letting herself and the police take credit for what we did even though journalists are supposed to tell the truth of things.'

'I thought you would have learned by now that the truth isn't always easy to swallow,' Ellen had said. 'And if she had told the truth, our faces could be all over the newspapers. Are you sure you would have liked that?'

'No. Flash cameras are too strong and they make a loud noise and I don't like how they block out people's faces.'

'Then maybe we should let sleeping dogs lie, this once,' she said, and laughed as her brother rolled his eyes.

She wondered if he was still sitting in the school corridor, filming another video of himself solving the cube. The one he'd uploaded two weeks ago had gained thirteen thousand views.

'Perhaps if I do it under thirty-five seconds and tell more jokes, I will get twenty thousand views. They say in the comments I have a good sense of humour,' he'd said and blushed.

If Camilla had her way, the article would be filed away in a folder forever. Niklas, though, was of a different opinion. *These things will always be at the forefront of our minds,* he'd said. *By pushing them away we only hurt ourselves. We must let them be where they need to be.*

Where they need to be.

Ellen brought her hand to her neck. She hadn't felt the sting since last summer, nor seen the ghost of Great-Granny Marit. It was as if Sapmi didn't need to alert them any more. The Blinds had accepted that life and history wanted to be remembered.

Ellen put the article back and shut the drawer. She put on her hat. Wandered into the hallway and gazed at her reflection in the mirror.

Studenten. The stepping-stone from school to adult life. Six months left.

Not for the first time, she wondered if she would be ready. There was still so much to do: the Gymnasium project, the national tests, the Swedish Scholastic Aptitude Test, university applications... She would barely have time to sit down before *studenten* came along and *whoosh*, one part of her life was ended.

A flash of light made her look into the living room. The setting sun, peering in through the window, lighting up the white lawn and making the frosted trees glitter. It reflected off the white tiles of the stove.

Ellen walked over to it. The iron tray beside the stove was stacked to the brim with logs. Dad had fetched more from the shed before leaving for work.

She knelt down and put in three logs. Picked two sheets of newspaper from the pile, scrunched them into balls and tucked them in amongst the wood. Soot lined the back of her hands when she pulled them out. Then she picked up the matches sitting at the edge of the tray and lit the fire.

The flames were slow at first. Newborn, they crawled over the ashes, up along the fresh wood, nibbling at one splinter at a time – making sense of their surroundings. As the flames grew taller the wood crackled and spat under the weight of them. That was all the sound there was.

Acknowledgements

In the summer of 2017, after my graduation from the University of Exeter, I went on a trip with my brother through northern Sweden on the *Inlandsbana* train. We spent three nights in the mining town on which Svartjokk is based, and went on a tour up Mount Dundret to see the midnight sun. The idea for *Embers* came from reading about a reindeer killing in the news, in which a circle of mutilated reindeer bodies had been discovered by two teenage girls in the forest. The location wasn't far from the town we were staying in, and the culprit was never found. I was shocked and horrified that such gruesome crimes could happen, and it opened my eyes to the hate crime that is committed against the Sami and their reindeer. I felt compelled to write a story in which the culprit was found, and used my own travels and relationship with my brother as the premise for the novel. Needless to say, if I hadn't gone on that trip and hadn't read about the killing in the news, *Embers* would never have happened.

Thanks to my father, Chris Greenland, who read and provided detailed feedback on the early drafts, and spent many hours going through the story with me, page after page.

To Dan Vyleta, my MA dissertation supervisor, who

guided me through the initial brainstorming and planning of the story and gave me invaluable advice on how to structure a novel. *Embers* would have taken a lot longer to complete without his help. To all staff at the creative writing departments of the University of Birmingham and the University of Exeter, who read my stories and helped me become the writer I am today.

To editor Victoria Millar, who helped bring the story up to a whole new level and make sure it realised its full potential. To copy editor Charlotte Norman, who had an excellent eye for detail. To Mark Ecob for the beautiful cover design.

Finally, huge thanks to Xander Cansell, Anna Simpson and the rest of the Unbound team for believing in this story and helping me bring it to life, and for providing the editorial services of Becca and Julia.

Unbound is the world's first crowdfunding publisher, established in 2011.

We believe that wonderful things can happen when you clear a path for people who share a passion. That's why we've built a platform that brings together readers and authors to crowdfund books they believe in – and give fresh ideas that don't fit the traditional mould the chance they deserve.

This book is in your hands because readers made it possible. Everyone who pledged their support is listed at the front of the book and below. Join them by visiting unbound.com and supporting a book today.

Amy Down
Ian and Catherine Downie
Lucy Elliott
Nadine Elroubi
Daisy Evered
James Evered
Enma Farnworth
Kerstin Fd Hassler
J E Flanagan
Rebecca Ford
Lucy Forsey
Tom Furnivall
Roman Gaev
Maggie Gellersjo
Alan Gillespie
Emma Grae
Bérengère Greenland
Hilary Greenland
Geoffrey Gudgion
Catarina Håkans
Cris Hale
Thomas Hametner
Maximilian Hawker
Natasha Hemmings
Pertti Honkanen
June Intana
Minna Isaksson
Melanie Jackson
Andrew Jardine
Marta Jez
Carolina Johansson
Emilie Lauren Jones
Eva-Lotta Jonsson
Wannapha Kaewkalong
Annalissa Kania
Hamoar Karim
Josh Kaye
John Keenan
Dan Kieran
Rosanna Kindersley
Domnika Krivas
Elisabetta Labella
Vanesa Lavado

Mary Lees
Noémie Léonard
Ellie Li
Miriam Loken
Åsa Lönn
Gunnar Mangsgård
Mary McGowan
Stefan Meyer
John Mitchinson
Daniel Morris
Rhel ná DecVandé
Carlo Navato
Jon Neil
Cheska Pallones
Hannah Parry
Linzi Paterson
Orla Patton
Esme Pears
Justin Pollard
Tamzin Reilly
Caroline Richards
Hannah Rixon
Cecee Rowland-Huss
K. S.
Oscar Sahlin
Edith Sandstrom
Bethany Savage
Elizabeth Savage
Sarah Selley
Katriina Seppänen
Esa Seth
Tom Shacklock
Ruth Sjöström
Rafael Solomon
Becky Springall
Harald Stokkeland
Dennis van Soest
Vera Vincent Almgren
Tom Ward
Paul Waters
Claire White
Jennie Widlund
Tom Wilson